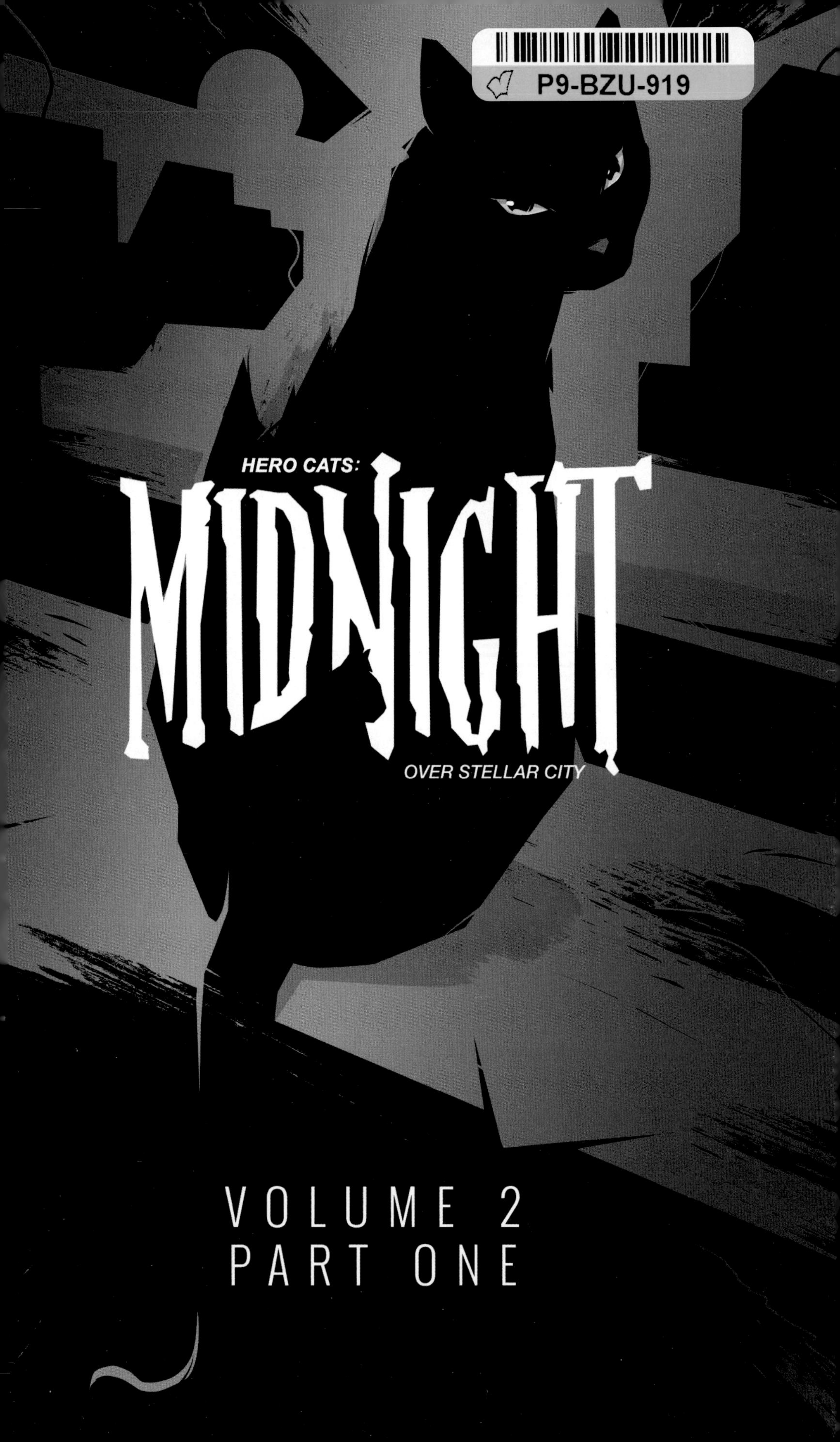
HERO CATS:
MIDNIGHT
OVER STELLAR CITY
VOLUME 2
PART ONE

THE CREATIVE TEAM

WRITTEN AND CREATED BY
KYLE PUTTKAMMER

ART AND LETTERS BY
ALEX OGLE

COLORS BY
JULIE HADDEN BARCLAY

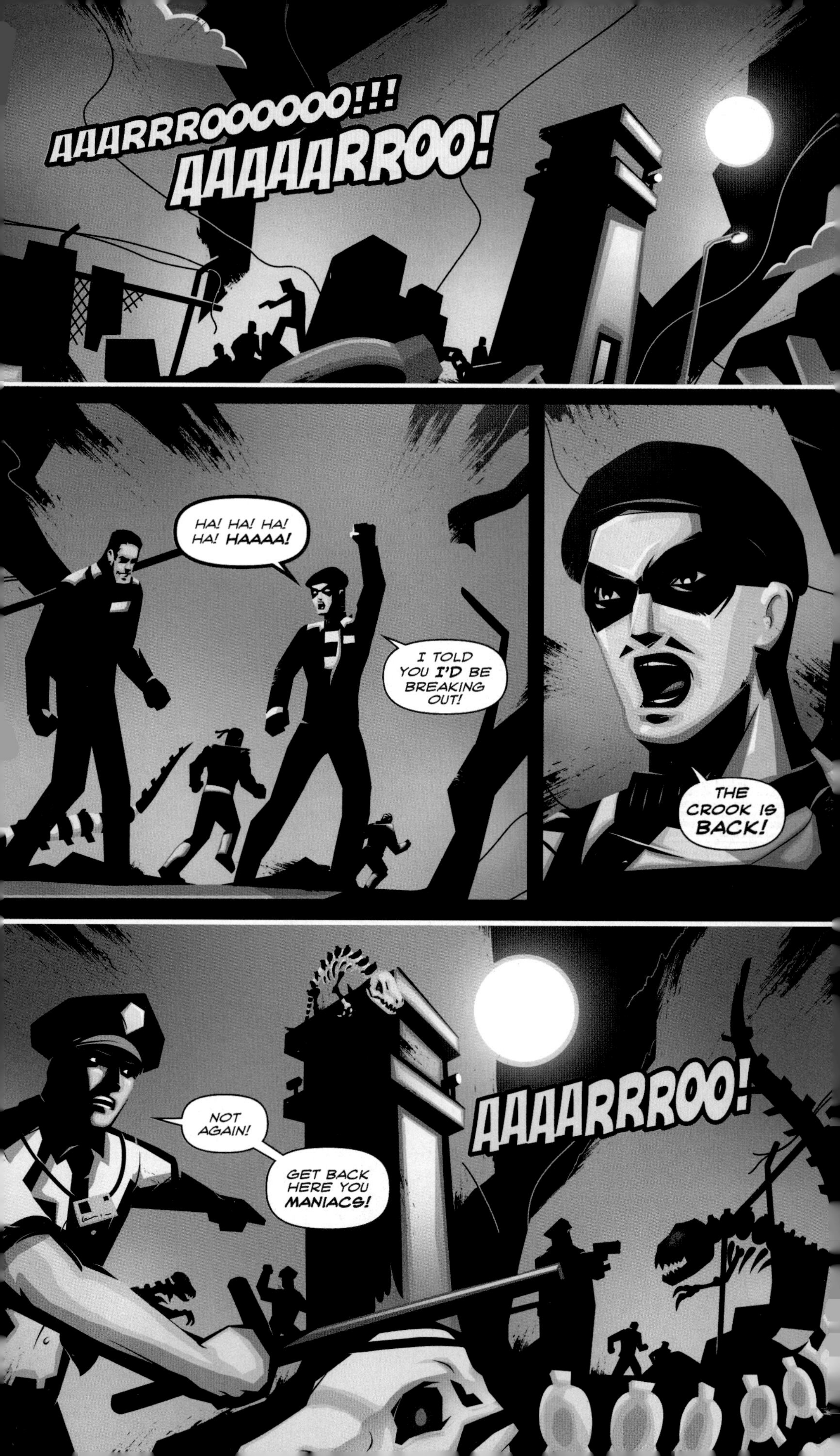
AAARRROOOOOO!!!
AAAAARROO!
HA! HA! HA! HA! HAAAA!
I TOLD YOU I'D BE BREAKING OUT!
THE CROOK IS BACK!
NOT AGAIN!
GET BACK HERE YOU MANIACS!
AAAARRROO!

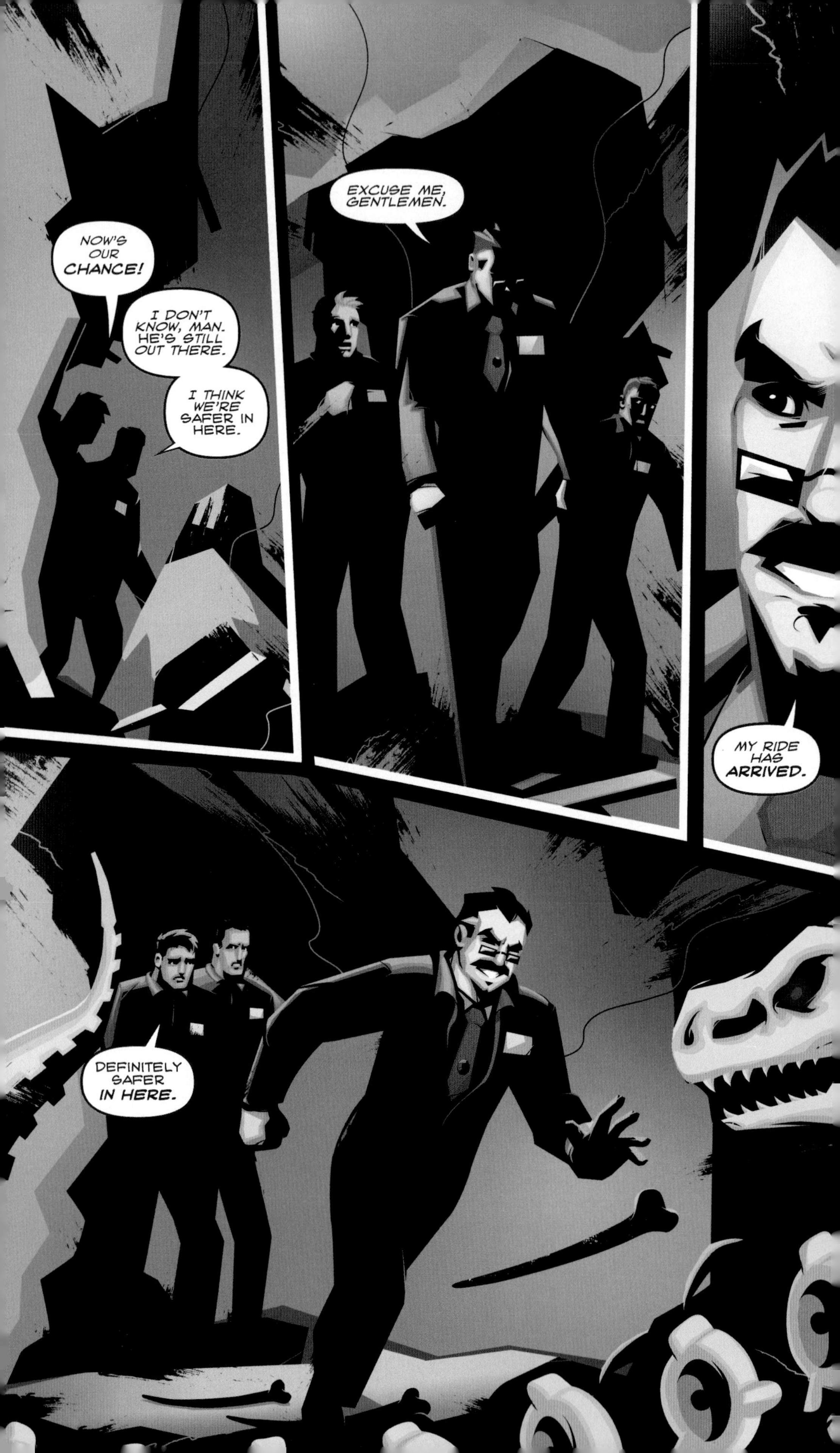
NOW'S OUR CHANCE!
I DON'T KNOW, MAN. HE'S STILL OUT THERE.
I THINK WE'RE SAFER IN HERE.
EXCUSE ME, GENTLEMEN.
MY RIDE HAS ARRIVED.
DEFINITELY SAFER IN HERE.

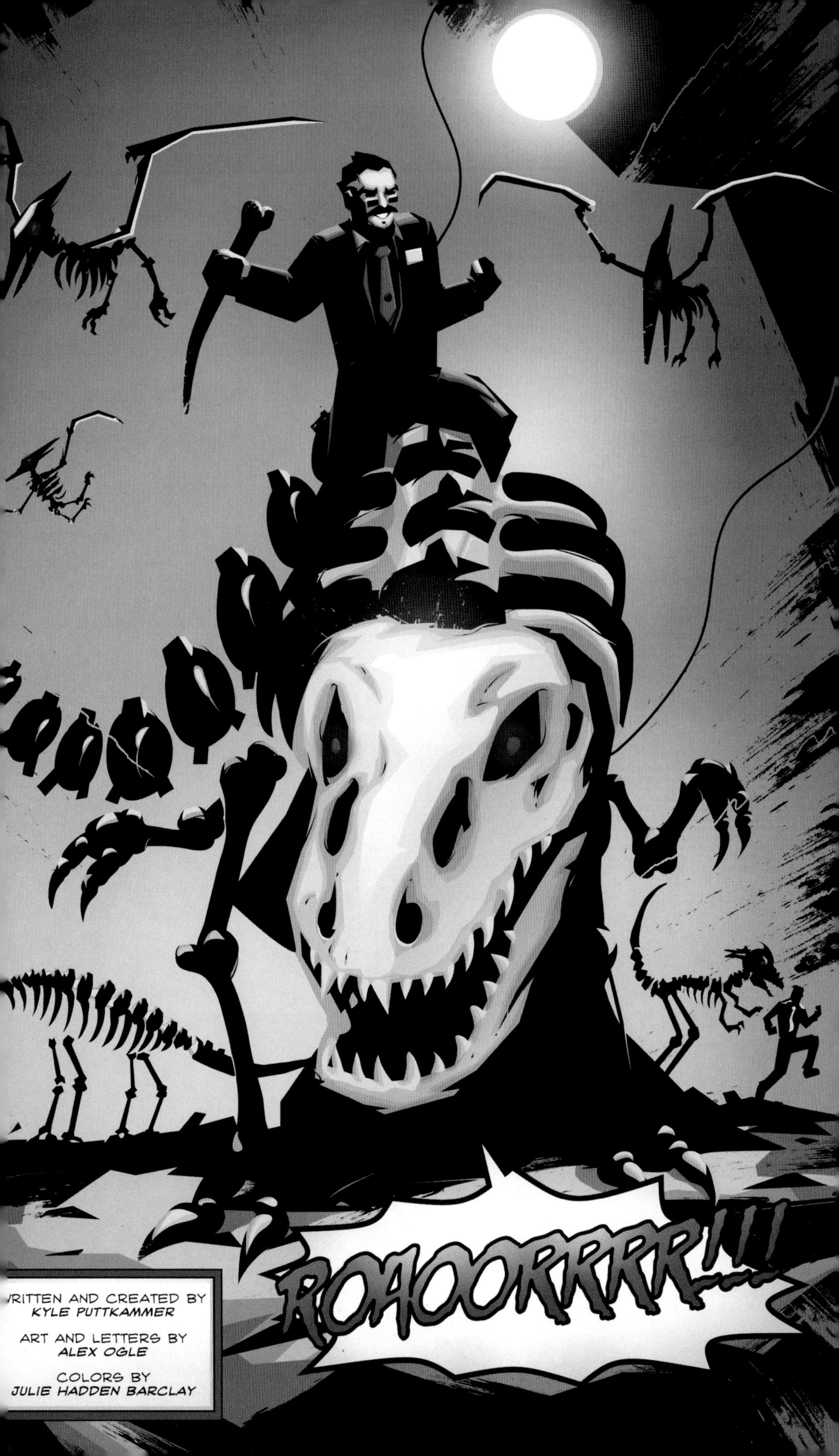
ROAOORRRR!!!
WRITTEN AND CREATED BY
KYLE PUTTKAMMER
ART AND LETTERS BY
ALEX OGLE
COLORS BY
JULIE HADDEN BARCLAY

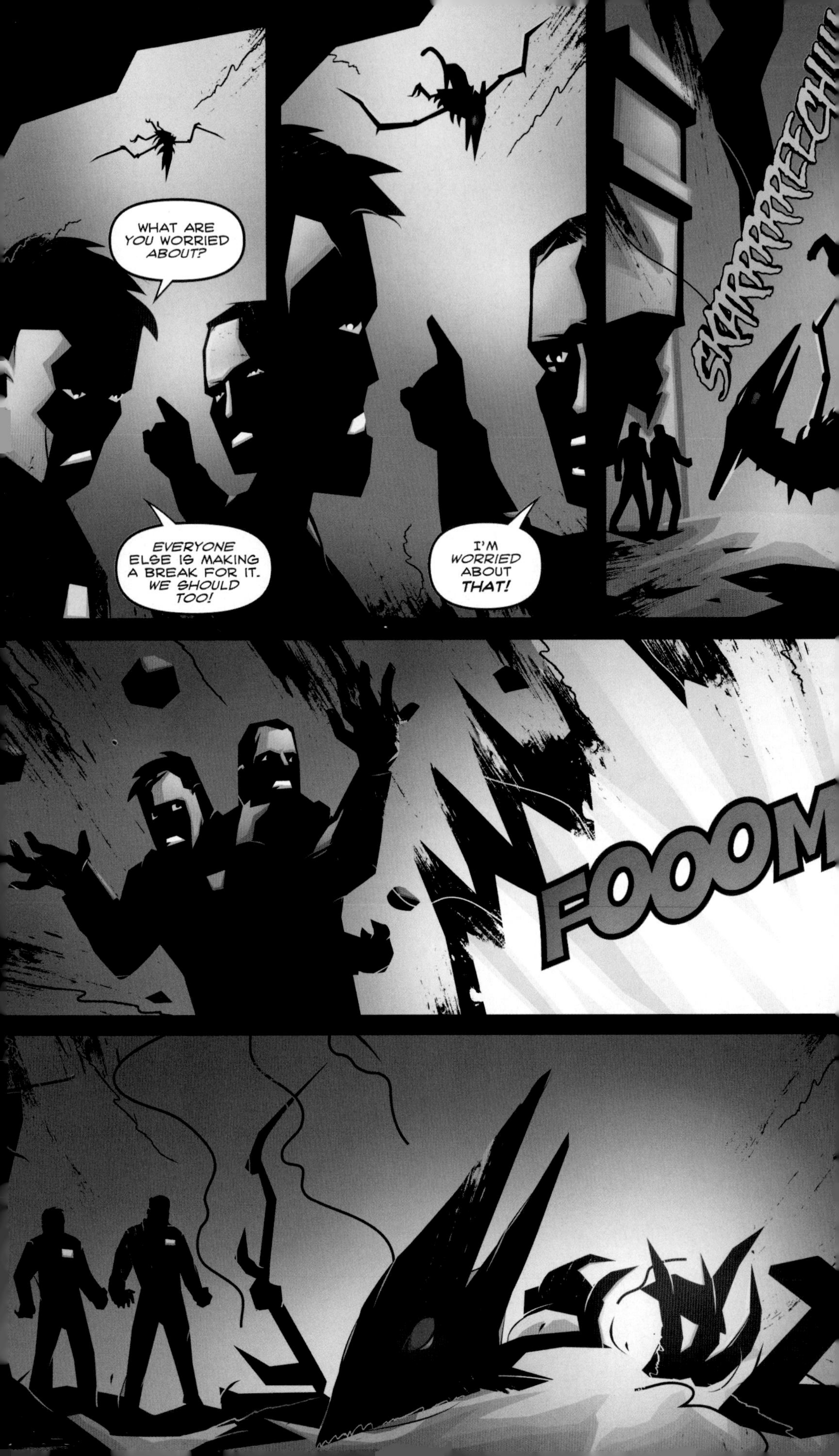
WHAT ARE YOU WORRIED ABOUT?
EVERYONE ELSE IS MAKING A BREAK FOR IT. WE SHOULD TOO!
I'M WORRIED ABOUT THAT!
SKARRRRREECHHH
FOOOM

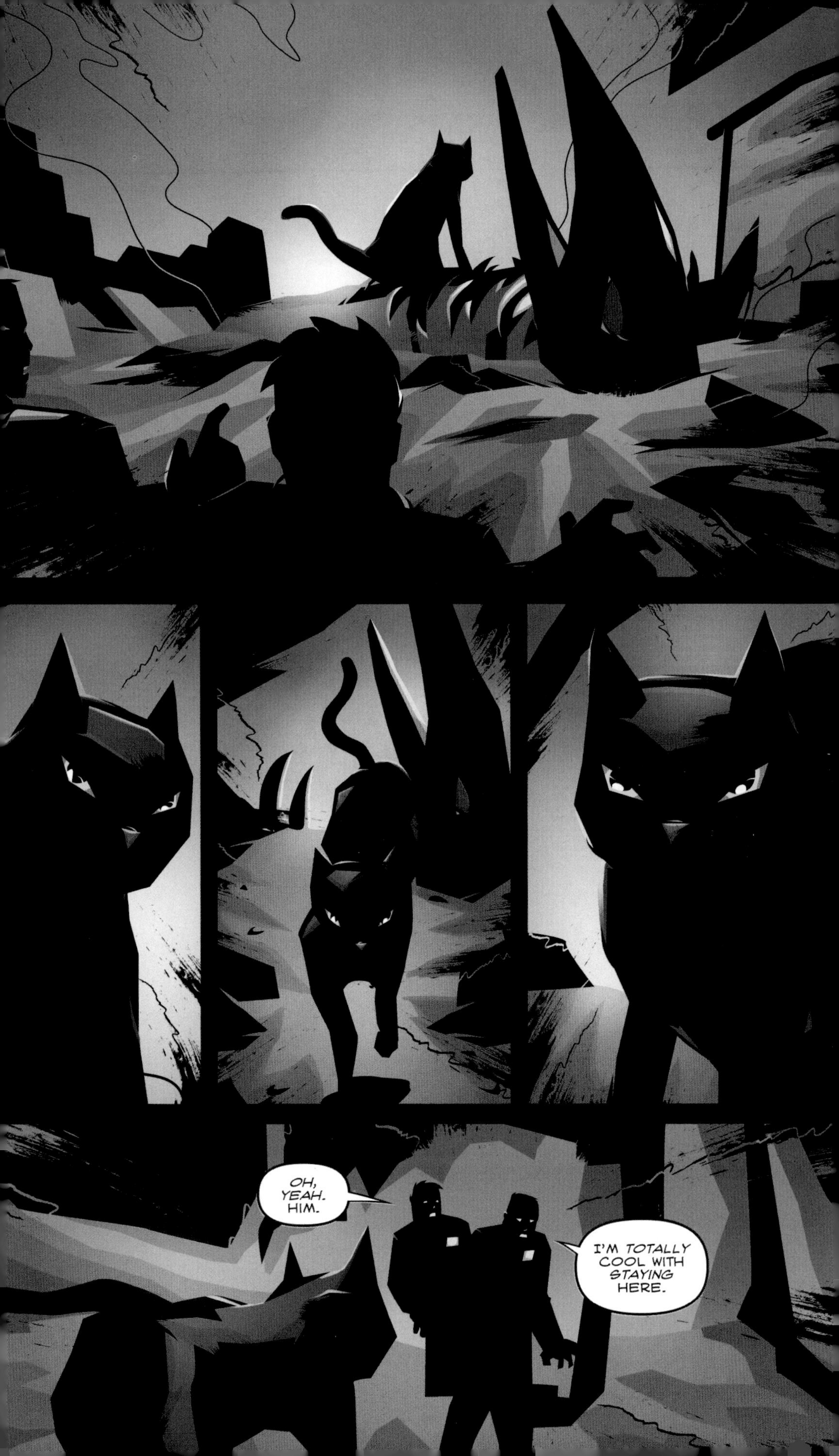
OH, YEAH. HIM.
I'M *TOTALLY* COOL WITH STAYING HERE.

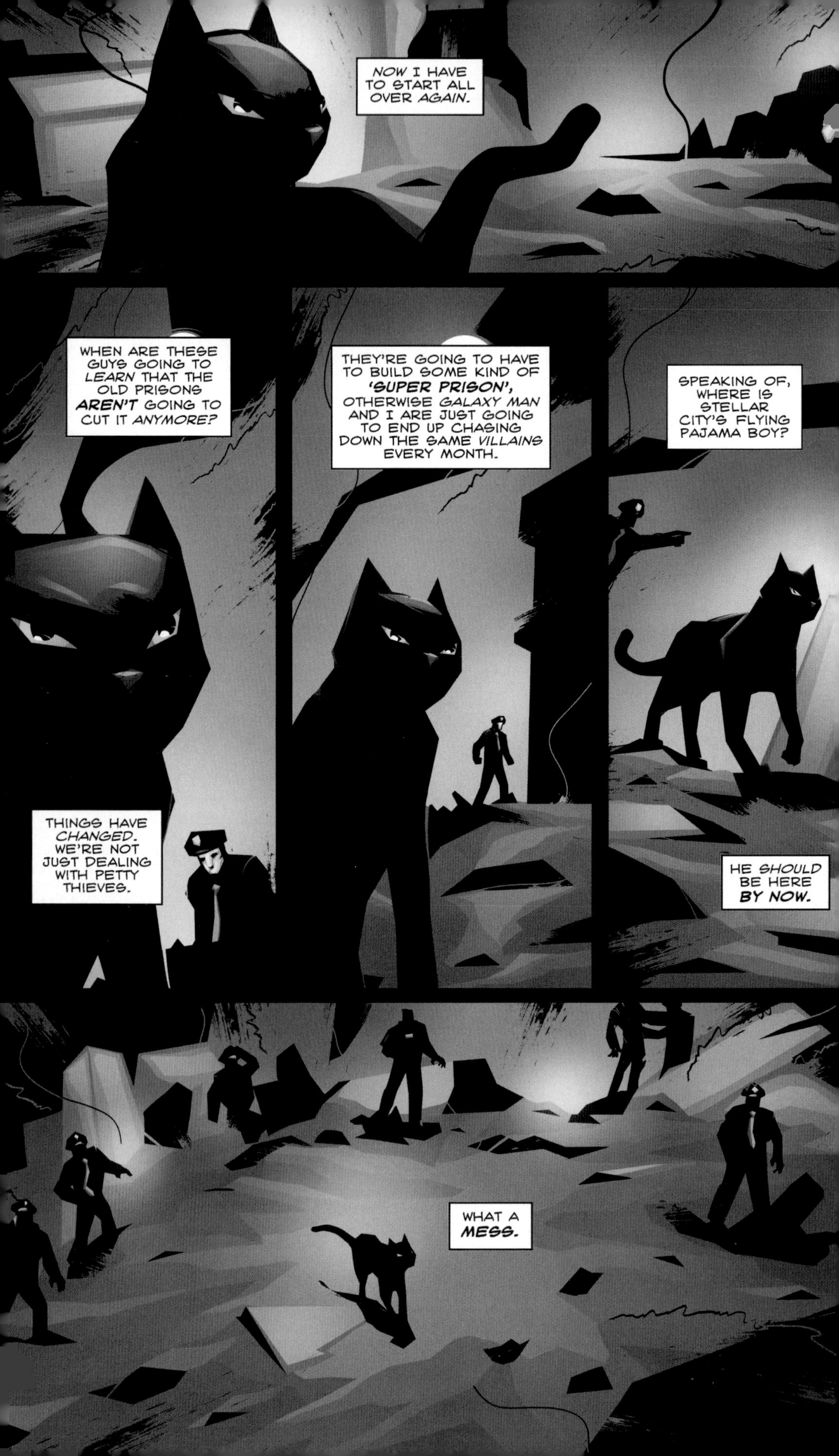
NOW I HAVE TO START ALL OVER AGAIN.
WHEN ARE THESE GUYS GOING TO LEARN THAT THE OLD PRISONS AREN'T GOING TO CUT IT ANYMORE?
THINGS HAVE CHANGED. WE'RE NOT JUST DEALING WITH PETTY THIEVES.
THEY'RE GOING TO HAVE TO BUILD SOME KIND OF 'SUPER PRISON', OTHERWISE GALAXY MAN AND I ARE JUST GOING TO END UP CHASING DOWN THE SAME VILLAINS EVERY MONTH.
SPEAKING OF, WHERE IS STELLAR CITY'S FLYING PAJAMA BOY?
HE SHOULD BE HERE BY NOW.
WHAT A MESS.

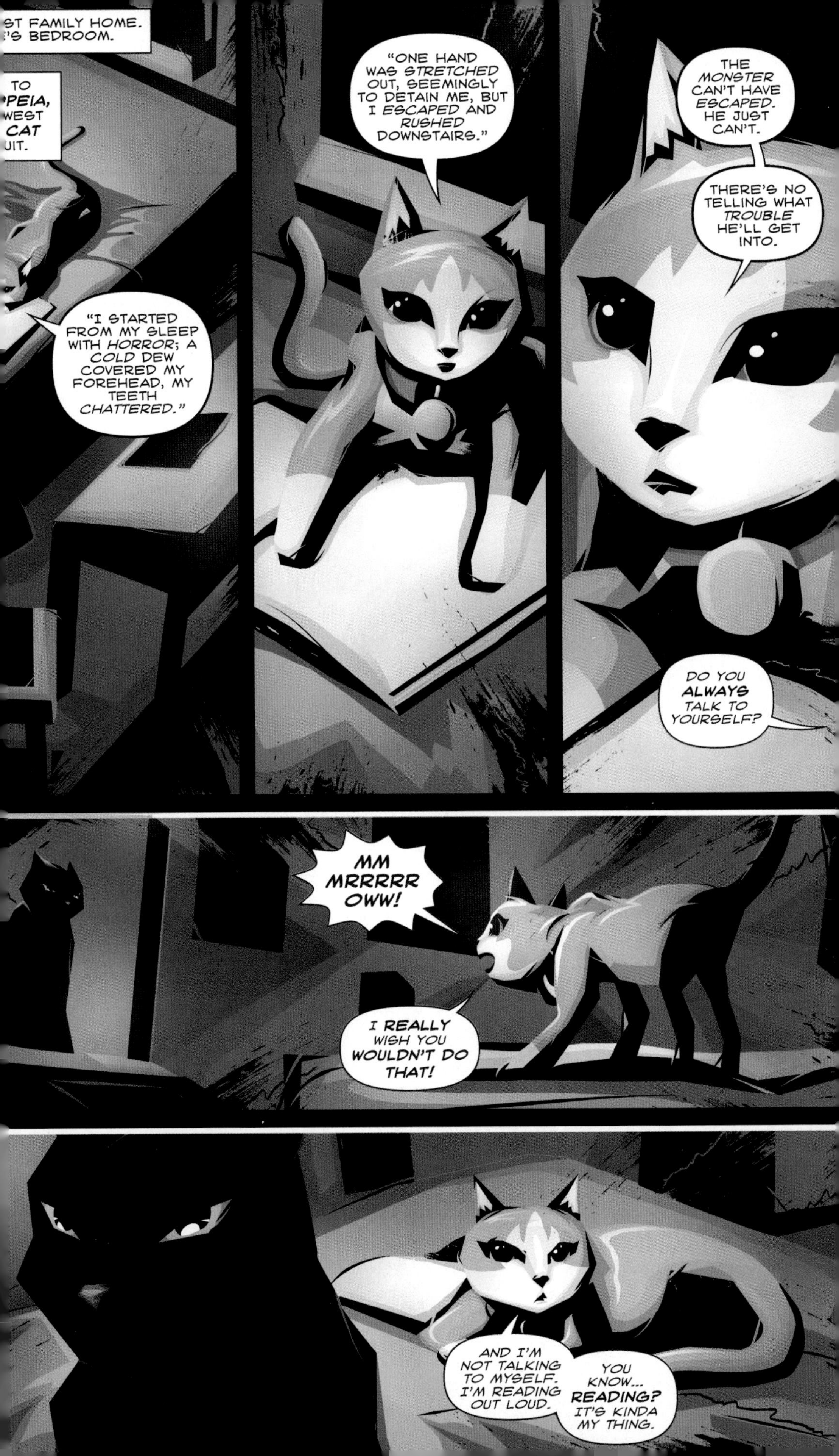
ST FAMILY HOME.
'S BEDROOM.
TO
PEIA,
WEST
CAT
UIT.
"I STARTED FROM MY SLEEP WITH HORROR; A COLD DEW COVERED MY FOREHEAD, MY TEETH CHATTERED."
"ONE HAND WAS STRETCHED OUT, SEEMINGLY TO DETAIN ME, BUT I ESCAPED AND RUSHED DOWNSTAIRS."
THE MONSTER CAN'T HAVE ESCAPED. HE JUST CAN'T.
THERE'S NO TELLING WHAT TROUBLE HE'LL GET INTO.
DO YOU ALWAYS TALK TO YOURSELF?
MM MRRRRR OWW!
I REALLY WISH YOU WOULDN'T DO THAT!
AND I'M NOT TALKING TO MYSELF. I'M READING OUT LOUD.
YOU KNOW... READING? IT'S KINDA MY THING.

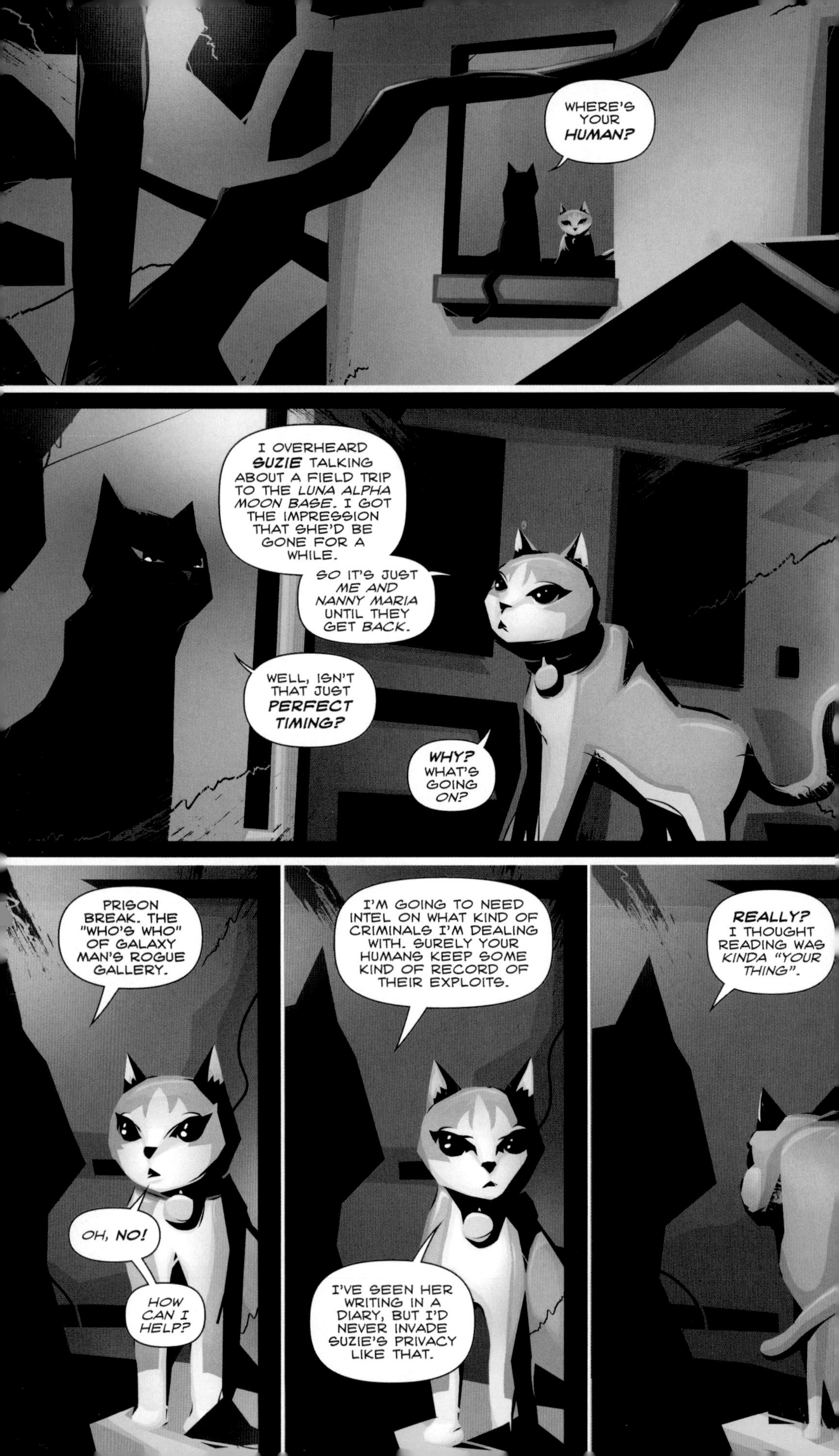
WHERE'S YOUR HUMAN?
I OVERHEARD SUZIE TALKING ABOUT A FIELD TRIP TO THE LUNA ALPHA MOON BASE. I GOT THE IMPRESSION THAT SHE'D BE GONE FOR A WHILE.
SO IT'S JUST ME AND NANNY MARIA UNTIL THEY GET BACK.
WELL, ISN'T THAT JUST PERFECT TIMING?
WHY? WHAT'S GOING ON?
PRISON BREAK. THE "WHO'S WHO" OF GALAXY MAN'S ROGUE GALLERY.
OH, NO!
HOW CAN I HELP?
I'M GOING TO NEED INTEL ON WHAT KIND OF CRIMINALS I'M DEALING WITH. SURELY YOUR HUMANS KEEP SOME KIND OF RECORD OF THEIR EXPLOITS.
I'VE SEEN HER WRITING IN A DIARY, BUT I'D NEVER INVADE SUZIE'S PRIVACY LIKE THAT.
REALLY? I THOUGHT READING WAS KINDA "YOUR THING".

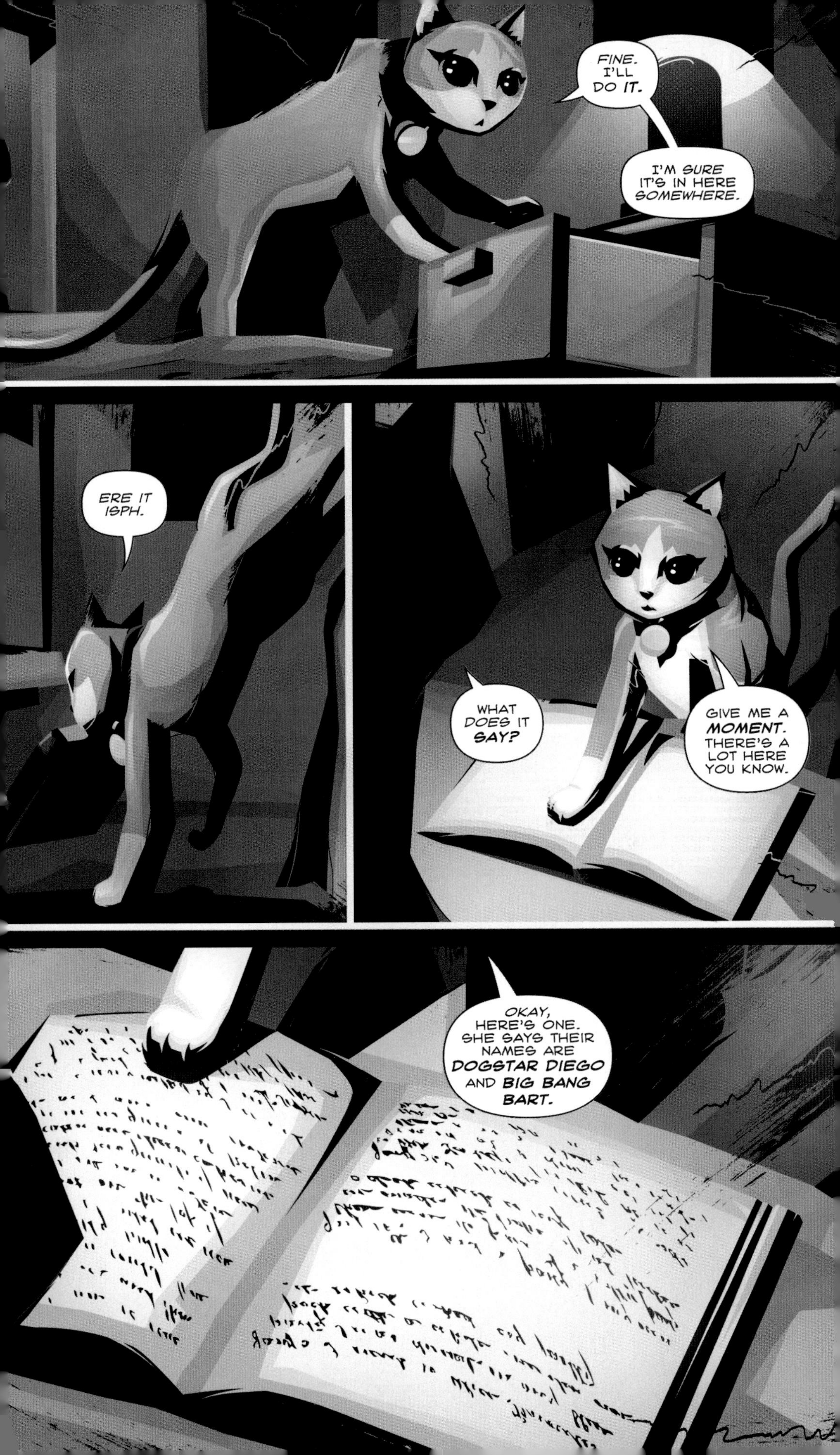
FINE. I'LL DO IT.
I'M SURE IT'S IN HERE SOMEWHERE.
ERE IT ISPH.
WHAT DOES IT SAY?
GIVE ME A MOMENT. THERE'S A LOT HERE YOU KNOW.
OKAY, HERE'S ONE. SHE SAYS THEIR NAMES ARE DOGSTAR DIEGO AND BIG BANG BART.

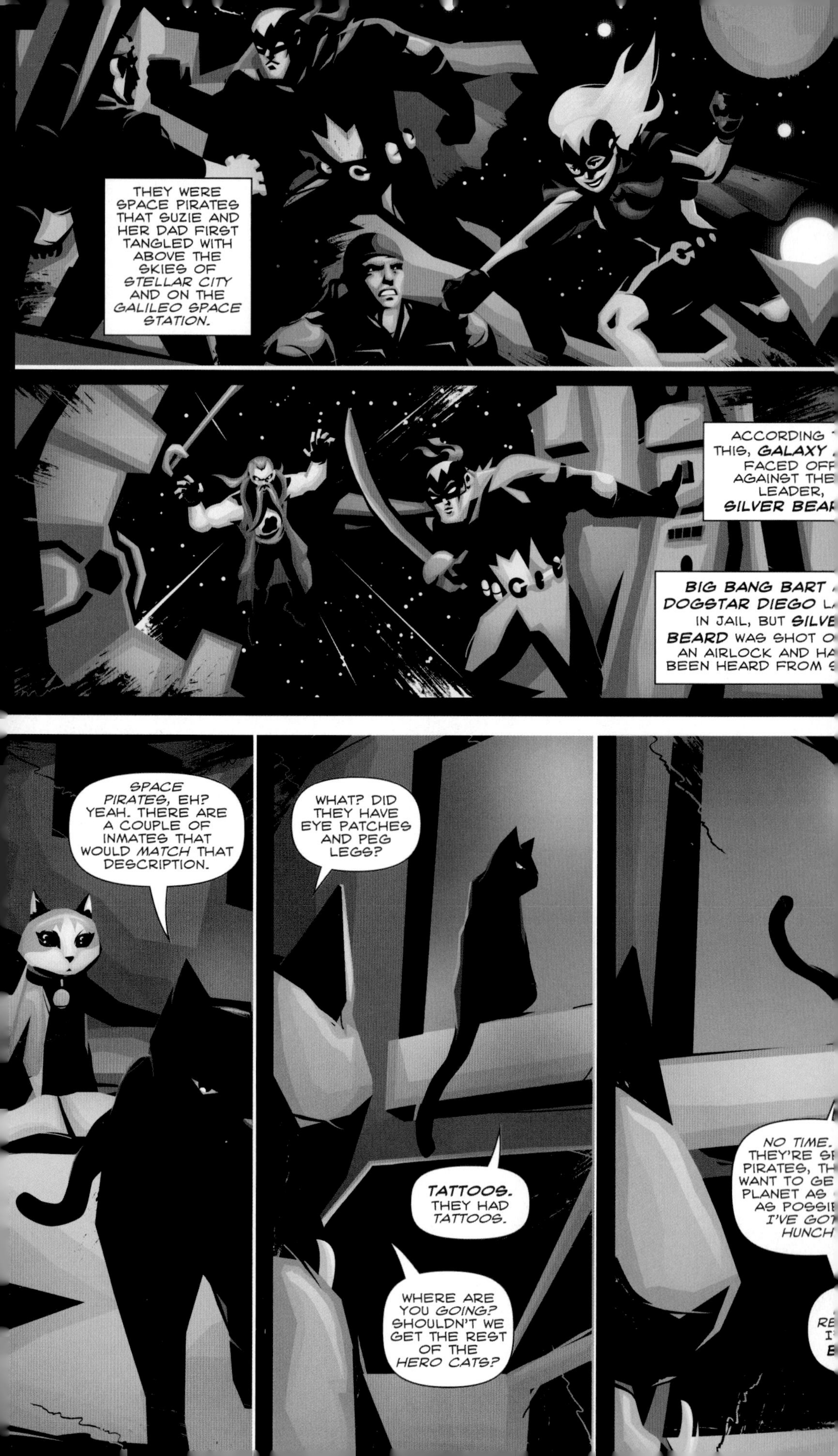
THEY WERE SPACE PIRATES THAT SUZIE AND HER DAD FIRST TANGLED WITH ABOVE THE SKIES OF *STELLAR CITY* AND ON THE *GALILEO SPACE STATION.*
ACCORDING THIS, **GALAXY** FACED OFF AGAINST THE LEADER, **SILVER BEA**
BIG BANG BART DOGSTAR DIEGO L IN JAIL, BUT **SILVE BEARD** WAS SHOT O AN AIRLOCK AND HA BEEN HEARD FROM
SPACE PIRATES, EH? YEAH. THERE ARE A COUPLE OF INMATES THAT WOULD *MATCH* THAT DESCRIPTION.
WHAT? DID THEY HAVE EYE PATCHES AND PEG LEGS?
TATTOOS. THEY HAD *TATTOOS.*
WHERE ARE YOU *GOING?* SHOULDN'T WE GET THE REST OF THE *HERO CATS?*
NO TIME. THEY'RE S PIRATES, TH WANT TO GE PLANET AS AS POSSI *I'VE GOT HUNCH*

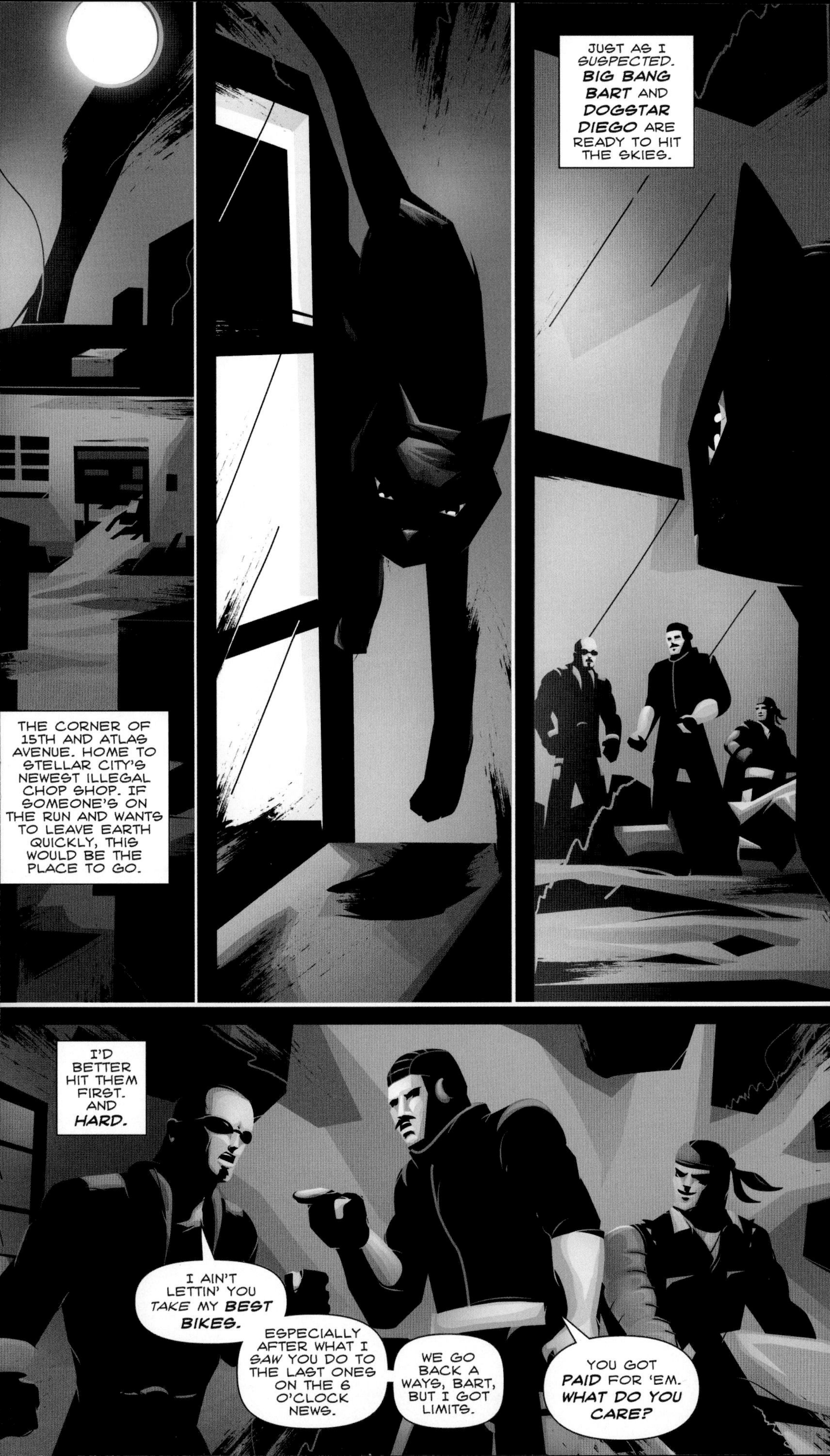
THE CORNER OF 15TH AND ATLAS AVENUE. HOME TO STELLAR CITY'S NEWEST ILLEGAL CHOP SHOP. IF SOMEONE'S ON THE RUN AND WANTS TO LEAVE EARTH QUICKLY, THIS WOULD BE THE PLACE TO GO.
JUST AS I SUSPECTED. BIG BANG BART AND DOGSTAR DIEGO ARE READY TO HIT THE SKIES.
I'D BETTER HIT THEM FIRST. AND HARD.
I AIN'T LETTIN' YOU TAKE MY BEST BIKES.
ESPECIALLY AFTER WHAT I SAW YOU DO TO THE LAST ONES ON THE 6 O'CLOCK NEWS.
WE GO BACK A WAYS, BART, BUT I GOT LIMITS.
YOU GOT PAID FOR 'EM. WHAT DO YOU CARE?

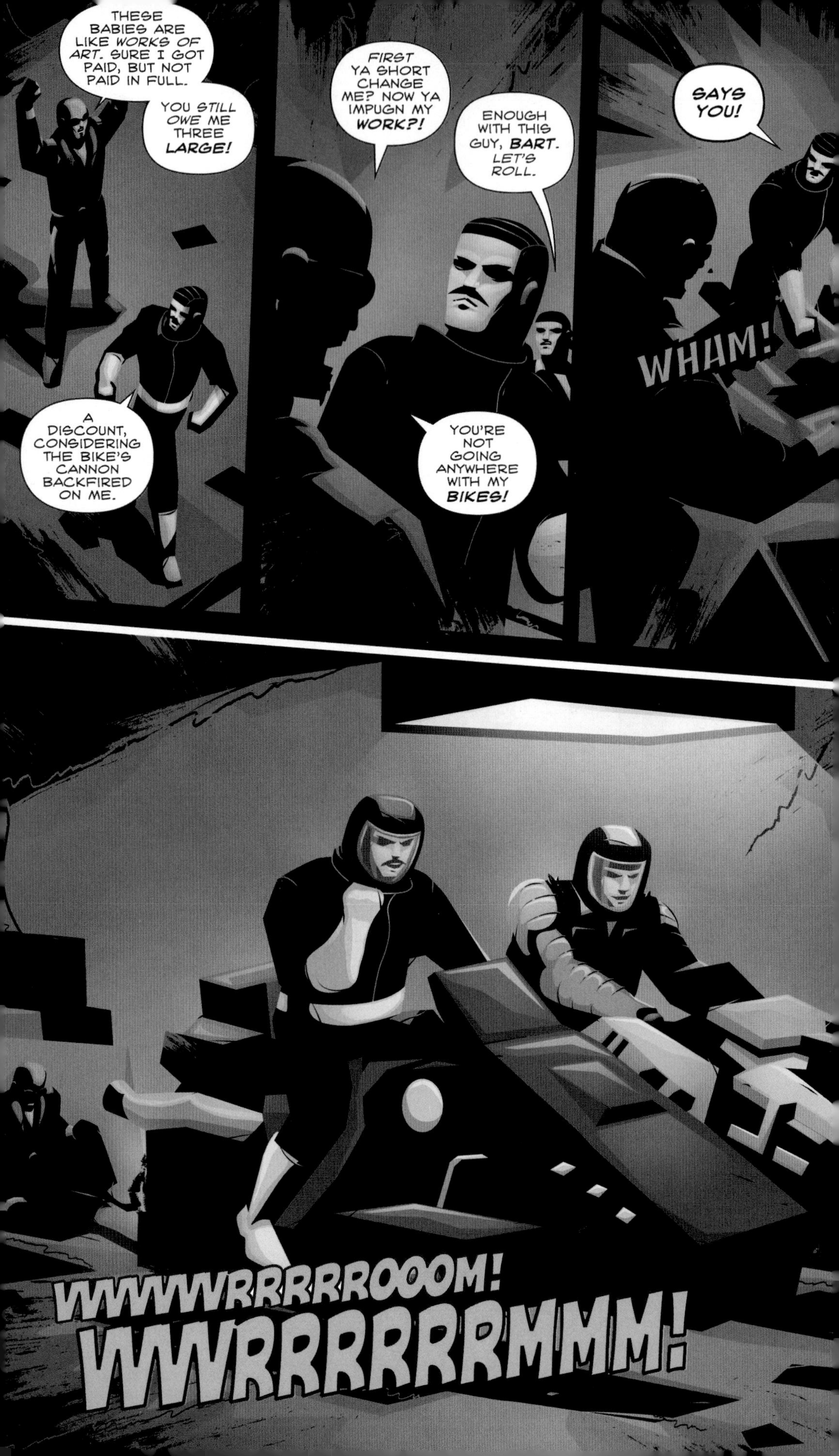
THESE BABIES ARE LIKE WORKS OF ART. SURE I GOT PAID, BUT NOT PAID IN FULL.
YOU STILL OWE ME THREE LARGE!
A DISCOUNT, CONSIDERING THE BIKE'S CANNON BACKFIRED ON ME.
FIRST YA SHORT CHANGE ME? NOW YA IMPUGN MY WORK?!
ENOUGH WITH THIS GUY, BART. LET'S ROLL.
YOU'RE NOT GOING ANYWHERE WITH MY BIKES!
SAYS YOU!
WHAM!
VVVVVVRRRRROOOM!
WWRRRRRRRMMM!

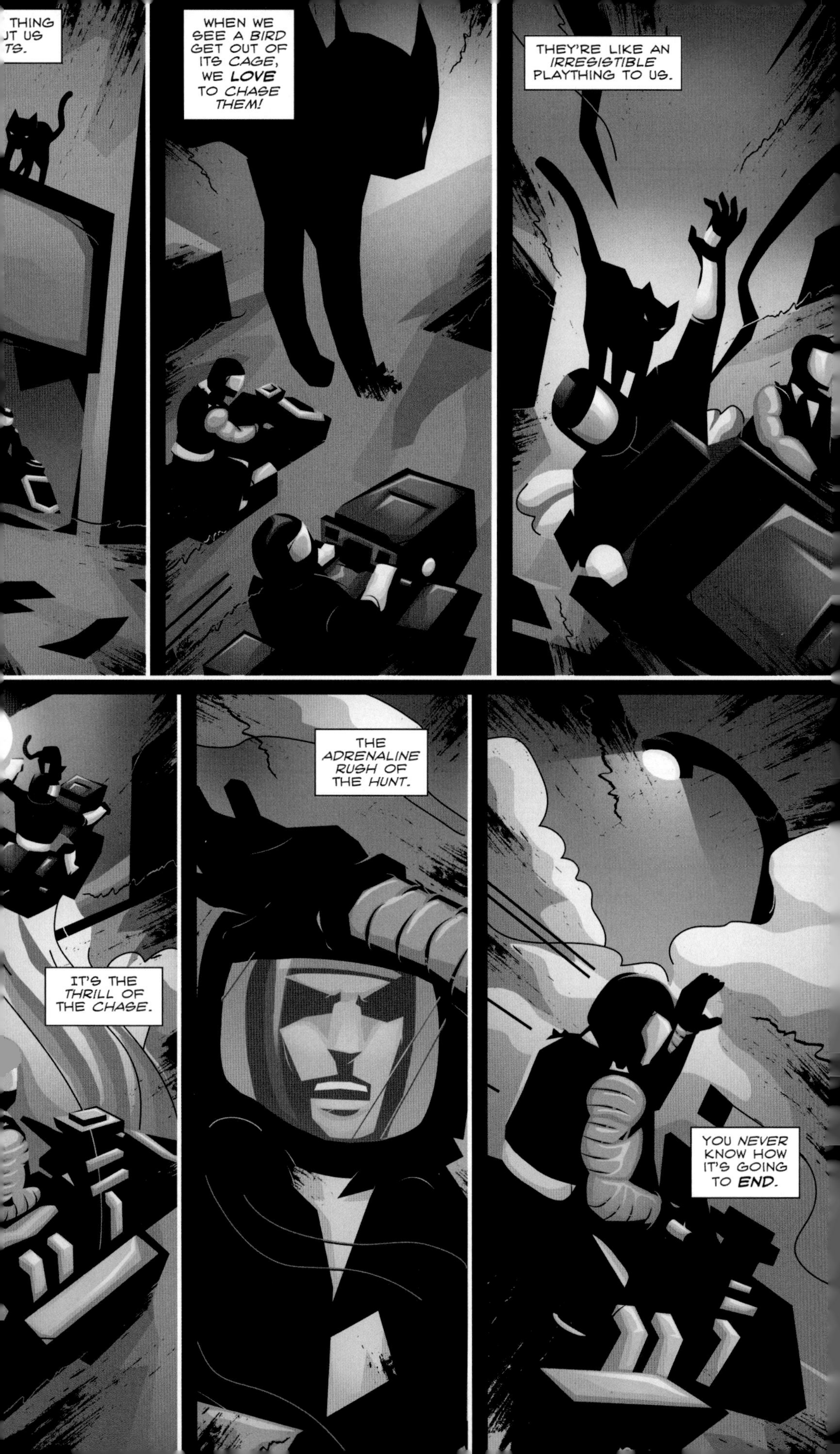
THING
UT US
TS.
WHEN WE SEE A *BIRD* GET OUT OF ITS *CAGE*, WE **LOVE** TO *CHASE THEM!*
THEY'RE LIKE AN *IRRESISTIBLE* PLAYTHING TO US.
IT'S THE *THRILL* OF THE *CHASE*.
THE *ADRENALINE RUSH* OF THE *HUNT*.
YOU *NEVER* KNOW HOW IT'S GOING TO **END**.

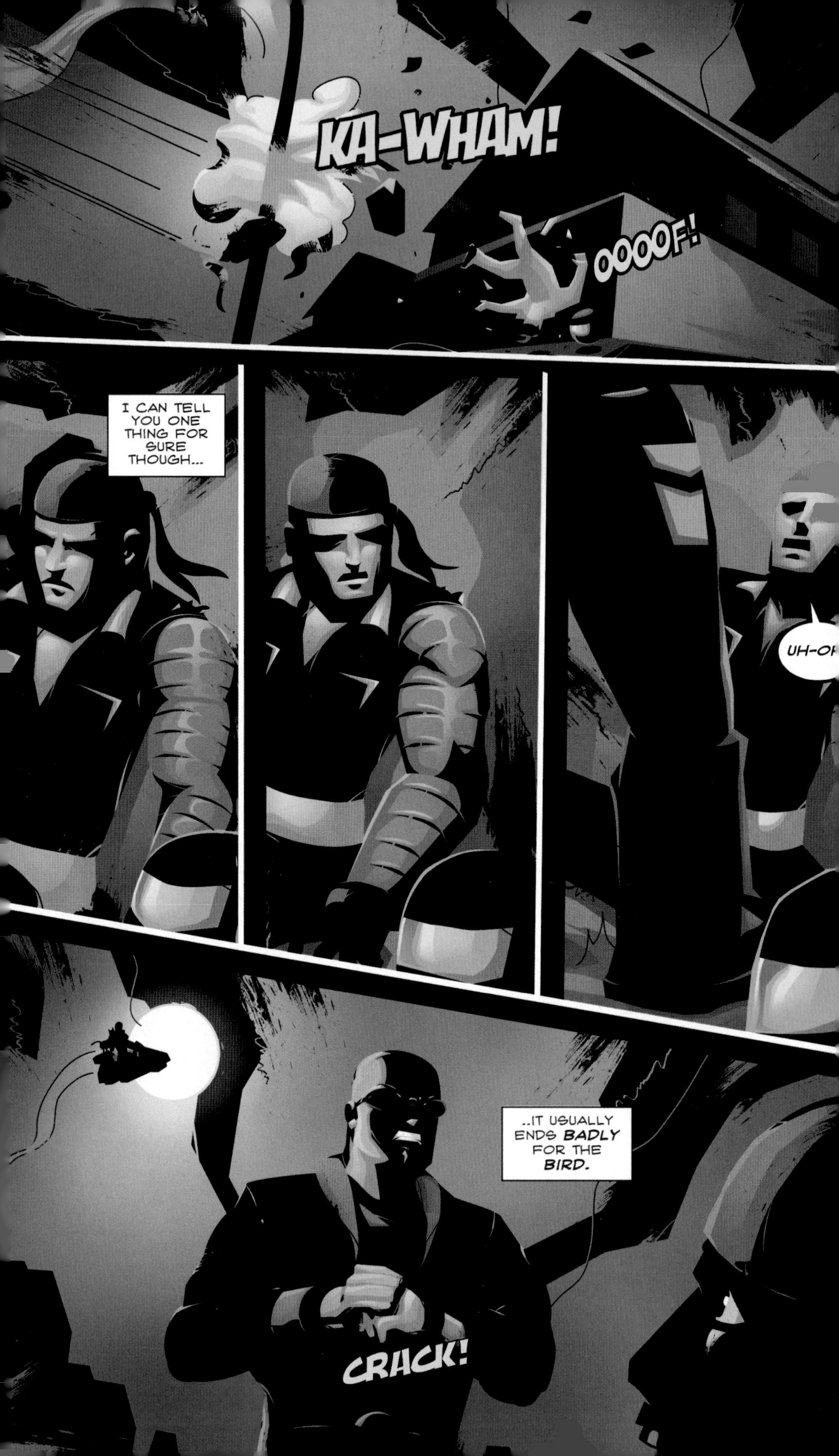
KA-WHAM!
OOOOF!
I CAN TELL YOU ONE THING FOR SURE THOUGH...
UH-OH
...IT USUALLY ENDS BADLY FOR THE BIRD.
CRACK!

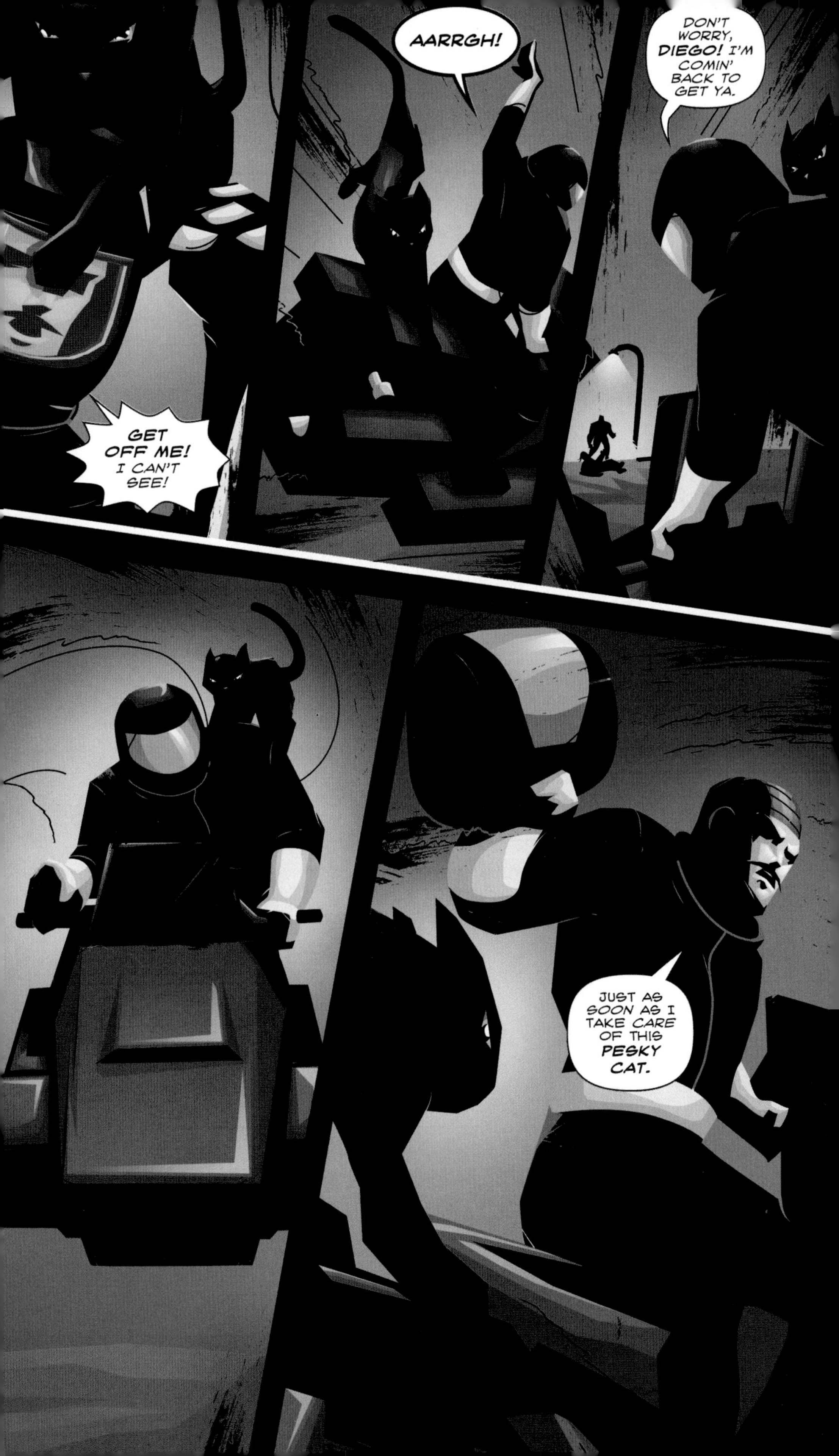
AARRGH!
DON'T WORRY, DIEGO! I'M COMIN' BACK TO GET YA.
GET OFF ME! I CAN'T SEE!
JUST AS SOON AS I TAKE CARE OF THIS PESKY CAT.

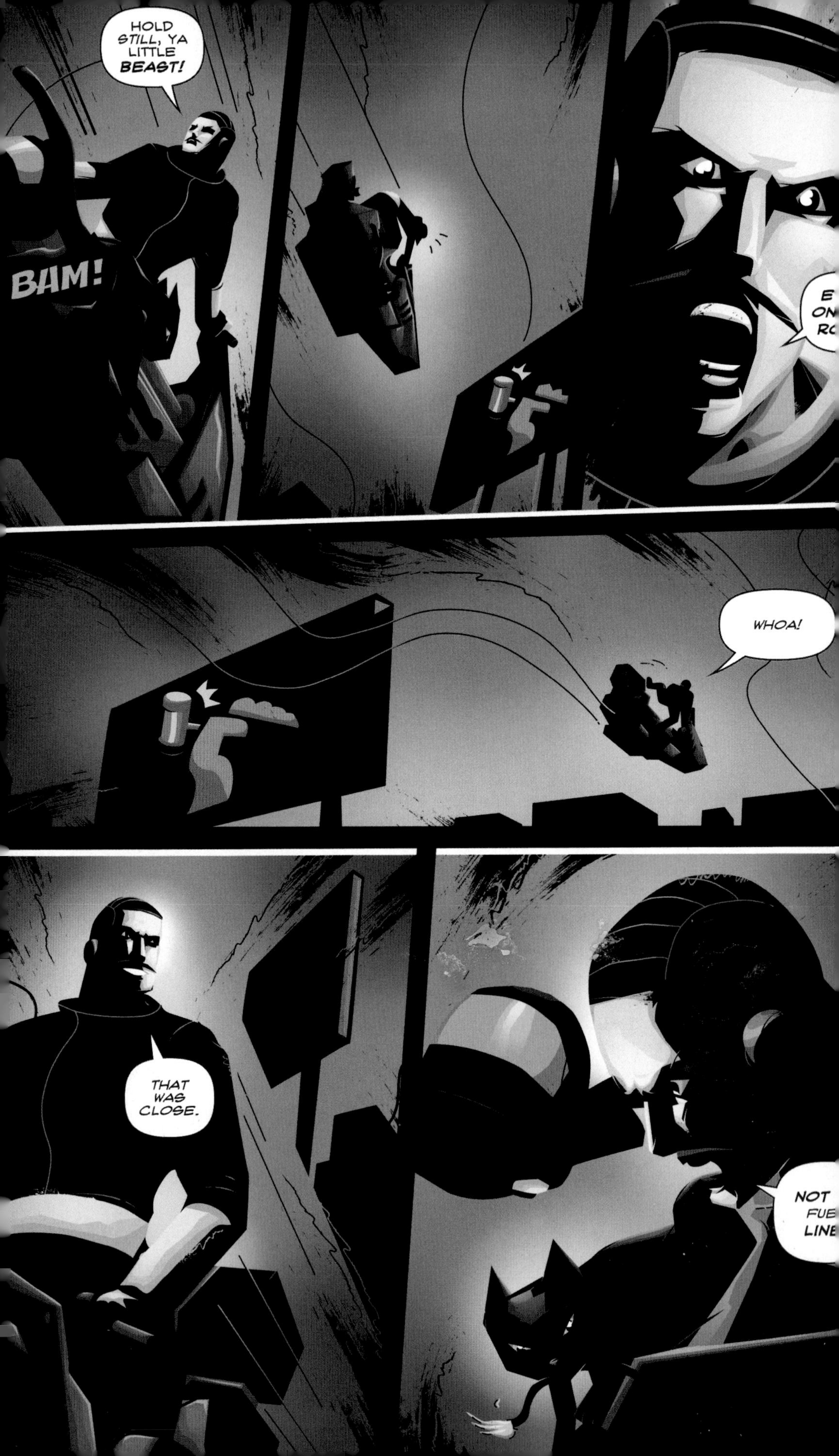
HOLD STILL, YA LITTLE BEAST!
BAM!
WHOA!
THAT WAS CLOSE.

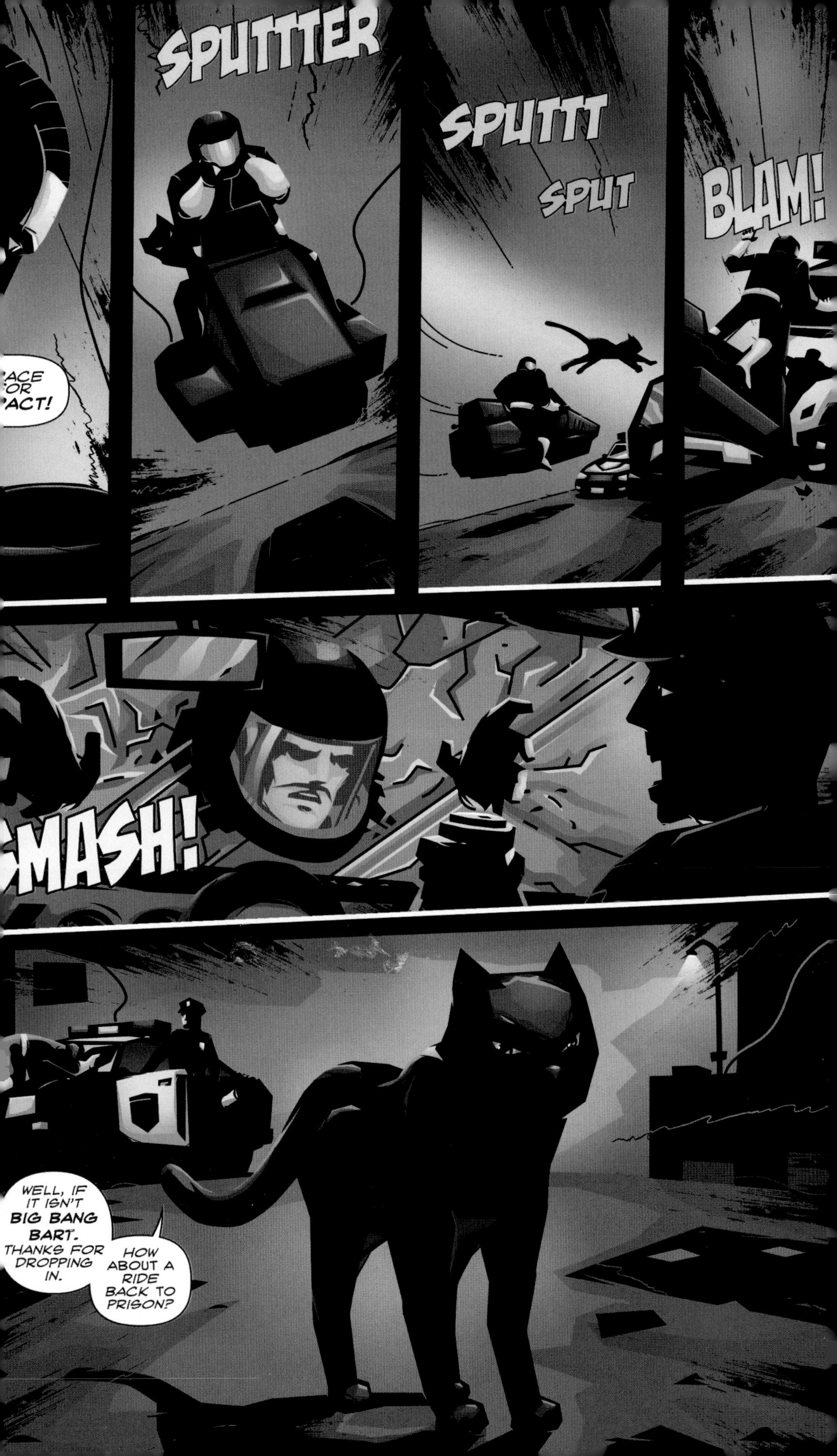
ACE
OR
ACT!
SPUTTTER
SPUTTT
SPUT
BLAM!
MASH!
WELL, IF IT ISN'T **BIG BANG BART**. THANKS FOR DROPPING IN.
HOW ABOUT A RIDE BACK TO PRISON?

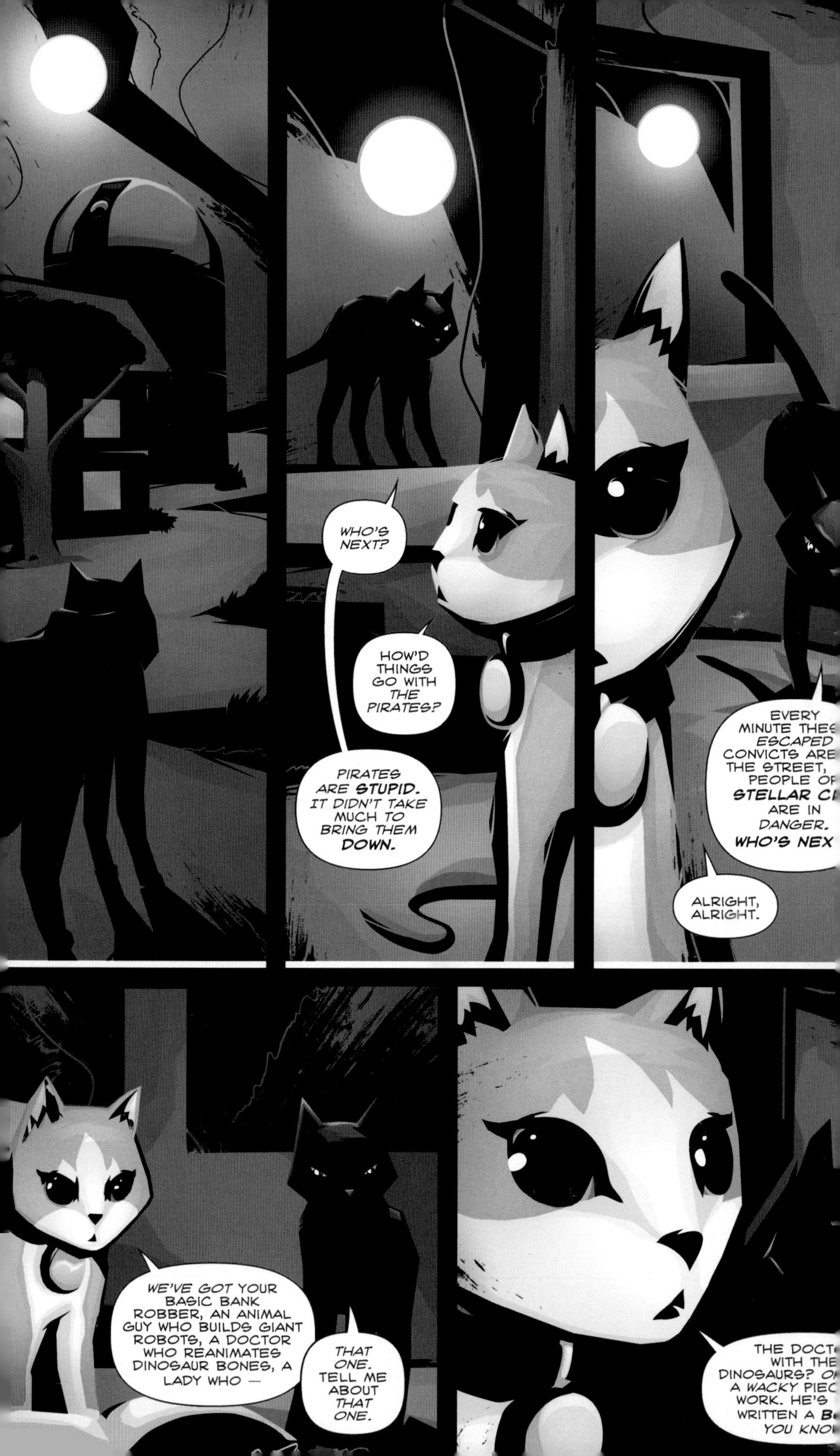
WHO'S NEXT?
HOW'D THINGS GO WITH THE PIRATES?
PIRATES ARE STUPID. IT DIDN'T TAKE MUCH TO BRING THEM DOWN.
EVERY MINUTE THES ESCAPED CONVICTS ARE THE STREET, PEOPLE OF STELLAR C ARE IN DANGER. WHO'S NEX
ALRIGHT, ALRIGHT.
WE'VE GOT YOUR BASIC BANK ROBBER, AN ANIMAL GUY WHO BUILDS GIANT ROBOTS, A DOCTOR WHO REANIMATES DINOSAUR BONES, A LADY WHO —
THAT ONE. TELL ME ABOUT THAT ONE.
THE DOCT WITH THE DINOSAURS? O A WACKY PIEC WORK. HE'S WRITTEN A B YOU KNO

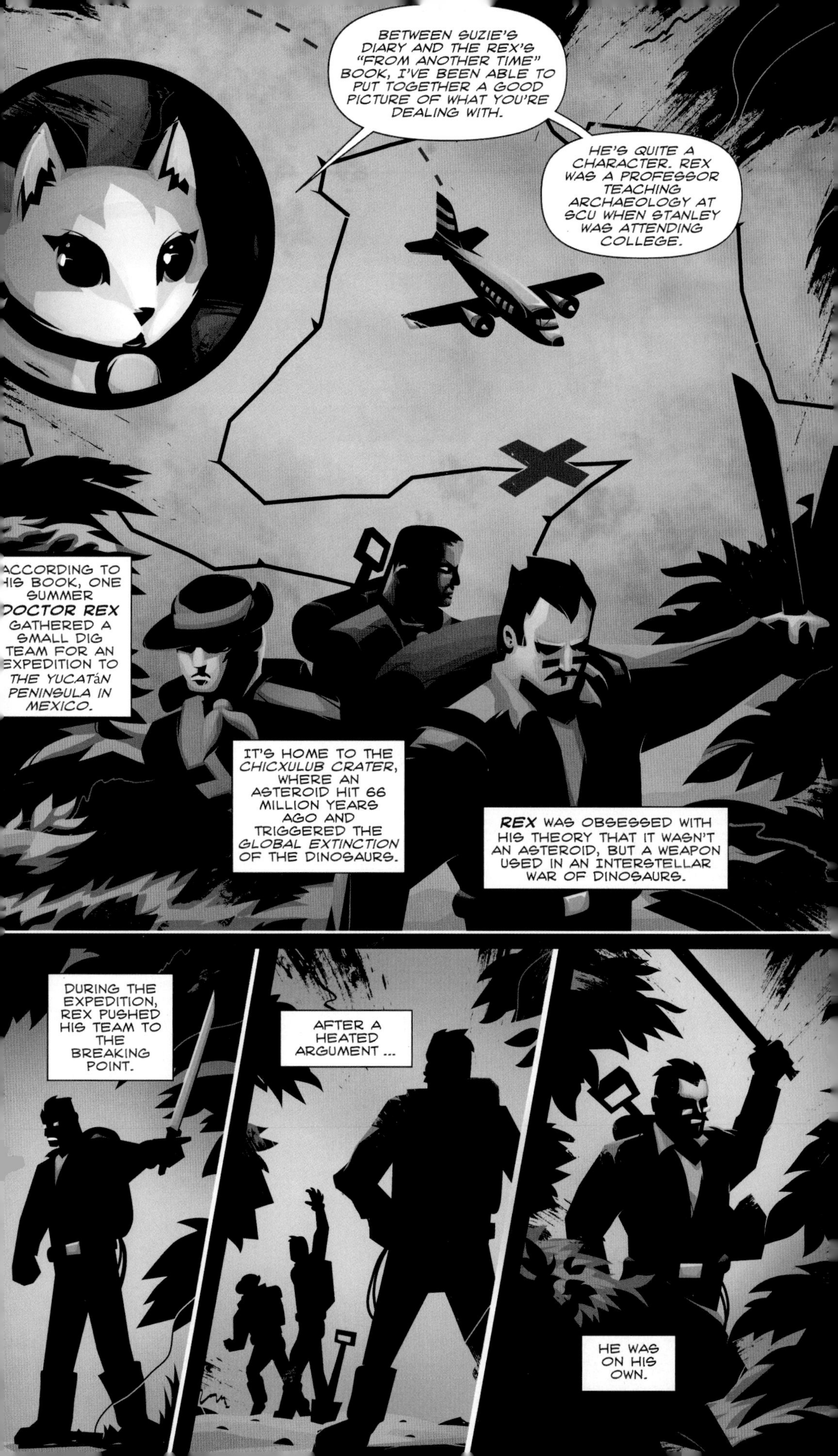

BETWEEN SUZIE'S DIARY AND THE REX'S "FROM ANOTHER TIME" BOOK, I'VE BEEN ABLE TO PUT TOGETHER A GOOD PICTURE OF WHAT YOU'RE DEALING WITH.
HE'S QUITE A CHARACTER. REX WAS A PROFESSOR TEACHING ARCHAEOLOGY AT SCU WHEN STANLEY WAS ATTENDING COLLEGE.
ACCORDING TO HIS BOOK, ONE SUMMER DOCTOR REX GATHERED A SMALL DIG TEAM FOR AN EXPEDITION TO THE YUCATÁN PENINSULA IN MEXICO.
IT'S HOME TO THE CHICXULUB CRATER, WHERE AN ASTEROID HIT 66 MILLION YEARS AGO AND TRIGGERED THE GLOBAL EXTINCTION OF THE DINOSAURS.
REX WAS OBSESSED WITH HIS THEORY THAT IT WASN'T AN ASTEROID, BUT A WEAPON USED IN AN INTERSTELLAR WAR OF DINOSAURS.
DURING THE EXPEDITION, REX PUSHED HIS TEAM TO THE BREAKING POINT.
AFTER A HEATED ARGUMENT ...
HE WAS ON HIS OWN.

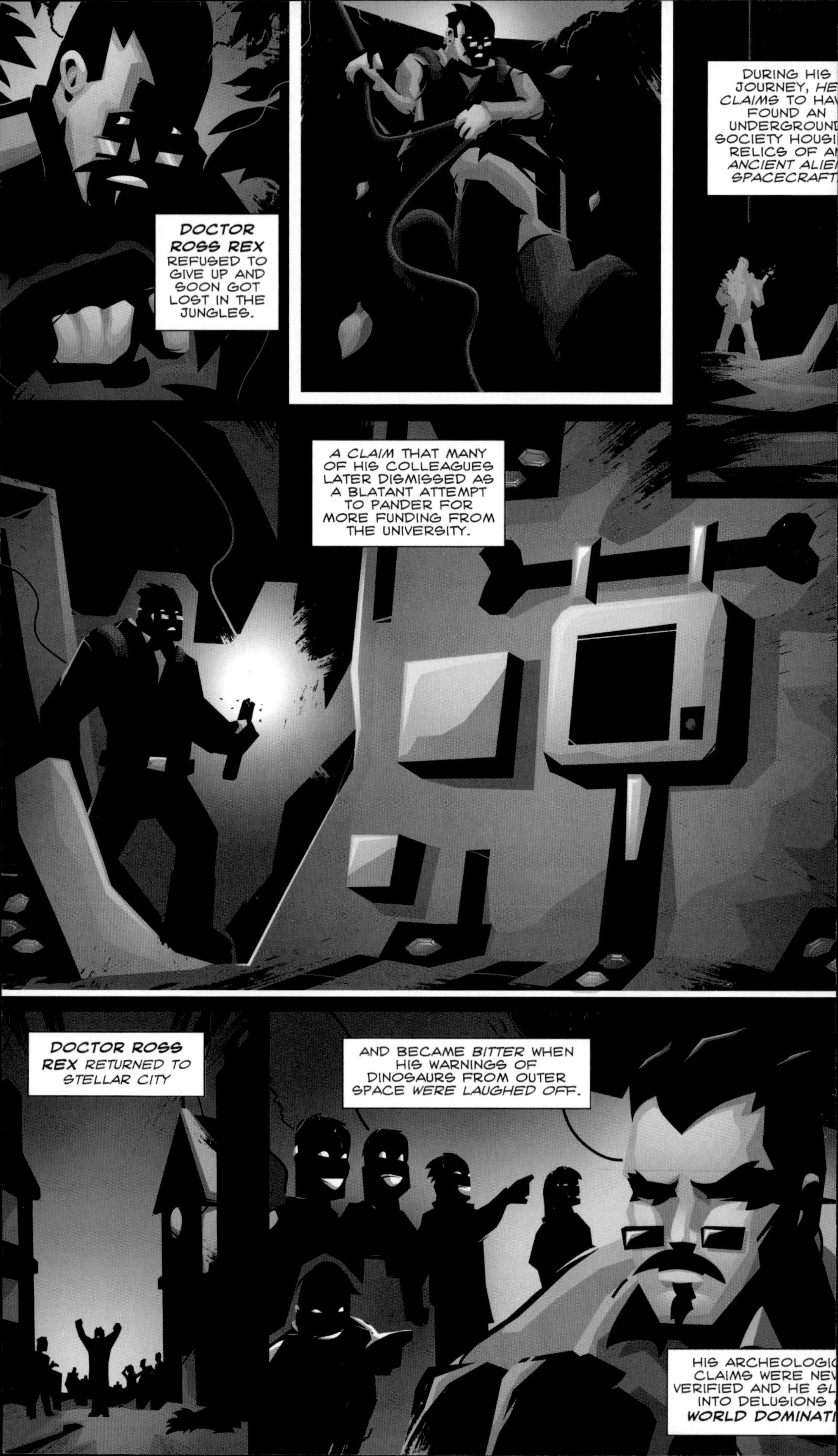
DOCTOR ROSS REX REFUSED TO GIVE UP AND SOON GOT LOST IN THE JUNGLES.
DURING HIS JOURNEY, HE CLAIMS TO HAV FOUND AN UNDERGROUND SOCIETY HOUSI RELICS OF AN ANCIENT ALIEN SPACECRAFT
A CLAIM THAT MANY OF HIS COLLEAGUES LATER DISMISSED AS A BLATANT ATTEMPT TO PANDER FOR MORE FUNDING FROM THE UNIVERSITY.
DOCTOR ROSS REX RETURNED TO STELLAR CITY
AND BECAME BITTER WHEN HIS WARNINGS OF DINOSAURS FROM OUTER SPACE WERE LAUGHED OFF.
HIS ARCHEOLOGIC CLAIMS WERE NEV VERIFIED AND HE SL INTO DELUSIONS WORLD DOMINATI

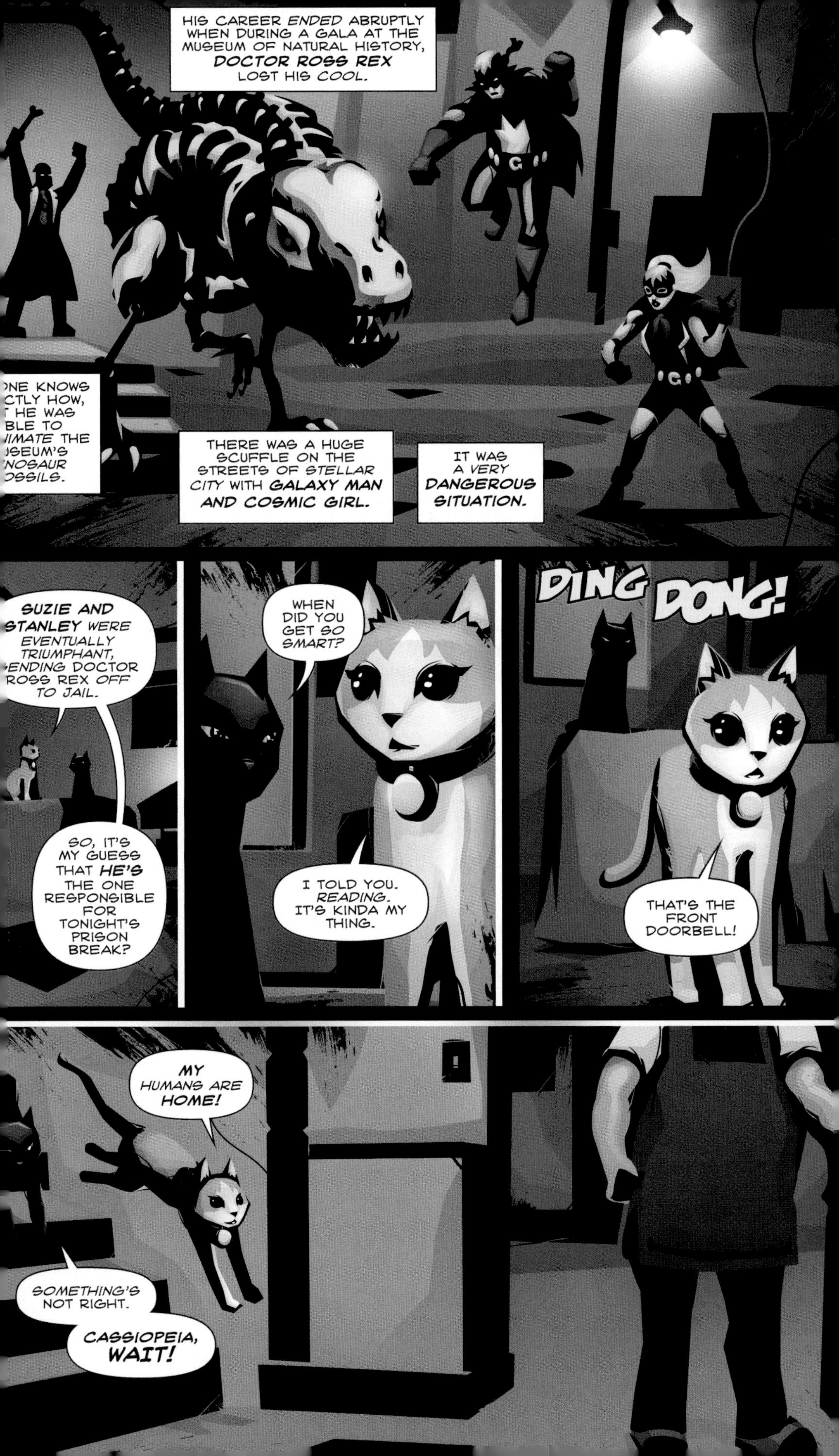
HIS CAREER ENDED ABRUPTLY WHEN DURING A GALA AT THE MUSEUM OF NATURAL HISTORY, DOCTOR ROSS REX LOST HIS COOL.
ONE KNOWS CTLY HOW, HE WAS BLE TO NIMATE THE USEUM'S NOSAUR OSSILS.
THERE WAS A HUGE SCUFFLE ON THE STREETS OF STELLAR CITY WITH GALAXY MAN AND COSMIC GIRL.
IT WAS A VERY DANGEROUS SITUATION.
SUZIE AND STANLEY WERE EVENTUALLY TRIUMPHANT, ENDING DOCTOR ROSS REX OFF TO JAIL.
SO, IT'S MY GUESS THAT HE'S THE ONE RESPONSIBLE FOR TONIGHT'S PRISON BREAK?
WHEN DID YOU GET SO SMART?
I TOLD YOU. READING. IT'S KINDA MY THING.
DING DONG!
THAT'S THE FRONT DOORBELL!
MY HUMANS ARE HOME!
SOMETHING'S NOT RIGHT.
CASSIOPEIA, WAIT!

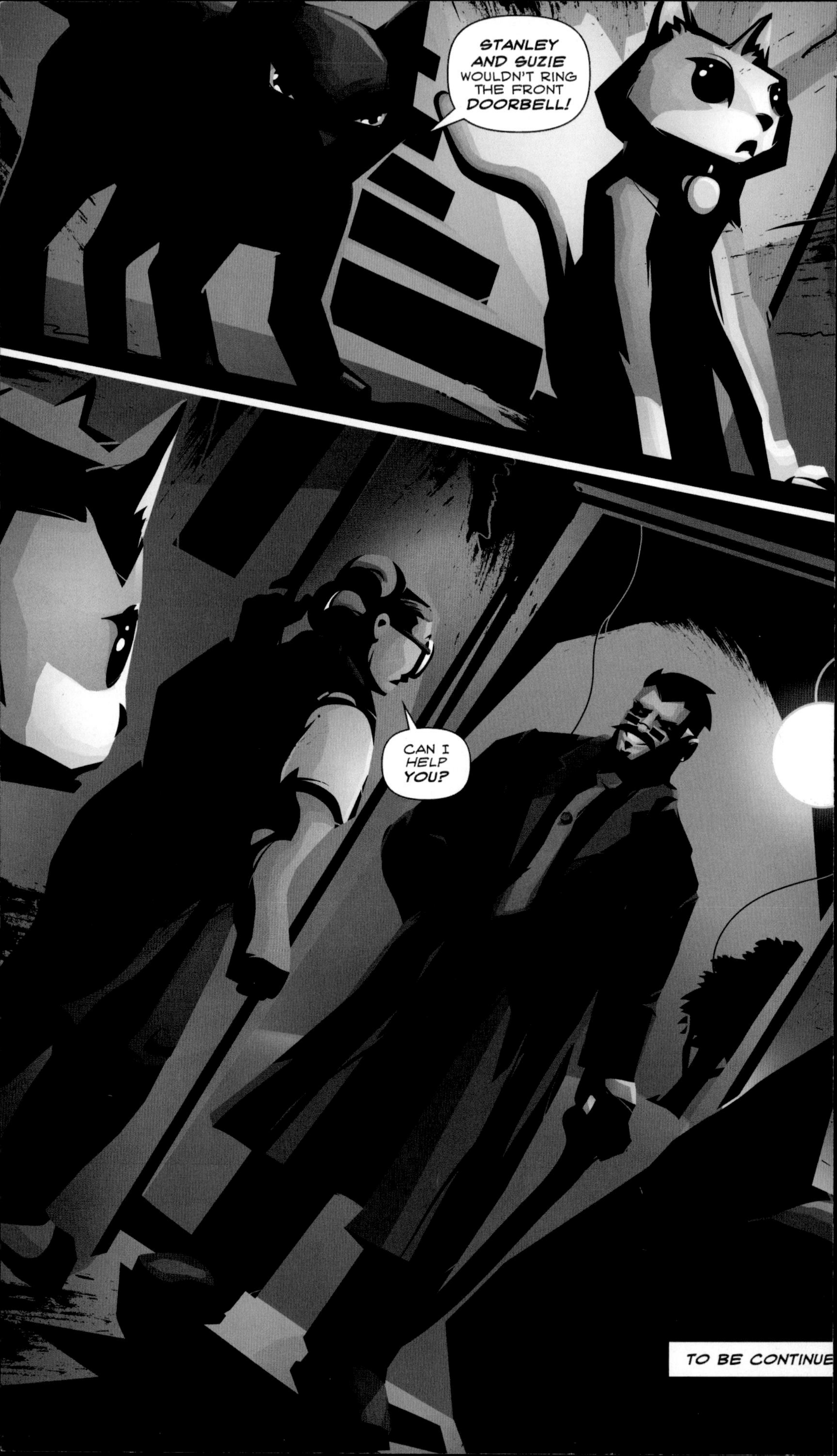
STANLEY AND SUZIE WOULDN'T RING THE FRONT DOORBELL!
CAN I HELP YOU?
TO BE CONTINUE

ER

IDNIGHT

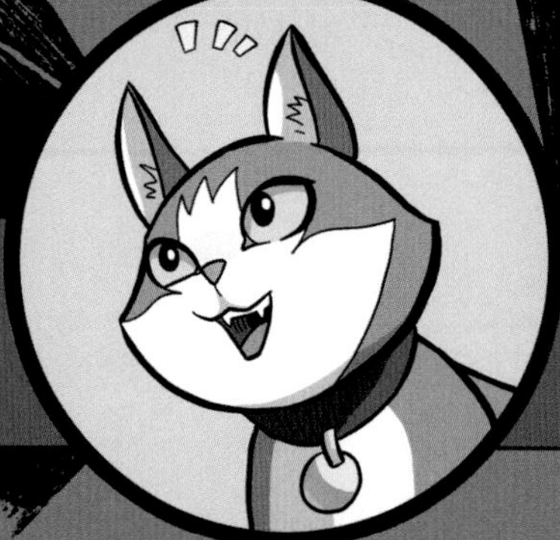

HERO CATS ARE HERE FOR COSMIC GIRL AND ALL THE
PLE OF STELLAR CITY. SUZIE'S SECRET DIARY SURE
) ME A LOT ABOUT HER ADVENTURES, BUT FIRST LET ME
YOU ABOUT OUR TEAM.

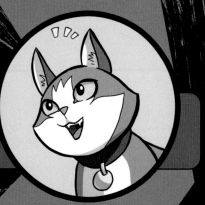

MEET MIDNIGHT'S TEAMMATES!

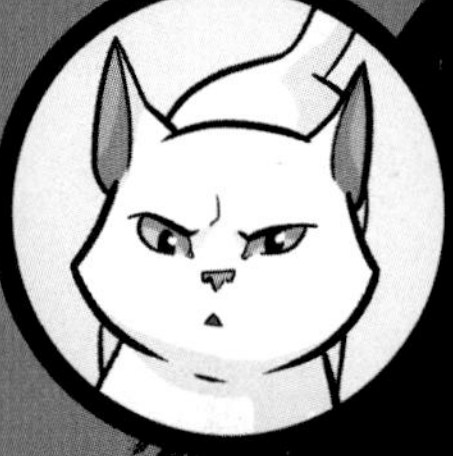

ACE IS ALWAYS READY FOR ACTION! HIS SUPERIOR OFFICER HAS TRAINED HIM WELL. NOW IT IS HIS DUTY TO LEAD THE HERO CATS AND PROTECT STELLAR CITY.

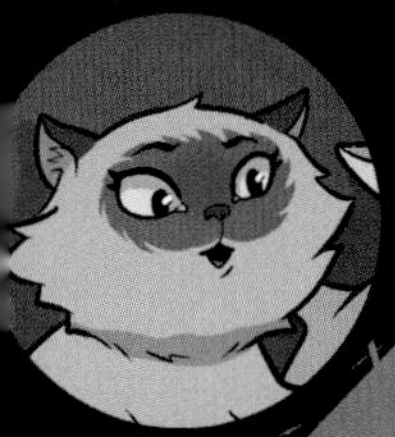

BELLE, DESPITE HER QUESTIONABLE PAST, IS A GREAT ASSET TO THE TEAM. SHE CAN READ THE HUMAN MIND. HER POWERS SEEM TO BE GROWING.

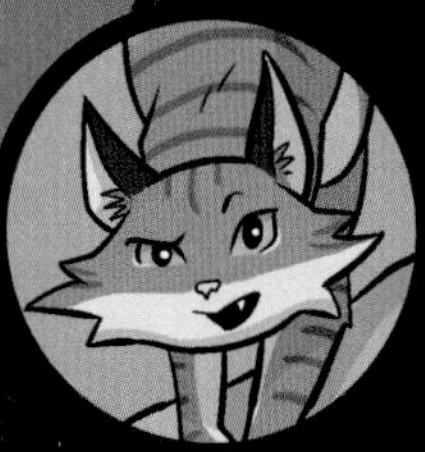

ROCKET IS THE FASTEST CAT ON EARTH AND HAS HIS OWN UFO. HE LOVES TO TINKER WITH MACHINES AND IS VERY RESOURCEFUL.

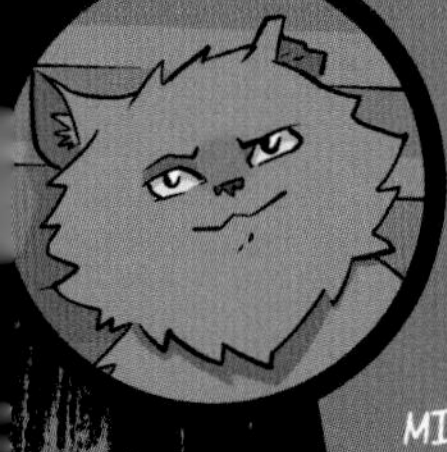

ROCCO NEVER LOSES A FIGHT AND LOVES MOVIES.

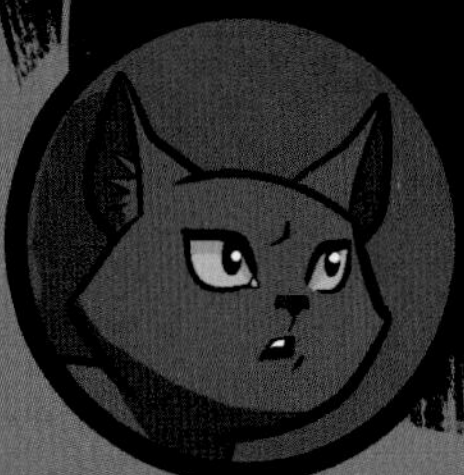

MIDNIGHT IS FOCUSED ON STOPPING CRIMINALS AND SOMETIMES STRIKES OUT ON HIS OWN PATH. SOMETHING'S BEEN BOTHERING HIM LATELY, BUT HE JUST WON'T OPEN UP TO THE REST OF THE TEAM.

OSMIC GIRL SURE KNOWS
HOW TO FIND TROUBLE.
SHE RECENTLY RAN INTO
SPACE PIRATES ON ONE
OF HER TRIPS TO THE
GALILEO SPACE STATION.

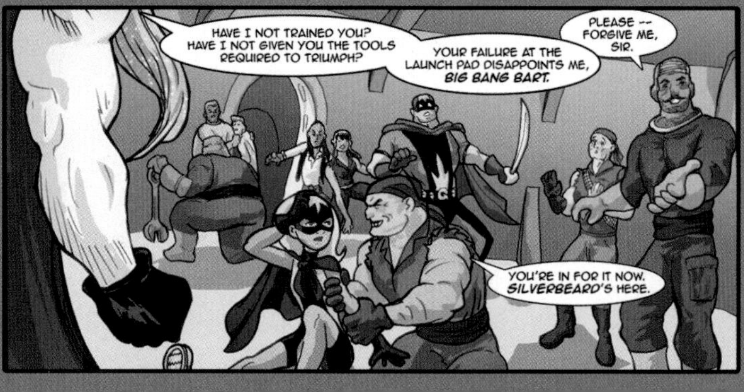
HAVE I NOT TRAINED YOU? HAVE I NOT GIVEN YOU THE TOOLS REQUIRED TO TRIUMPH?
YOUR FAILURE AT THE LAUNCH PAD DISAPPOINTS ME, BIG BANG BART.
PLEASE -- FORGIVE ME, SIR.
YOU'RE IN FOR IT NOW. SILVERBEARD'S HERE.

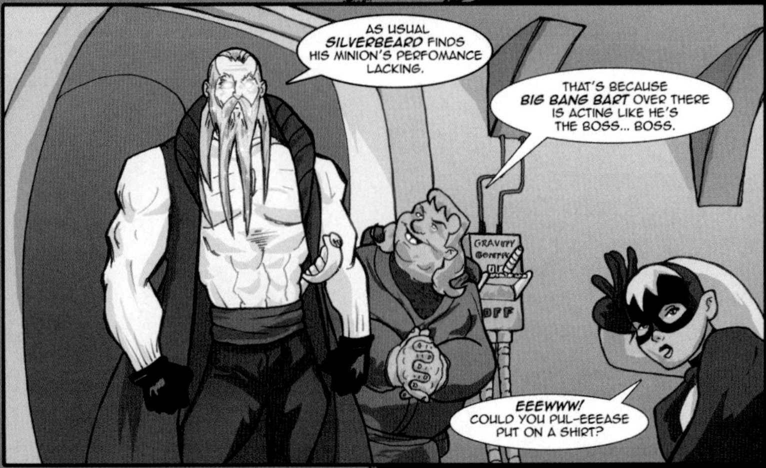
AS USUAL **SILVERBEARD** FINDS HIS MINION'S PERFOMANCE LACKING.
THAT'S BECAUSE **BIG BANG BART** OVER THERE IS ACTING LIKE HE'S THE BOSS... BOSS.
OFF
EEEWWW! COULD YOU PUL-EEEASE PUT ON A SHIRT?

COSMIC GIRL DID HER BEST TO HELP HER DAD, BUT SILVER BEARD WAS DETERMINED TO FIND OUT WHERE GALAXY MAN GOT HIS POWERS.

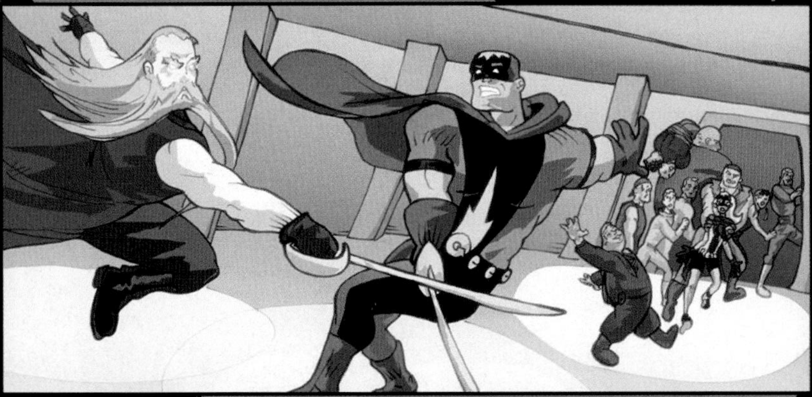

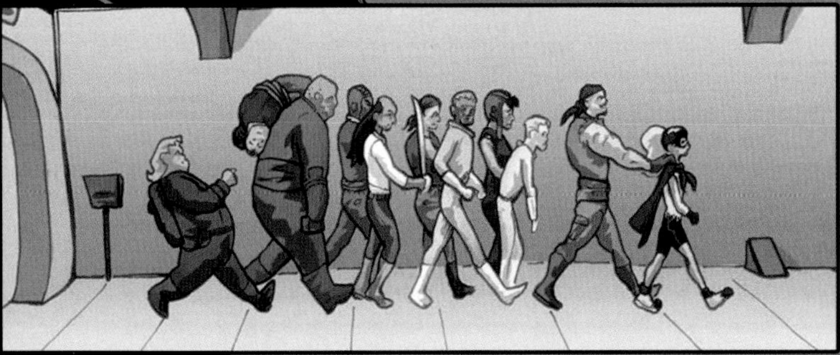

EVENTUALLY SHE WAS CAPTURED WITH THE RES THE STATION'S CREW.

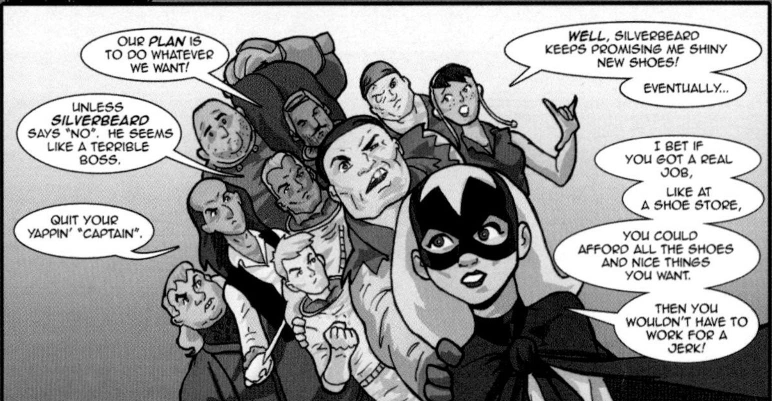
OUR **PLAN** IS TO DO WHATEVER WE WANT!
WELL, SILVERBEARD KEEPS PROMISING ME SHINY NEW SHOES!
EVENTUALLY...
UNLESS **SILVERBEARD** SAYS "NO". HE SEEMS LIKE A TERRIBLE BOSS.
I BET IF YOU GOT A REAL JOB,
LIKE AT A SHOE STORE,
QUIT YOUR YAPPIN' "CAPTAIN".
YOU COULD AFFORD ALL THE SHOES AND NICE THINGS YOU WANT.
THEN YOU WOULDN'T HAVE TO WORK FOR A JERK!

BUT COMIC GIRL FO A WAY TO TALK HERS OUT OF A DIFFICUL SITUATION.

*Galaxy Man #4 is published through Galactic Press and available at www.herocatsonline.com

ALAXY MAN EVENTUALLY
FEATED SILVER BEARD,
IIS PIRATES ENDED UP
AIL, THAT IS UNTIL DR
ROSS REX HELPED
THEM ESCAPE.

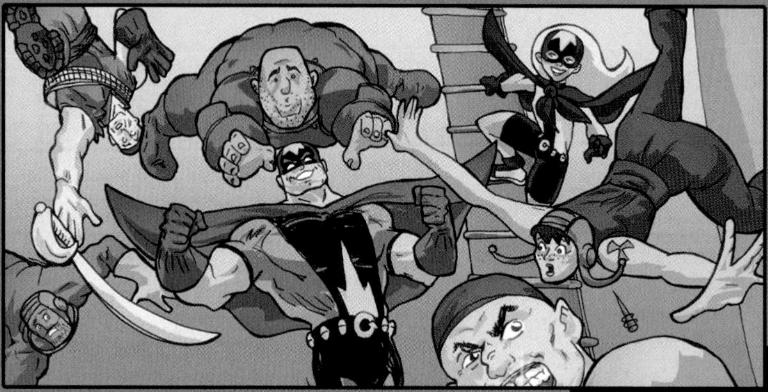

GOOD THING MIDNIGHT STOPPED BOTH
BIG BANG BART AND DOGSTAR DIEGO.
THE HERO CATS ARE ON THE JOB.

THE STORY CONTINUES IN
HERO CATS: MIDNIGHT
OVER STELLAR CITY #2
VOLUME 2.

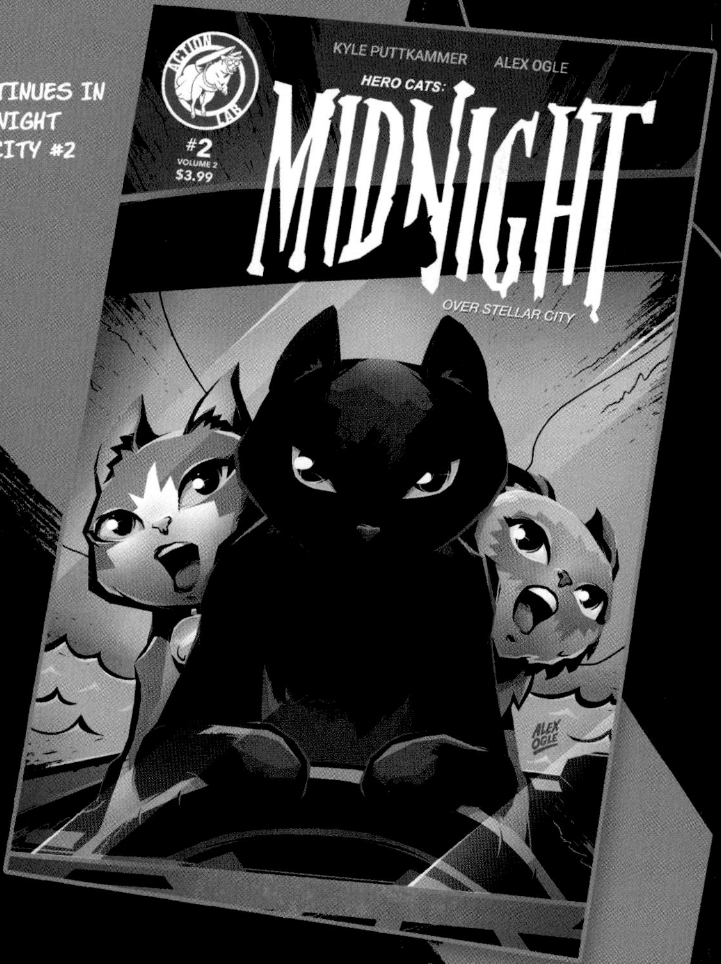
KYLE PUTTKAMMER
ALEX OGLE
HERO CATS:
MIDNIGHT
OVER STELLAR CITY
#2
VOLUME 2
$3.99
ALEX OGLE

TION LAB ENTERTAINMENT
an Seaton - Publisher
ve Dwonch - President of Marketing
awn Gabborin - Editor in Chief
on Martin - Publisher - Danger Zone
cole D'Andria - Marking Director
n Dietz - Social Media Manager
tt Bradley - CFO
ad Cicconi - Over the moon

o Cats: Midnight Over Stellar City #1 Volume 2, June 2017

ted in Canada.

t Printing.

VOLUME ONE
COVER GALLERY

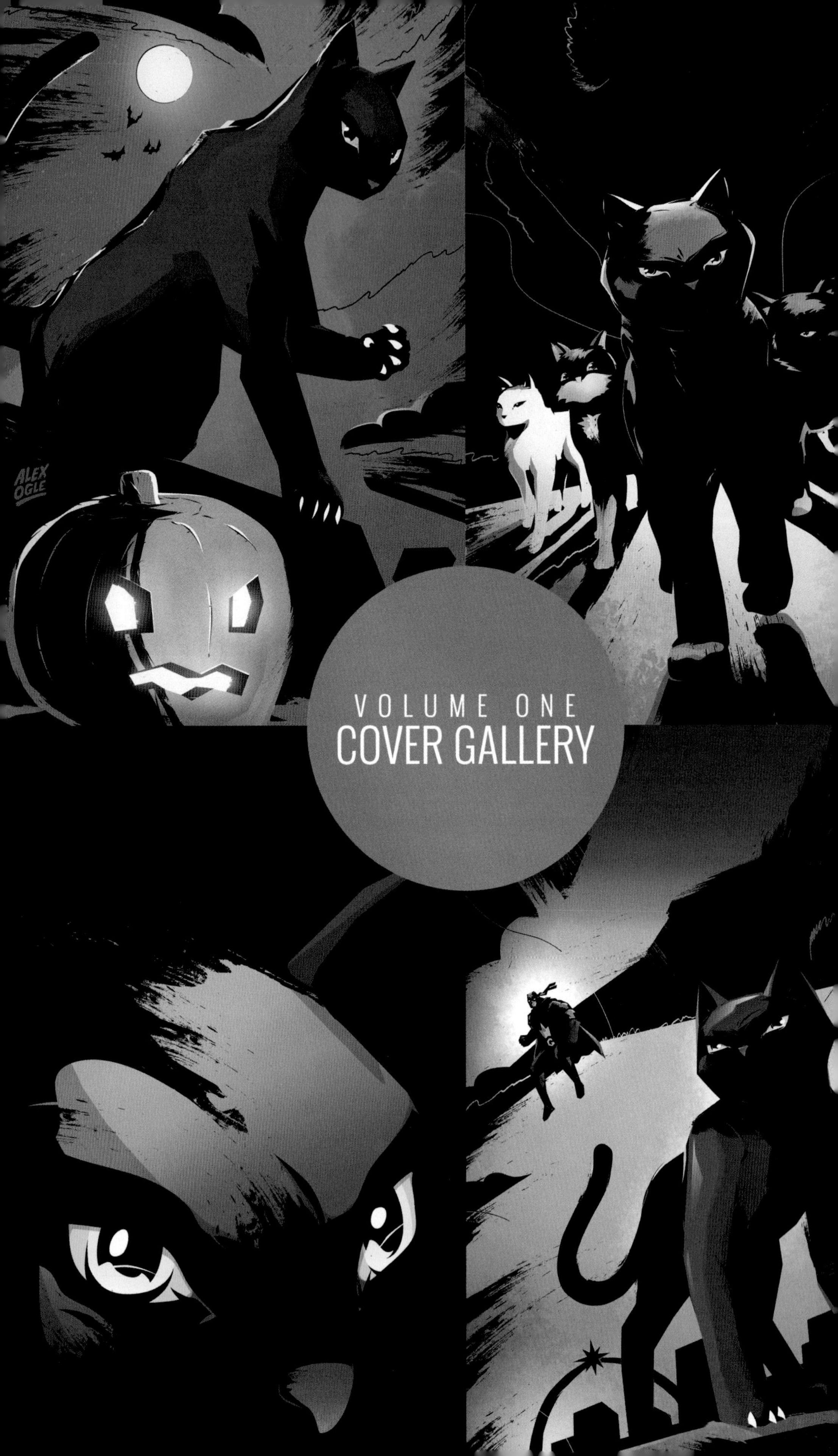
ALEX
OGLE

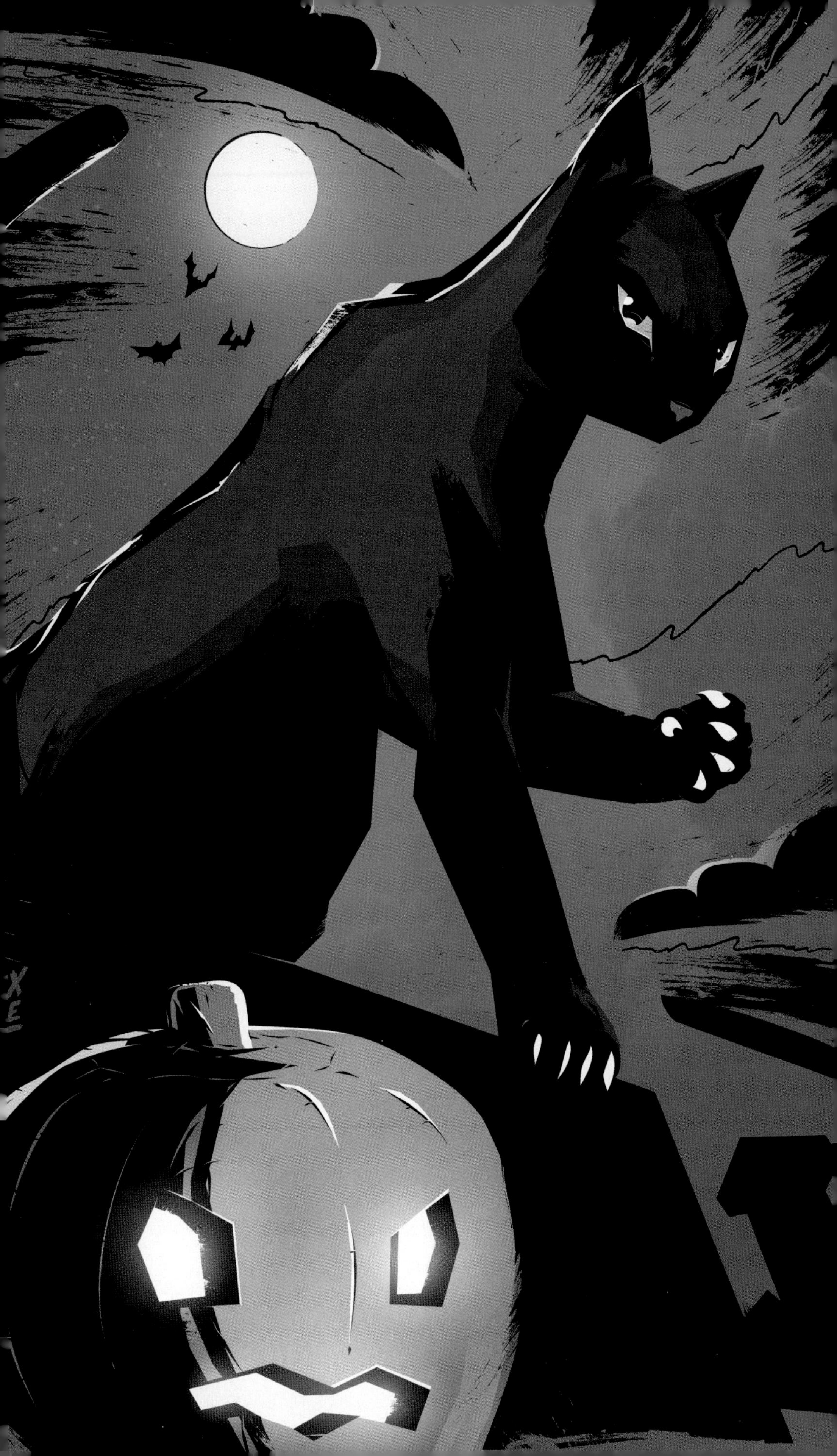

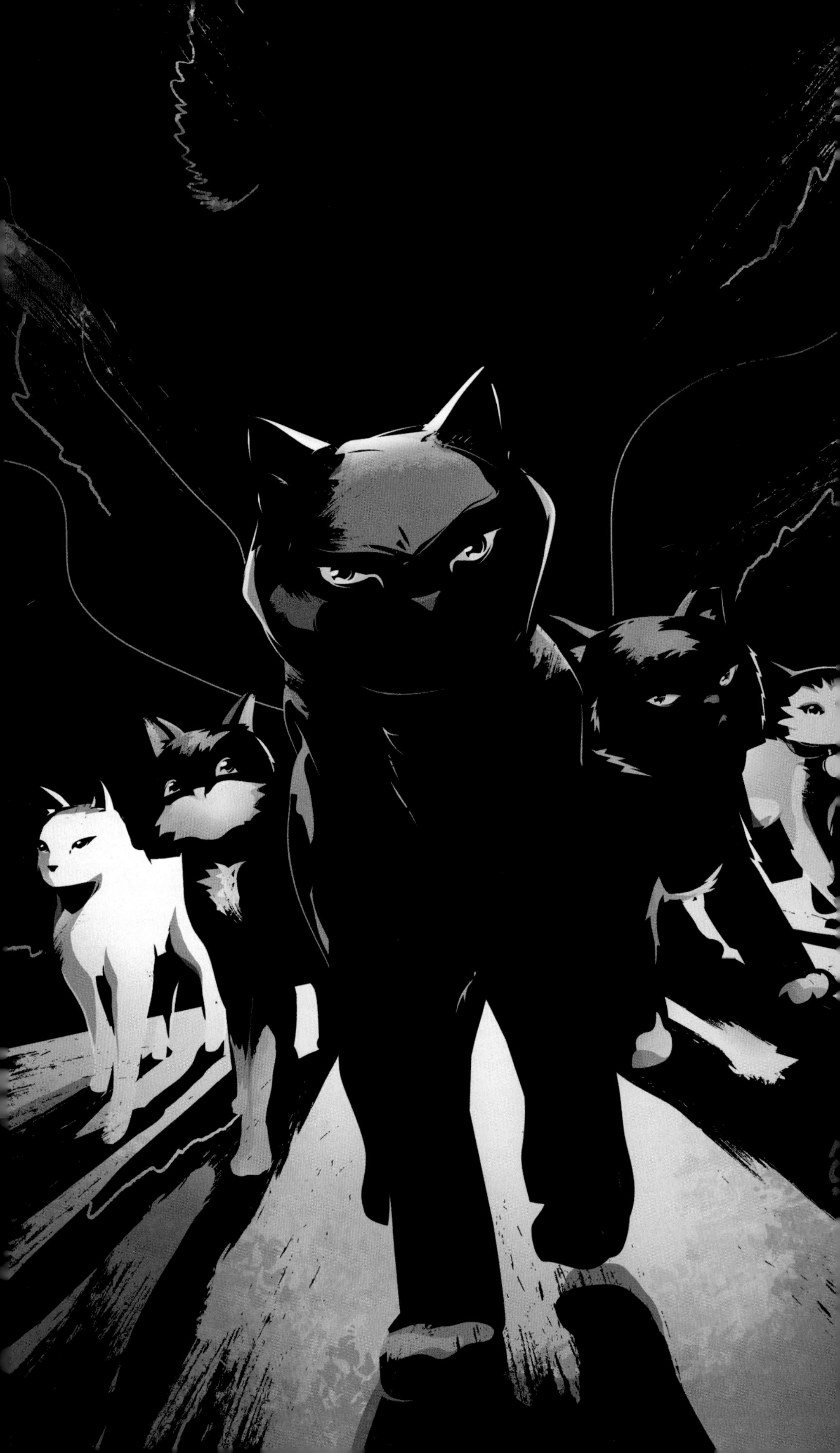

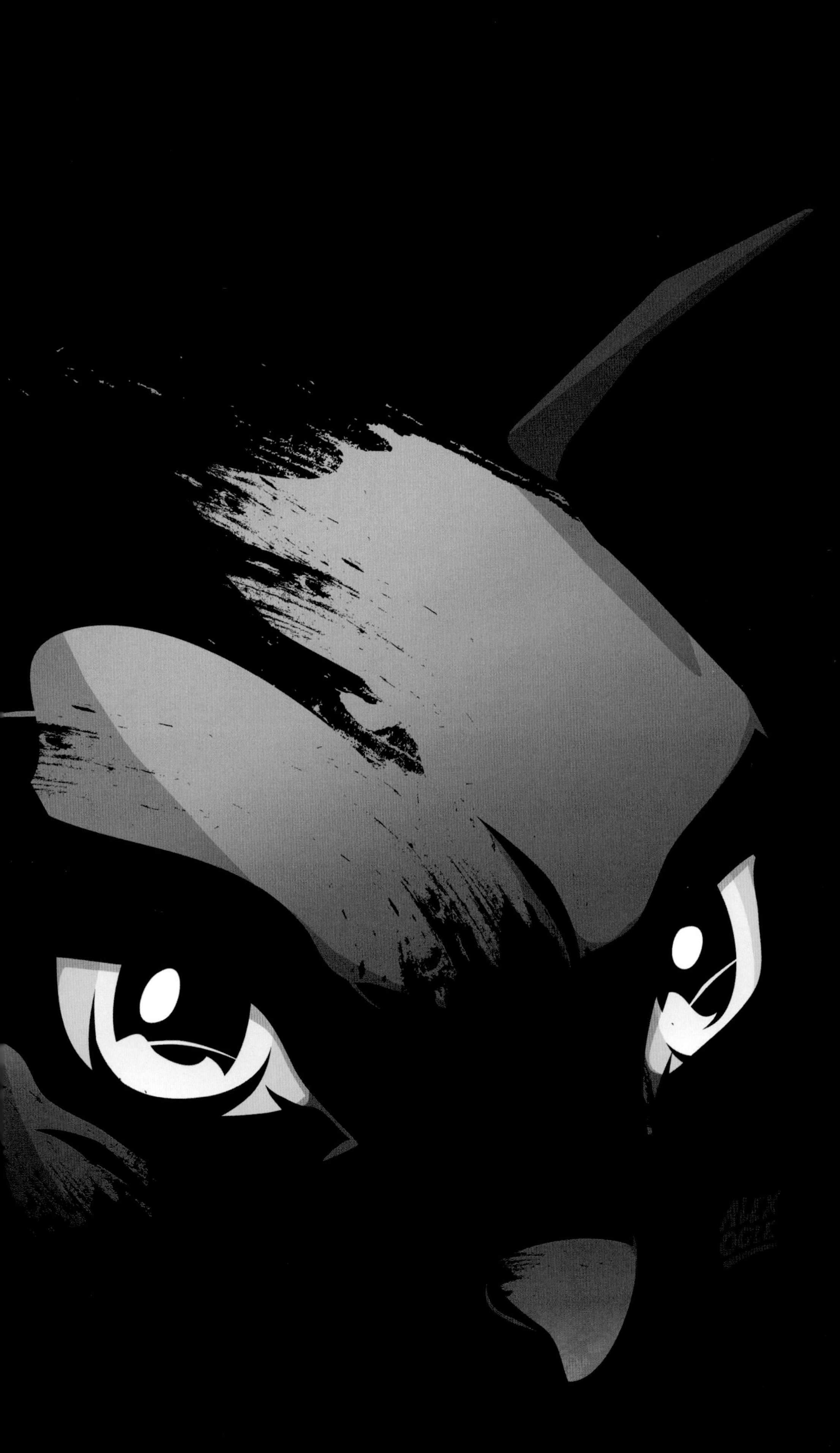
ALEX OGLE

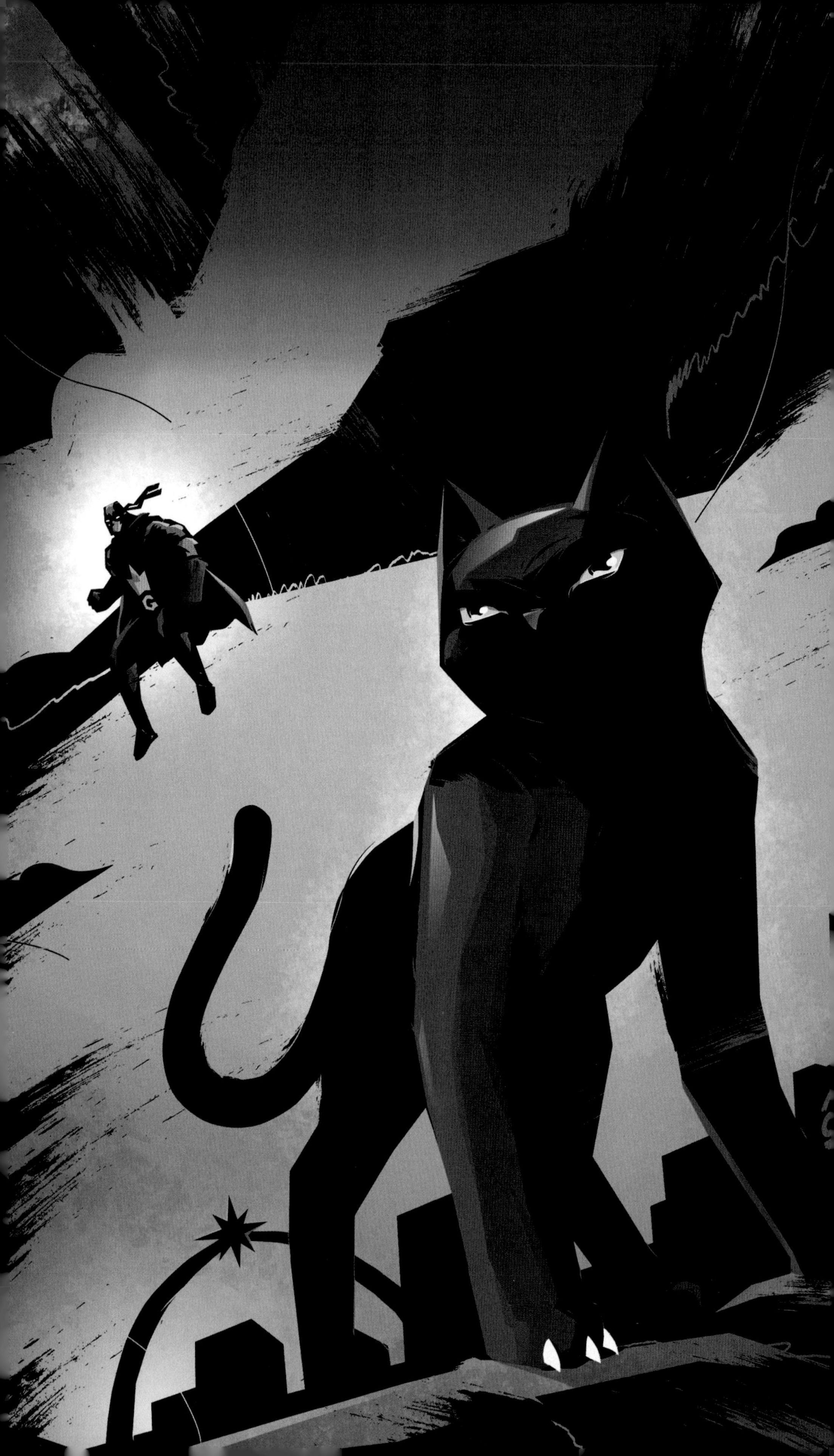

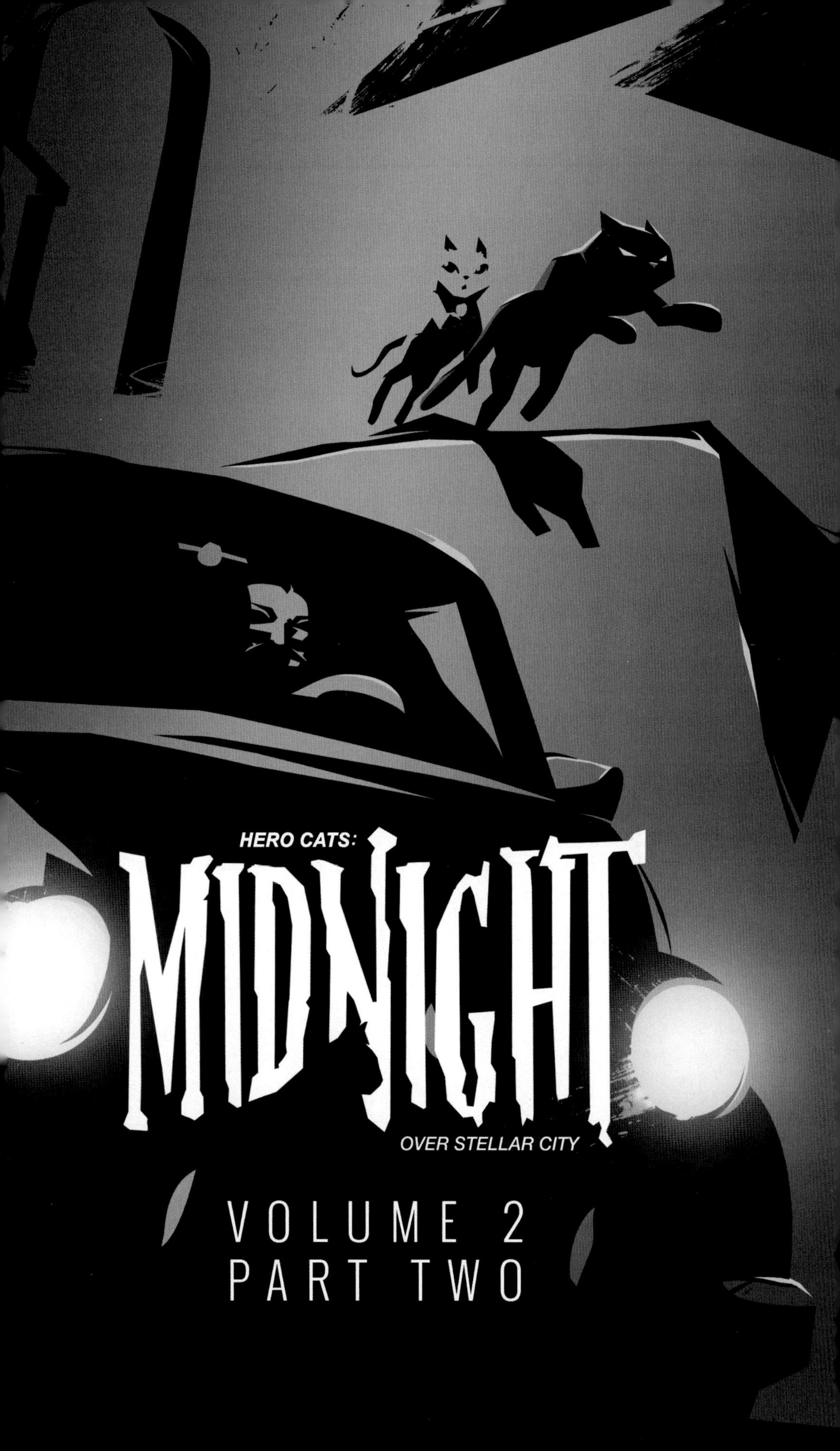
HERO CATS:
MIDNIGHT
OVER STELLAR CITY
VOLUME 2
PART TWO

THE CREATIVE TEAM

WRITTEN AND CREATED BY
KYLE PUTTKAMMER

ART AND LETTERS BY
ALEX OGLE

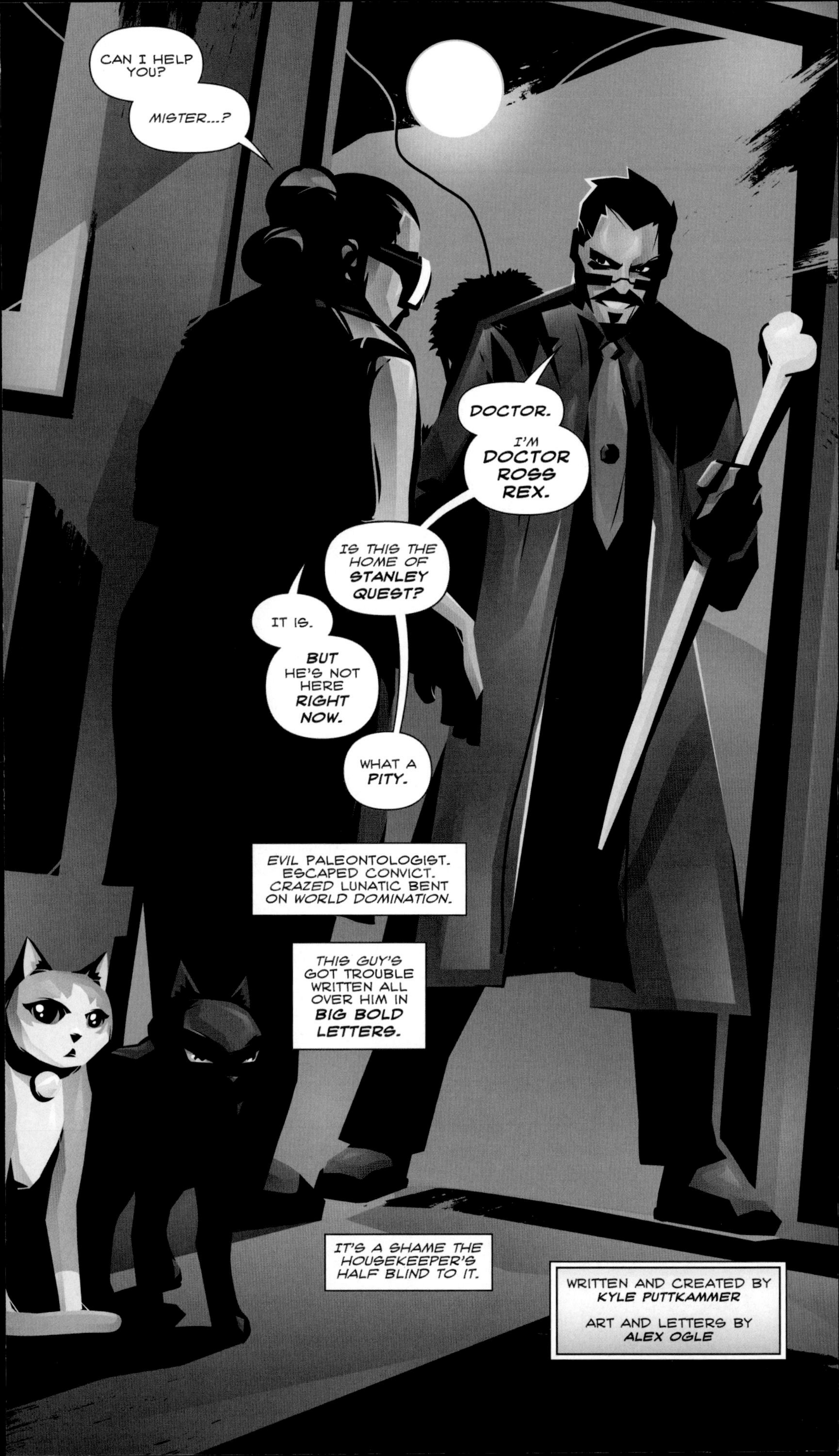
CAN I HELP YOU?
MISTER...?
DOCTOR.
I'M DOCTOR ROSS REX.
IS THIS THE HOME OF STANLEY QUEST?
IT IS.
BUT HE'S NOT HERE RIGHT NOW.
WHAT A PITY.
EVIL PALEONTOLOGIST. ESCAPED CONVICT. CRAZED LUNATIC BENT ON WORLD DOMINATION.
THIS GUY'S GOT TROUBLE WRITTEN ALL OVER HIM IN BIG BOLD LETTERS.
IT'S A SHAME THE HOUSEKEEPER'S HALF BLIND TO IT.
WRITTEN AND CREATED BY KYLE PUTTKAMMER
ART AND LETTERS BY ALEX OGLE

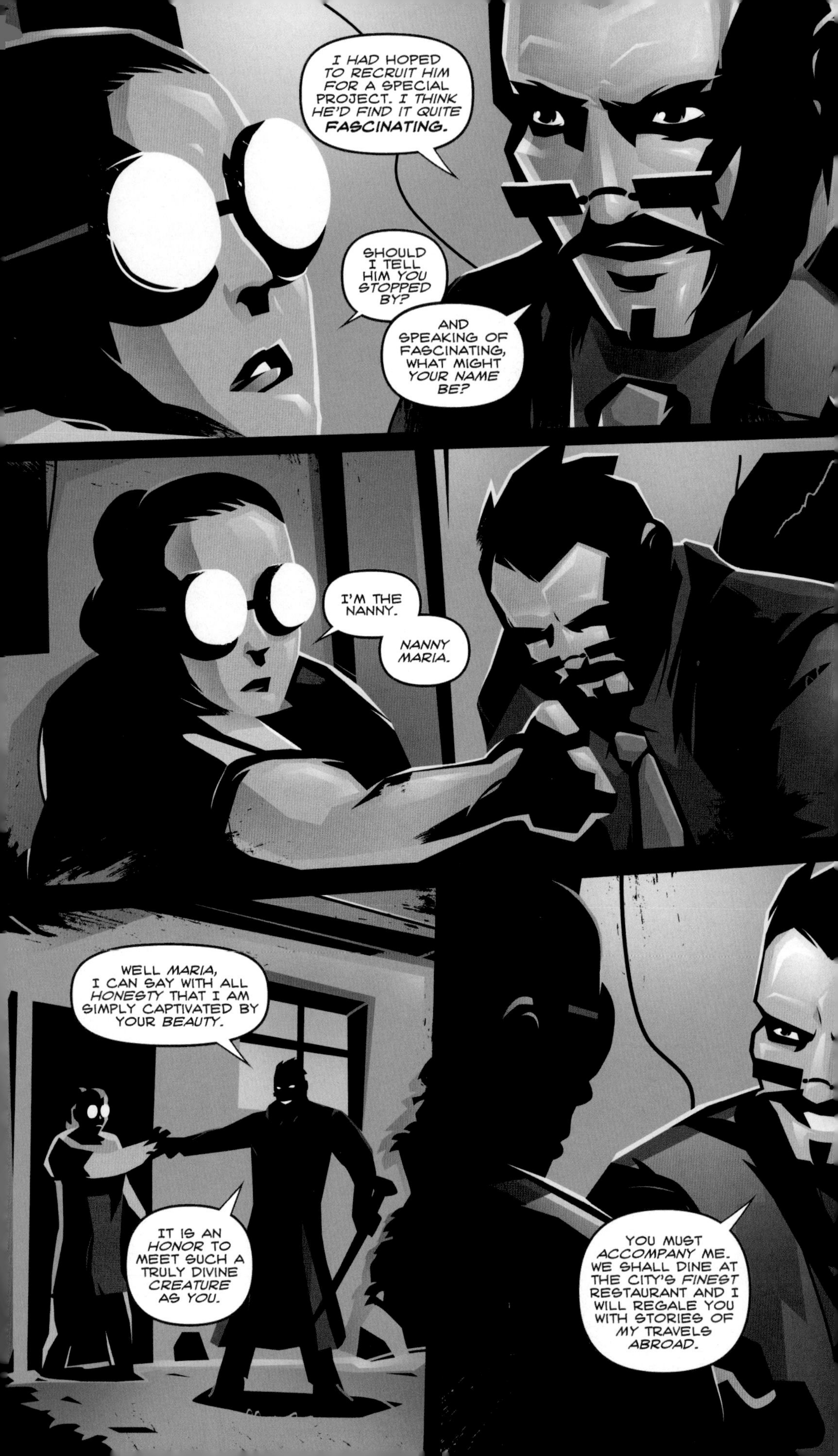
I HAD HOPED TO RECRUIT HIM FOR A SPECIAL PROJECT. I THINK HE'D FIND IT QUITE **FASCINATING.**
SHOULD I TELL HIM *YOU* STOPPED BY?
AND SPEAKING OF FASCINATING, WHAT MIGHT *YOUR NAME* BE?
I'M THE NANNY.
NANNY MARIA.
WELL *MARIA*, I CAN SAY WITH ALL *HONESTY* THAT I AM SIMPLY CAPTIVATED BY YOUR *BEAUTY*.
IT IS AN *HONOR* TO MEET SUCH A TRULY DIVINE *CREATURE* AS YOU.
YOU MUST *ACCOMPANY* ME. WE SHALL DINE AT THE CITY'S *FINEST* RESTAURANT AND I WILL REGALE YOU WITH STORIES OF *MY TRAVELS ABROAD*.

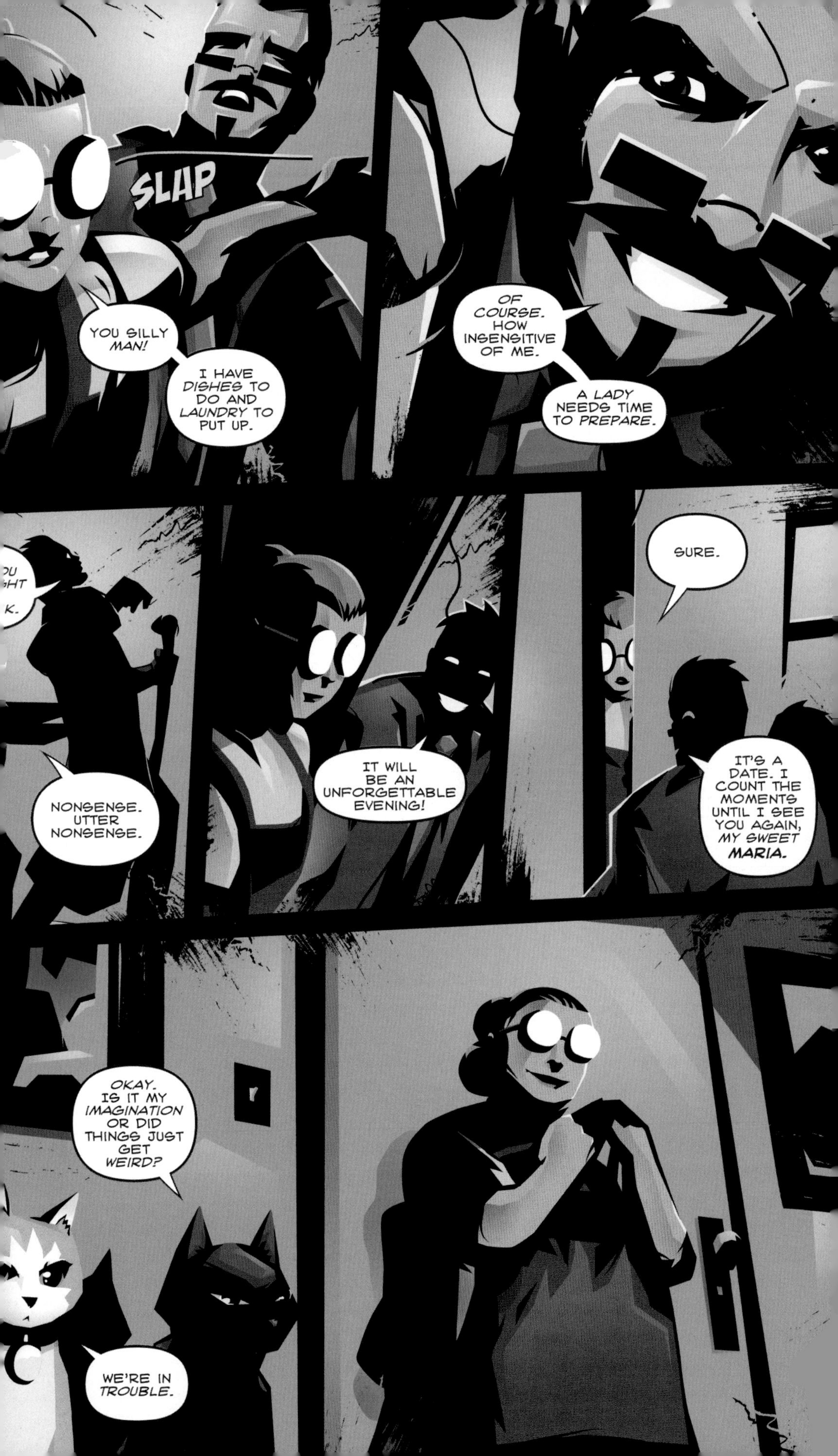
SLAP
YOU SILLY MAN!
I HAVE DISHES TO DO AND LAUNDRY TO PUT UP.
OF COURSE. HOW INSENSITIVE OF ME.
A LADY NEEDS TIME TO PREPARE.
NONSENSE. UTTER NONSENSE.
IT WILL BE AN UNFORGETTABLE EVENING!
SURE.
IT'S A DATE. I COUNT THE MOMENTS UNTIL I SEE YOU AGAIN, MY SWEET MARIA.
OKAY. IS IT MY IMAGINATION OR DID THINGS JUST GET WEIRD?
WE'RE IN TROUBLE.

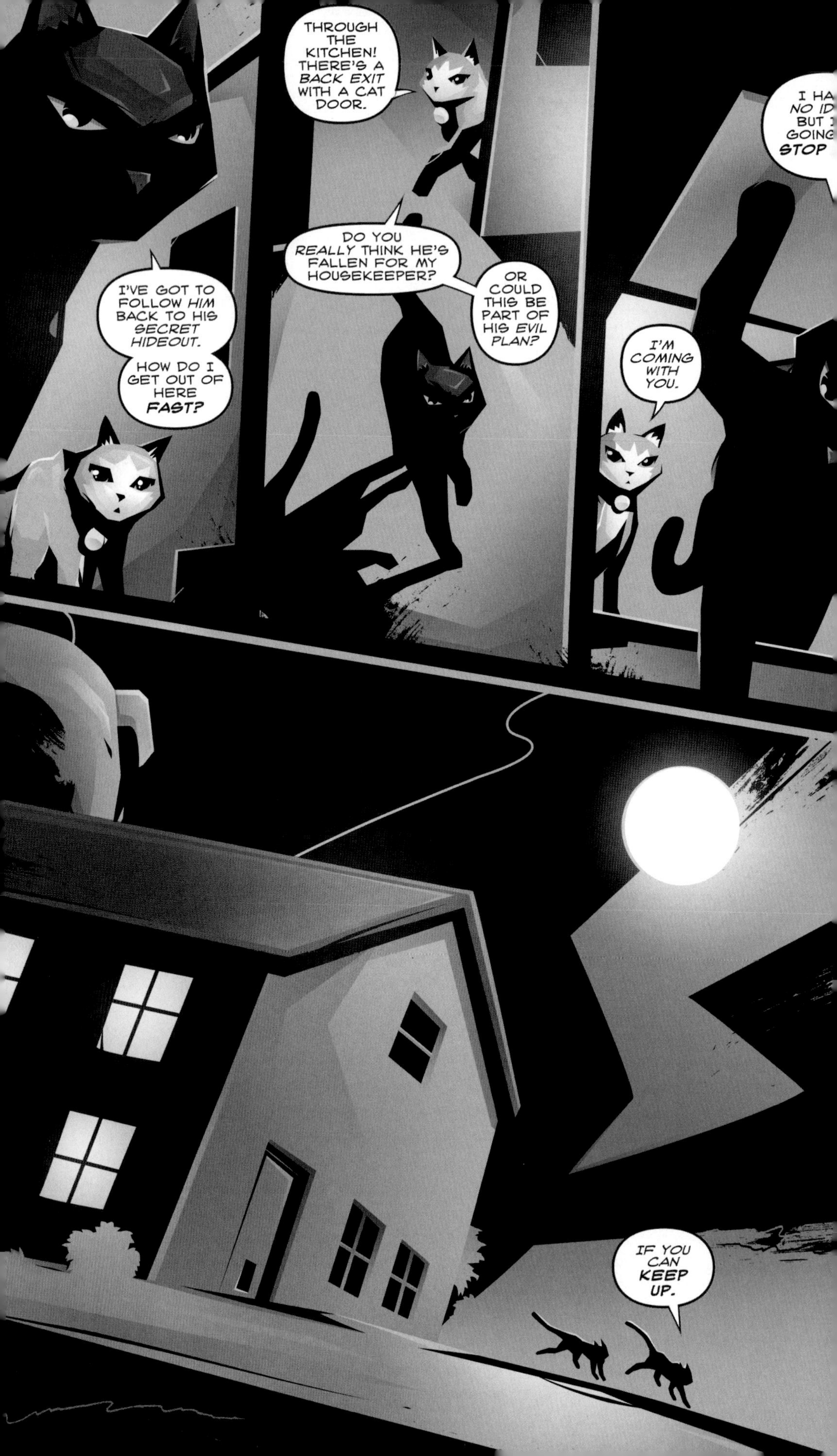
I'VE GOT TO FOLLOW *HIM* BACK TO HIS *SECRET HIDEOUT.*
HOW DO I GET OUT OF HERE **FAST?**
THROUGH THE KITCHEN! THERE'S A *BACK EXIT* WITH A CAT DOOR.
DO YOU *REALLY* THINK HE'S FALLEN FOR MY HOUSEKEEPER?
OR COULD THIS BE PART OF HIS *EVIL PLAN?*
I'M COMING WITH YOU.
IF YOU CAN **KEEP UP.**

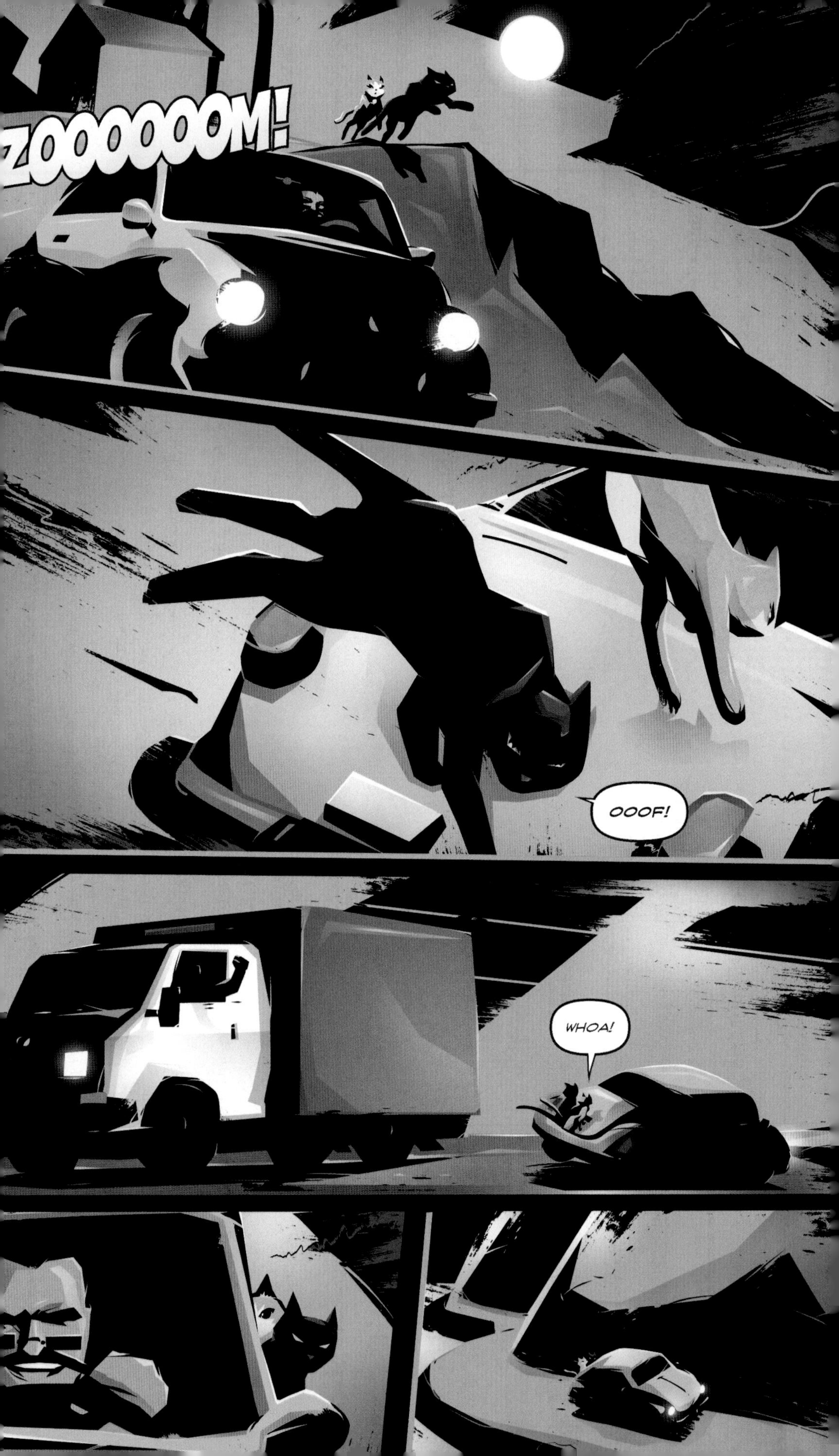
ZOOOOOOM!
OOOF!
WHOA!

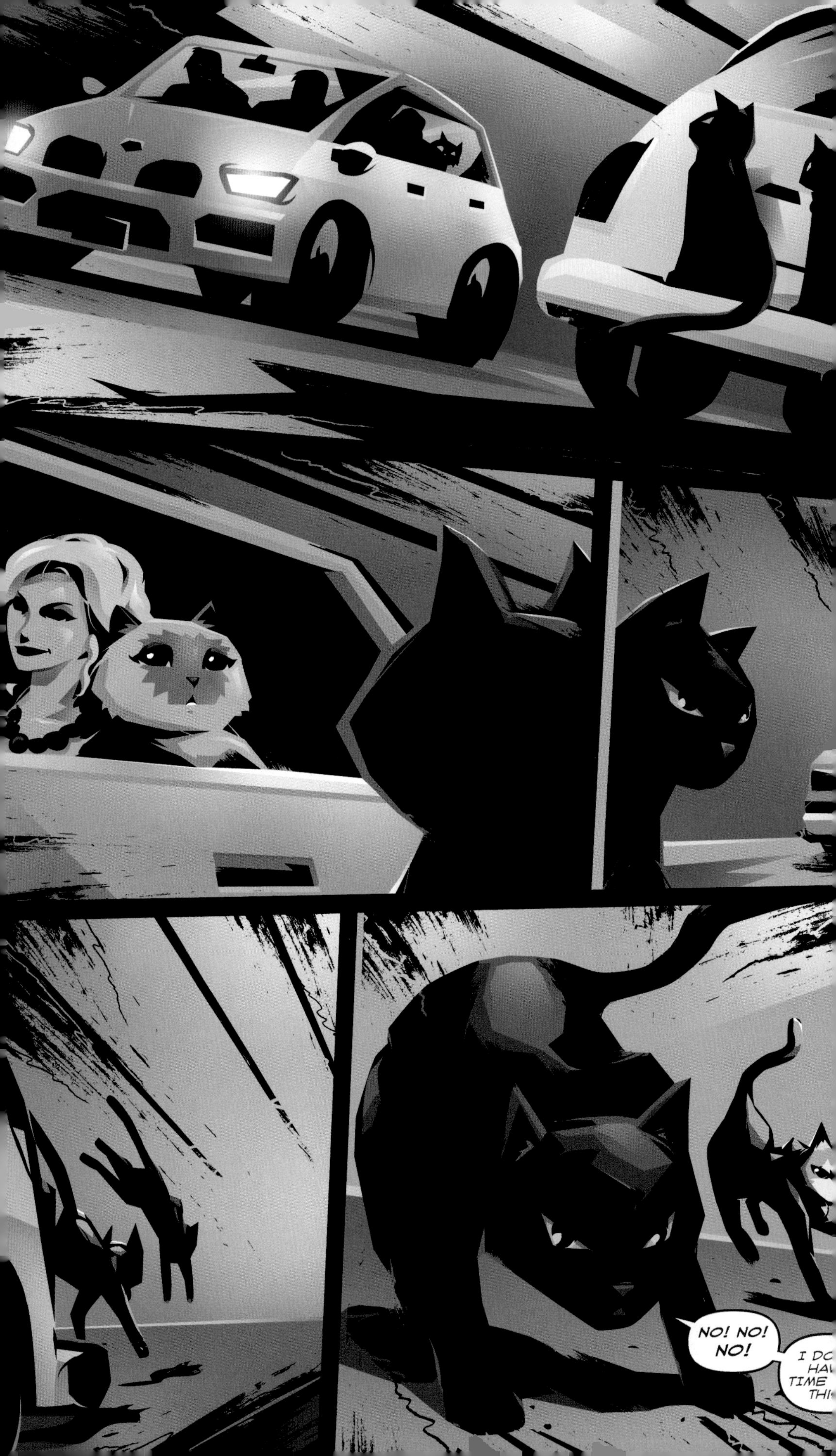
NO! NO! NO!

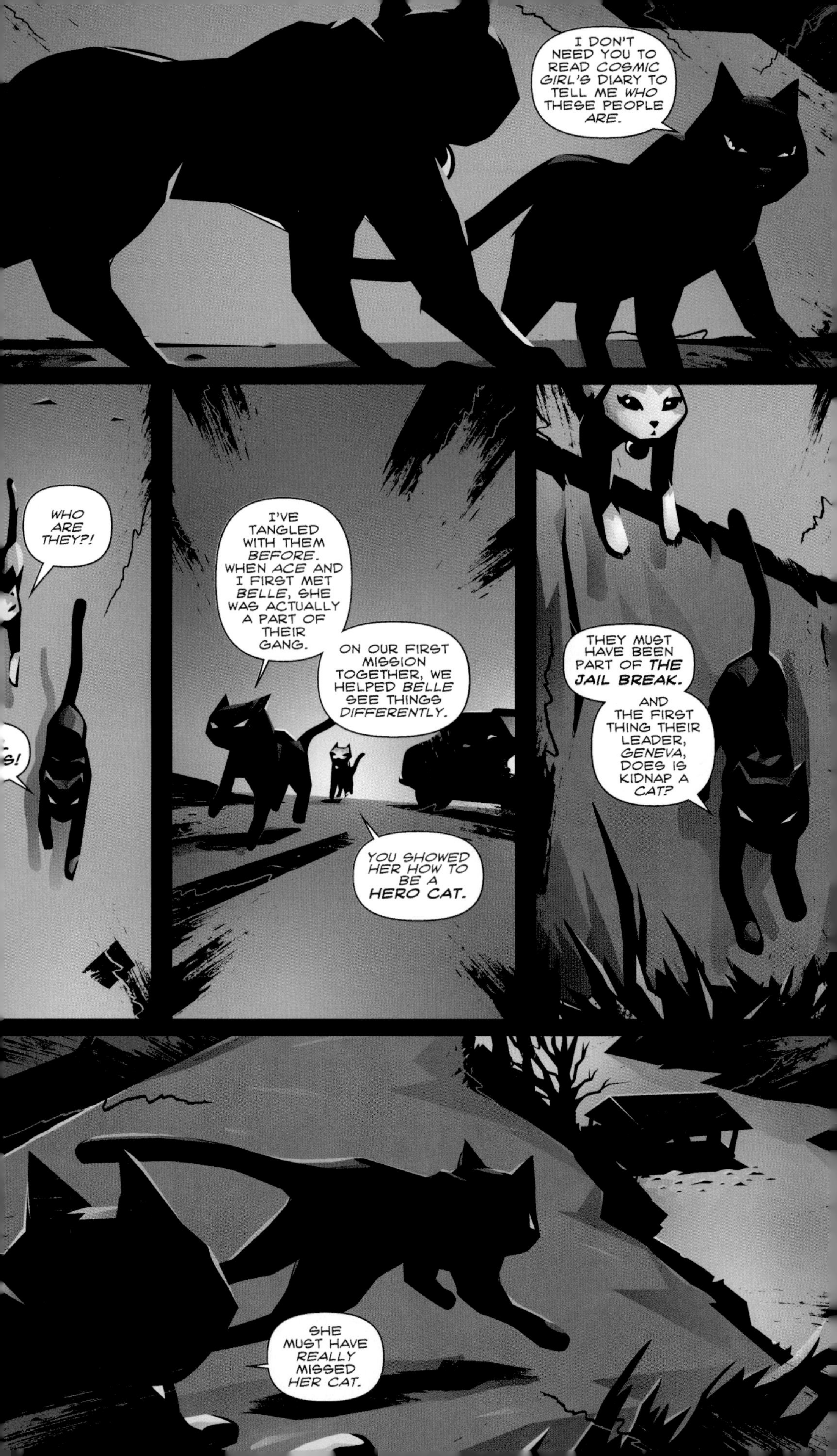
I DON'T NEED YOU TO READ COSMIC GIRL'S DIARY TO TELL ME WHO THESE PEOPLE ARE.
WHO ARE THEY?!
I'VE TANGLED WITH THEM BEFORE. WHEN ACE AND I FIRST MET BELLE, SHE WAS ACTUALLY A PART OF THEIR GANG.
ON OUR FIRST MISSION TOGETHER, WE HELPED BELLE SEE THINGS DIFFERENTLY.
YOU SHOWED HER HOW TO BE A HERO CAT.
THEY MUST HAVE BEEN PART OF THE JAIL BREAK.
AND THE FIRST THING THEIR LEADER, GENEVA, DOES IS KIDNAP A CAT?
SHE MUST HAVE REALLY MISSED HER CAT.

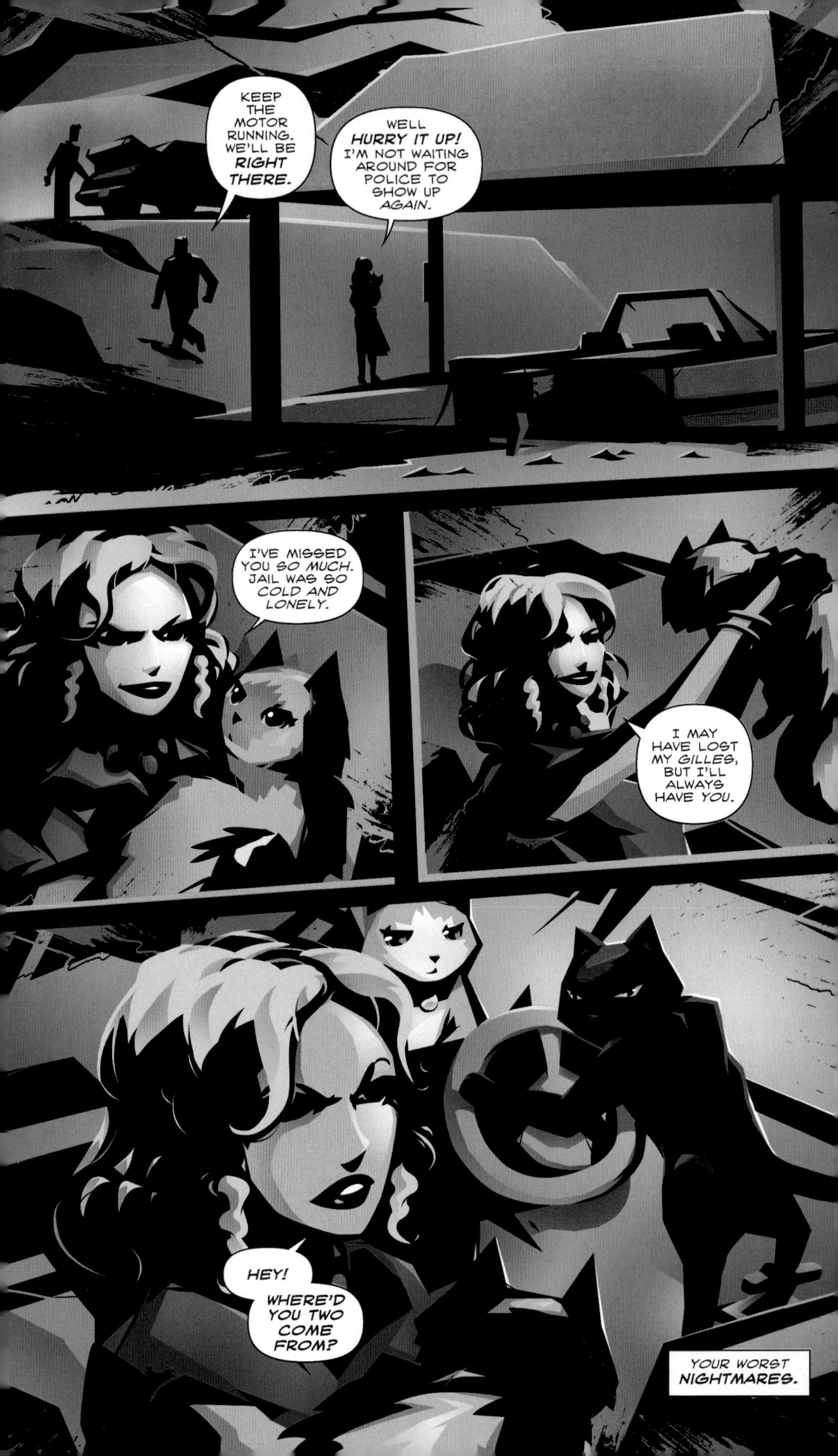
KEEP THE MOTOR RUNNING. WE'LL BE RIGHT THERE.
WELL HURRY IT UP! I'M NOT WAITING AROUND FOR POLICE TO SHOW UP AGAIN.
I'VE MISSED YOU SO MUCH. JAIL WAS SO COLD AND LONELY.
I MAY HAVE LOST MY GILLES, BUT I'LL ALWAYS HAVE YOU.
HEY!
WHERE'D YOU TWO COME FROM?
YOUR WORST NIGHTMARES.

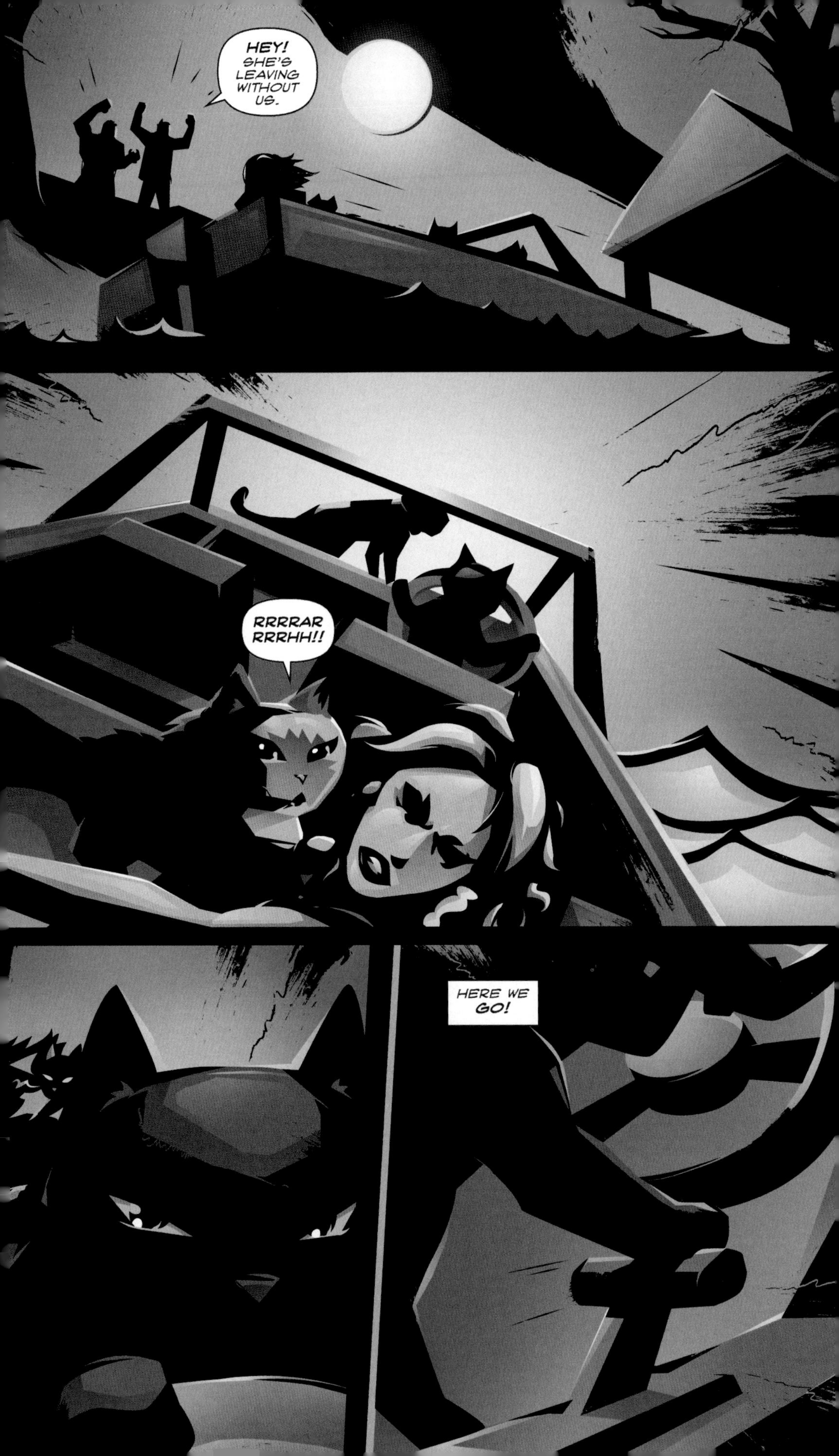
HEY! SHE'S LEAVING WITHOUT US.
RRRRAR RRRHH!!
HERE WE GO!

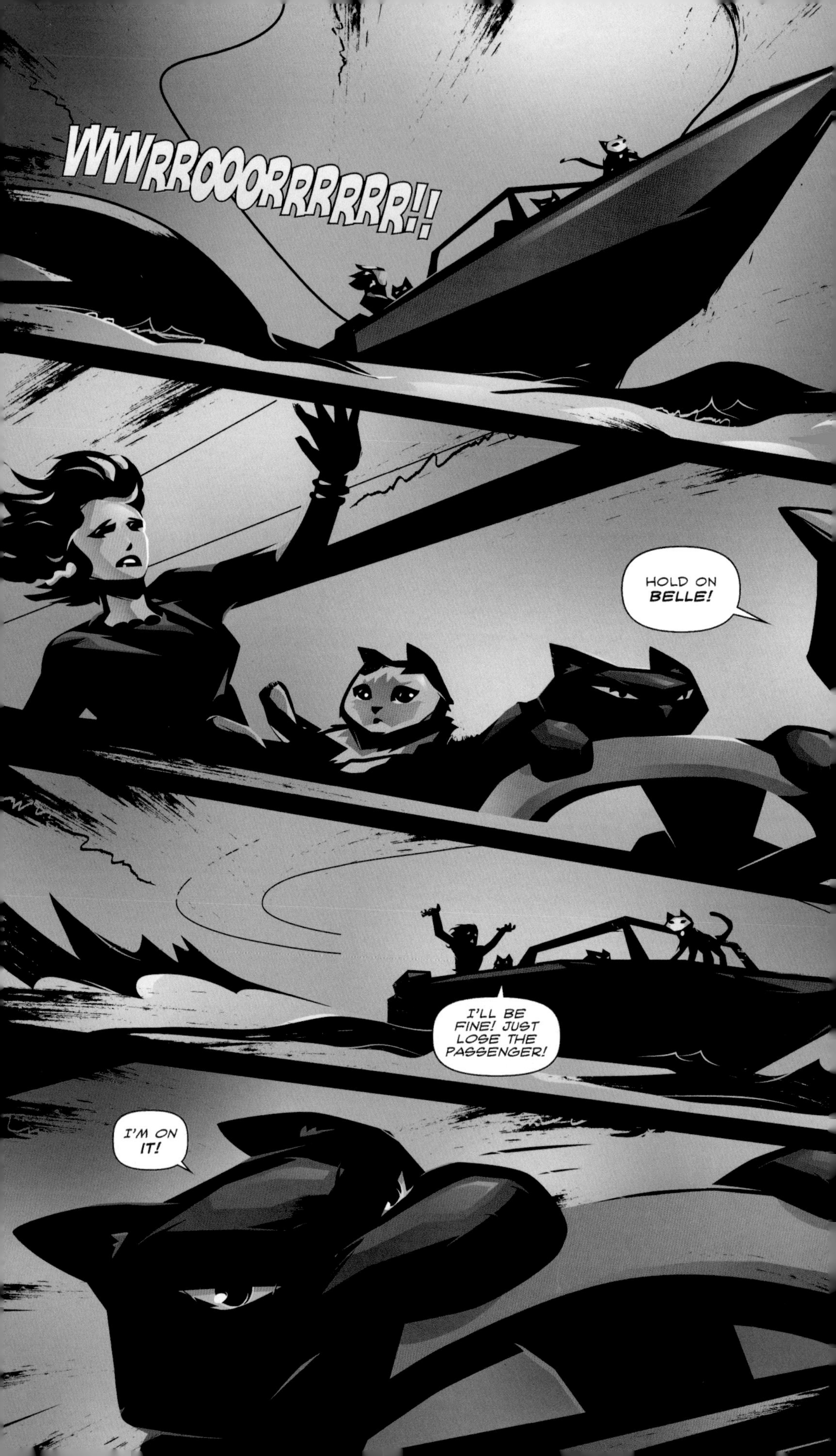
WWRROOORRRRRR!!
HOLD ON BELLE!
I'LL BE FINE! JUST LOSE THE PASSENGER!
I'M ON IT!

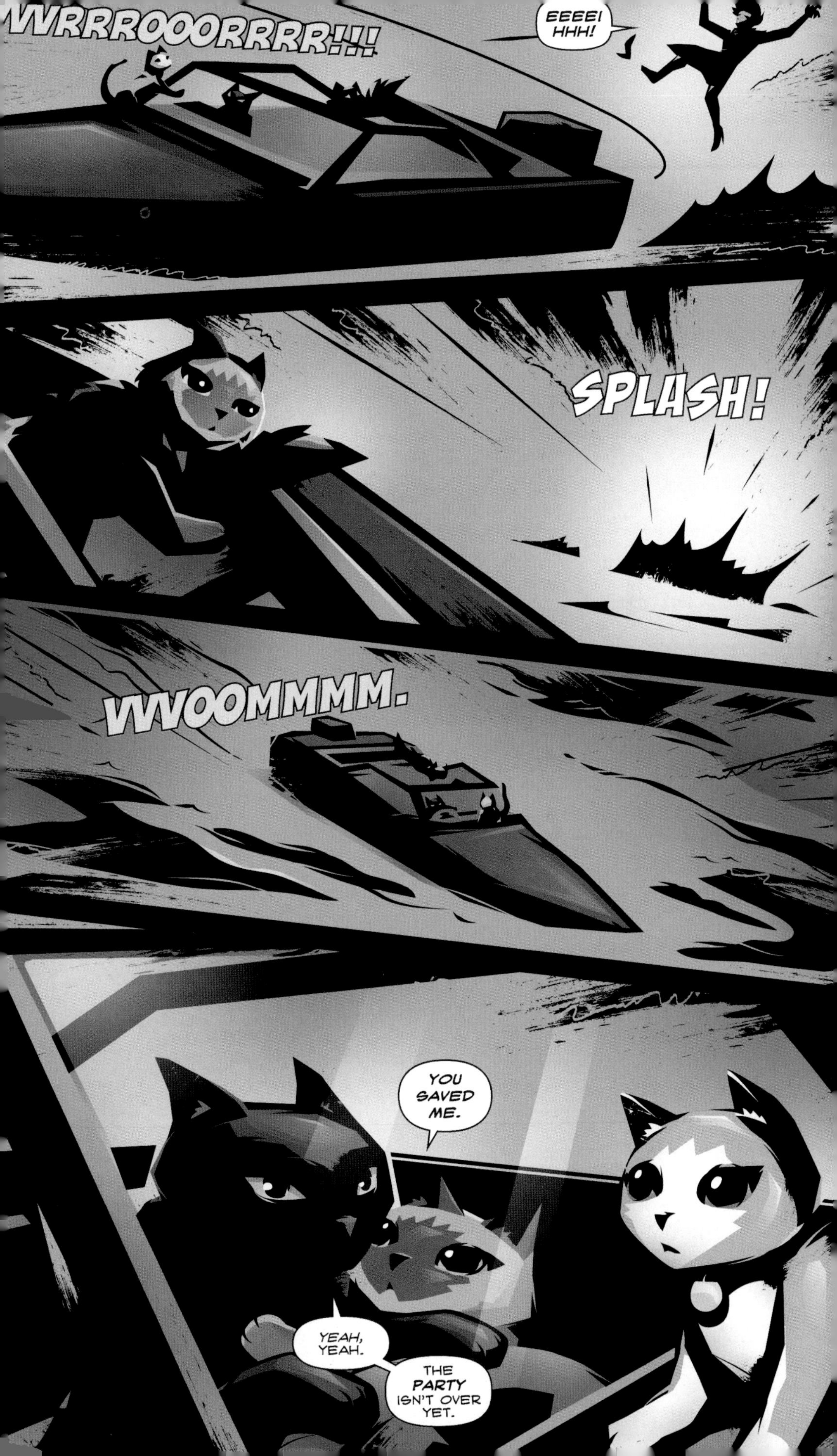
VVRRROOORRRR!!!
EEEEI HHH!
SPLASH!
VVVOOMMMM.
YOU SAVED ME.
YEAH, YEAH.
THE PARTY ISN'T OVER YET.

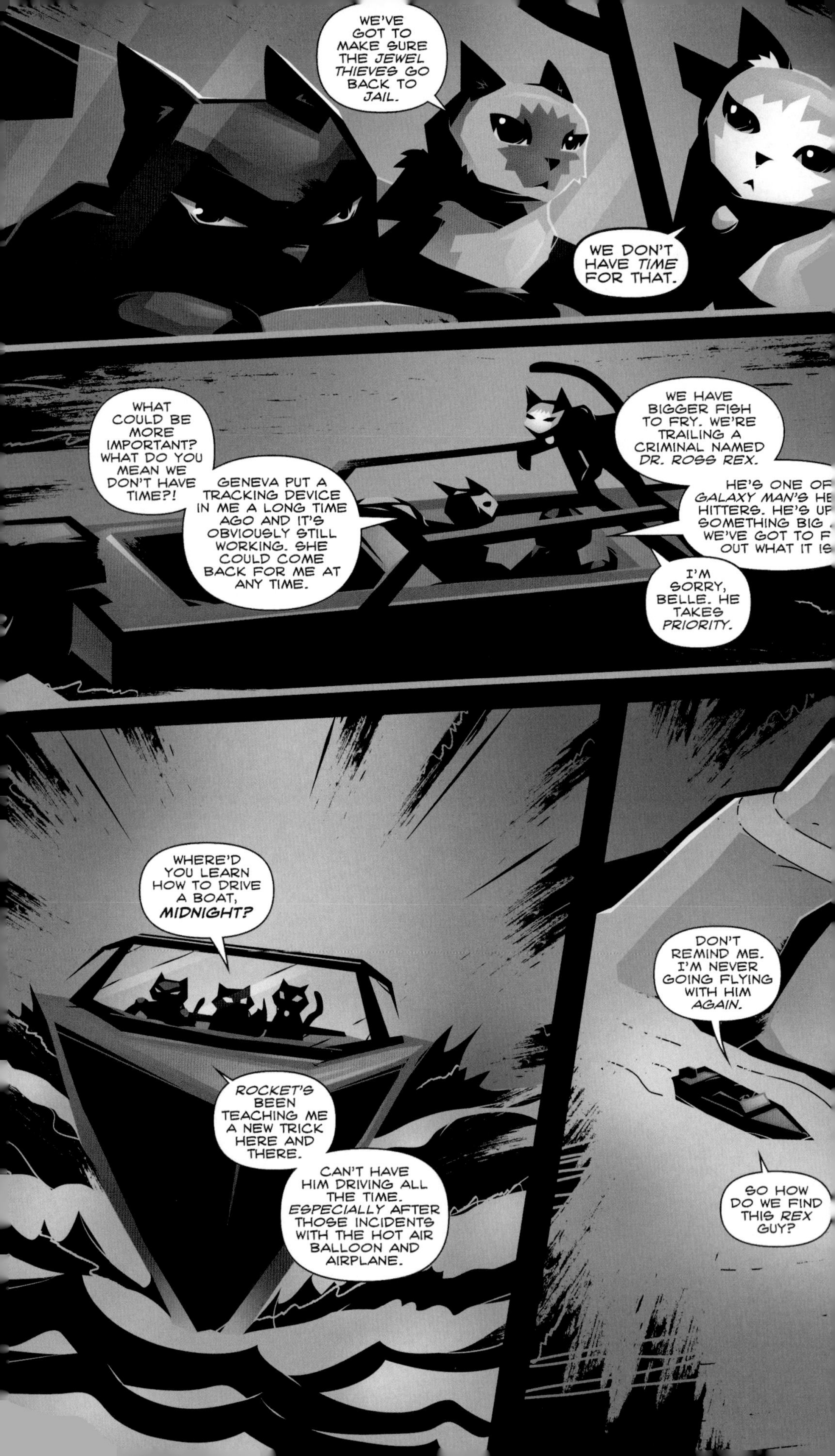
WE'VE GOT TO MAKE SURE THE JEWEL THIEVES GO BACK TO JAIL.
WE DON'T HAVE TIME FOR THAT.
WHAT COULD BE MORE IMPORTANT? WHAT DO YOU MEAN WE DON'T HAVE TIME?!
WE HAVE BIGGER FISH TO FRY. WE'RE TRAILING A CRIMINAL NAMED DR. ROSS REX.
HE'S ONE OF GALAXY MAN'S HE HITTERS. HE'S UP SOMETHING BIG WE'VE GOT TO F OUT WHAT IT IS
GENEVA PUT A TRACKING DEVICE IN ME A LONG TIME AGO AND IT'S OBVIOUSLY STILL WORKING. SHE COULD COME BACK FOR ME AT ANY TIME.
I'M SORRY, BELLE. HE TAKES PRIORITY.
WHERE'D YOU LEARN HOW TO DRIVE A BOAT, MIDNIGHT?
ROCKET'S BEEN TEACHING ME A NEW TRICK HERE AND THERE.
CAN'T HAVE HIM DRIVING ALL THE TIME. ESPECIALLY AFTER THOSE INCIDENTS WITH THE HOT AIR BALLOON AND AIRPLANE.
DON'T REMIND ME. I'M NEVER GOING FLYING WITH HIM AGAIN.
SO HOW DO WE FIND THIS REX GUY?

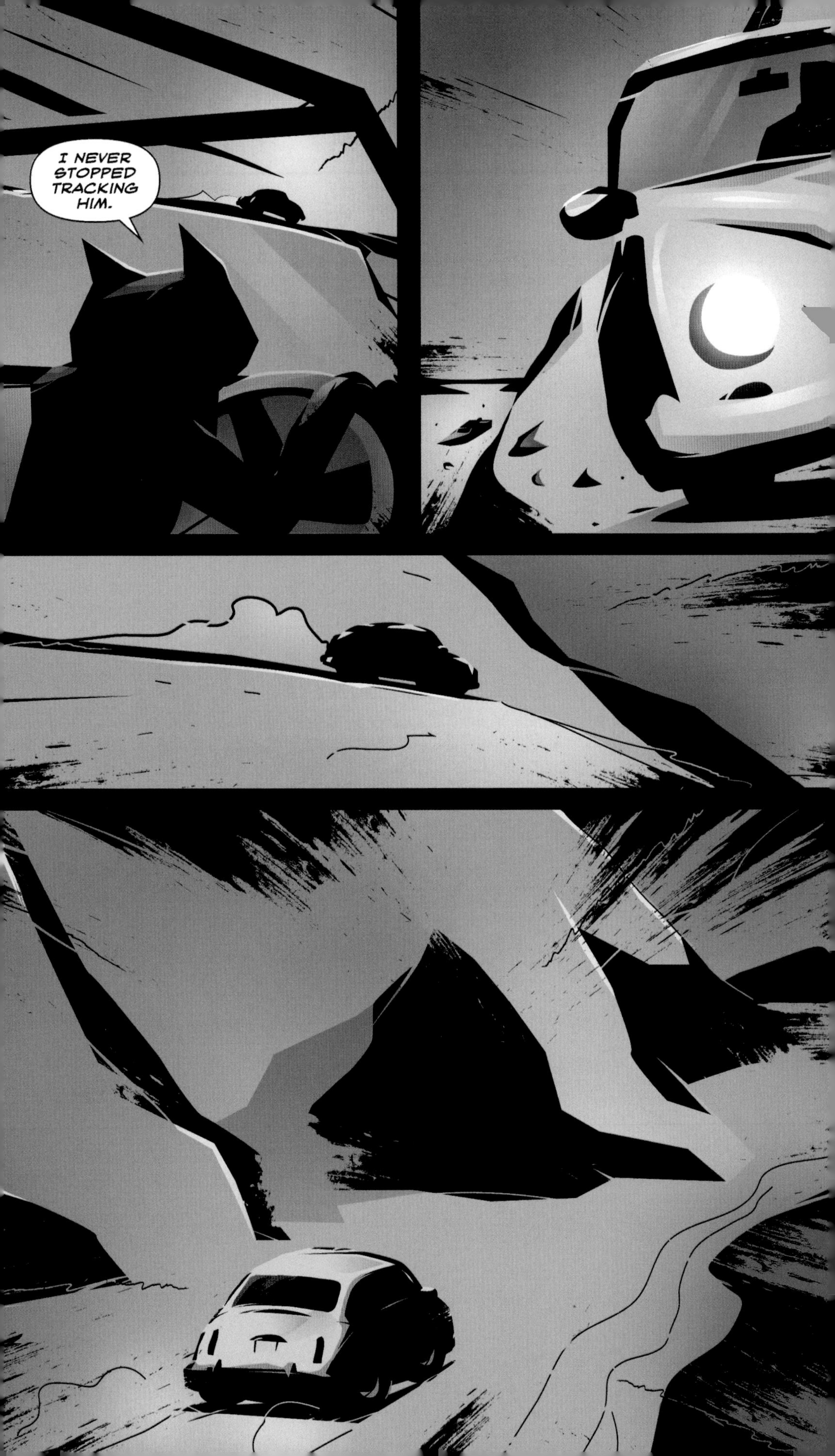
I NEVER STOPPED TRACKING HIM.

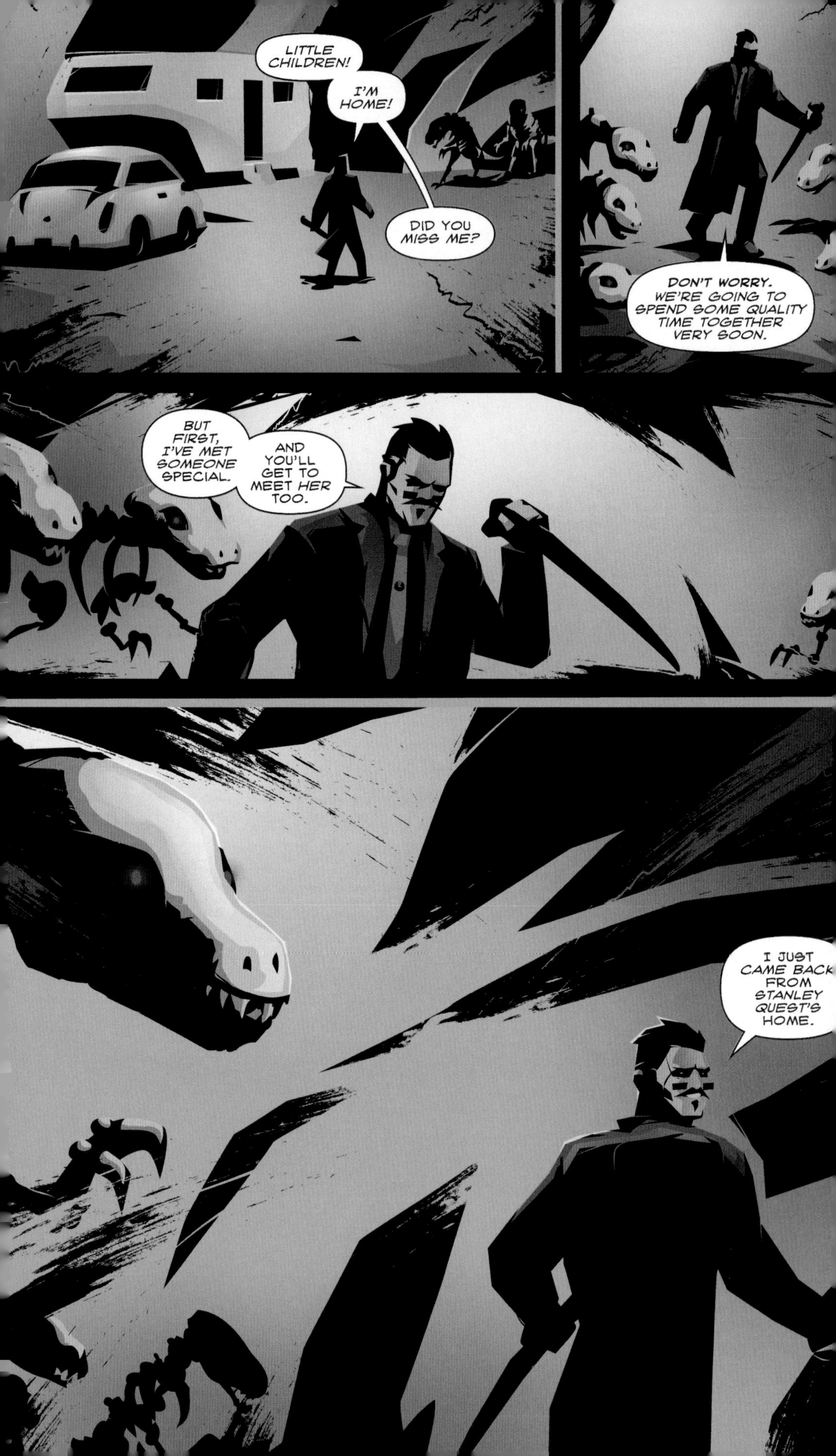
LITTLE CHILDREN!
I'M HOME!
DID YOU MISS ME?
DON'T WORRY. WE'RE GOING TO SPEND SOME QUALITY TIME TOGETHER VERY SOON.
BUT FIRST, I'VE MET SOMEONE SPECIAL.
AND YOU'LL GET TO MEET HER TOO.
I JUST CAME BACK FROM STANLEY QUEST'S HOME.

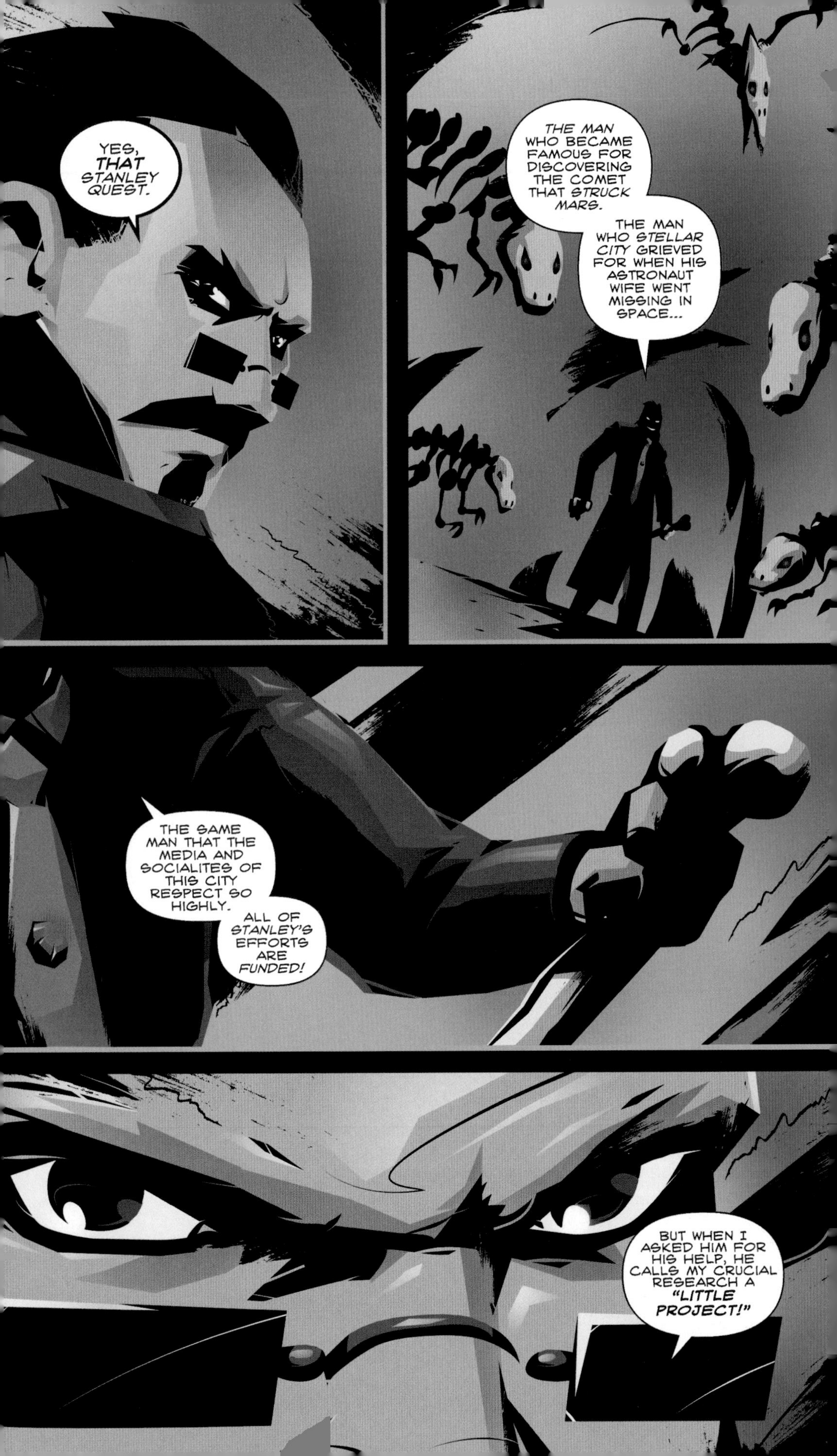
YES, THAT STANLEY QUEST.
THE MAN WHO BECAME FAMOUS FOR DISCOVERING THE COMET THAT STRUCK MARS.
THE MAN WHO STELLAR CITY GRIEVED FOR WHEN HIS ASTRONAUT WIFE WENT MISSING IN SPACE...
THE SAME MAN THAT THE MEDIA AND SOCIALITES OF THIS CITY RESPECT SO HIGHLY.
ALL OF STANLEY'S EFFORTS ARE FUNDED!
BUT WHEN I ASKED HIM FOR HIS HELP, HE CALLS MY CRUCIAL RESEARCH A "LITTLE PROJECT!"

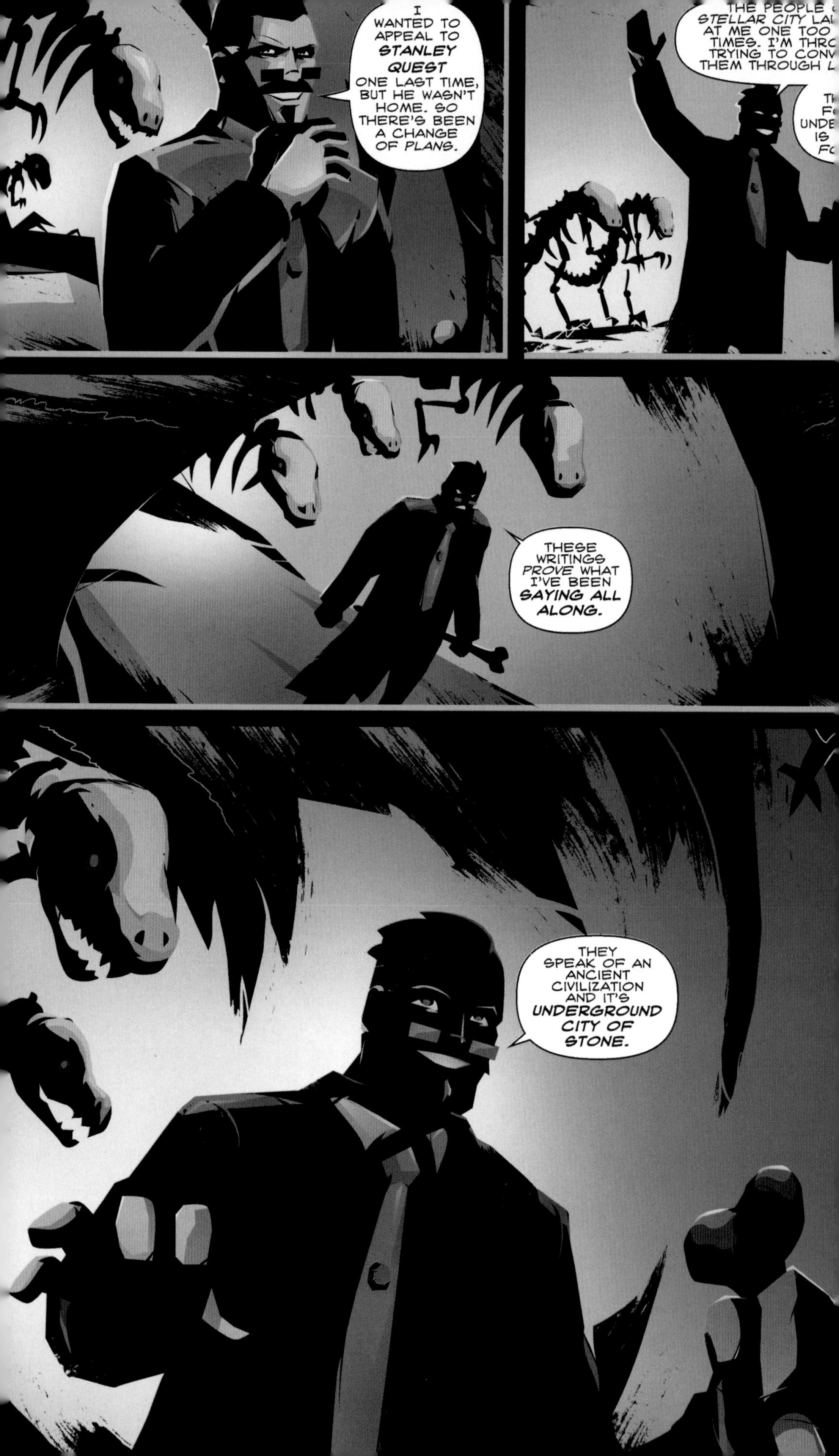
I WANTED TO APPEAL TO STANLEY QUEST ONE LAST TIME, BUT HE WASN'T HOME. SO THERE'S BEEN A CHANGE OF PLANS.
THE PEOPLE STELLAR CITY AT ME ONE TOO TIMES. I'M TRYING TO THEM THROUGH
THESE WRITINGS PROVE WHAT I'VE BEEN SAYING ALL ALONG.
THEY SPEAK OF AN ANCIENT CIVILIZATION AND IT'S UNDERGROUND CITY OF STONE.

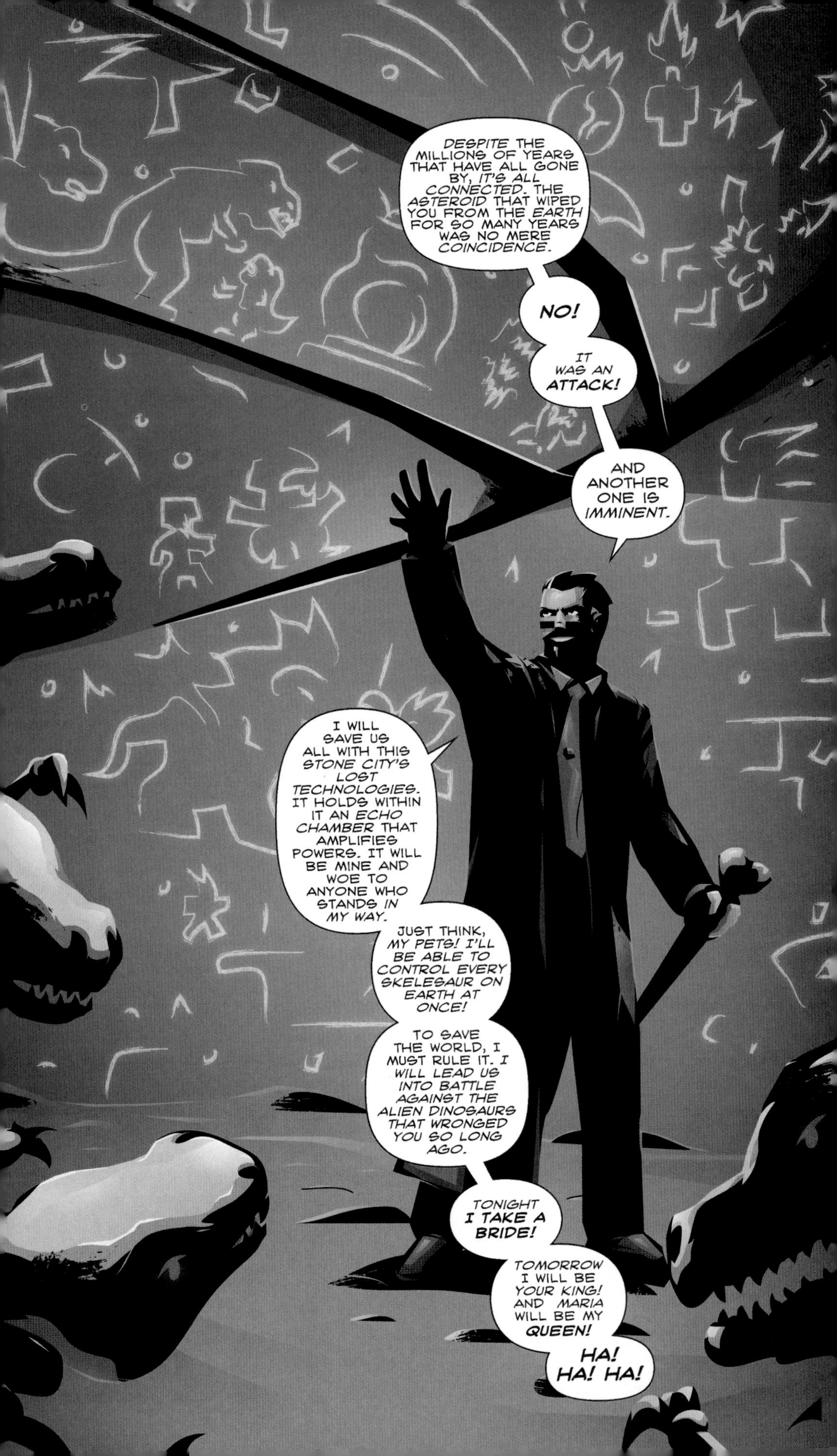
DESPITE THE MILLIONS OF YEARS THAT HAVE ALL GONE BY, IT'S ALL CONNECTED. THE ASTEROID THAT WIPED YOU FROM THE EARTH FOR SO MANY YEARS WAS NO MERE COINCIDENCE.
NO!
IT WAS AN ATTACK!
AND ANOTHER ONE IS IMMINENT.
I WILL SAVE US ALL WITH THIS STONE CITY'S LOST TECHNOLOGIES. IT HOLDS WITHIN IT AN ECHO CHAMBER THAT AMPLIFIES POWERS. IT WILL BE MINE AND WOE TO ANYONE WHO STANDS IN MY WAY.
JUST THINK, MY PETS! I'LL BE ABLE TO CONTROL EVERY SKELESAUR ON EARTH AT ONCE!
TO SAVE THE WORLD, I MUST RULE IT. I WILL LEAD US INTO BATTLE AGAINST THE ALIEN DINOSAURS THAT WRONGED YOU SO LONG AGO.
TONIGHT I TAKE A BRIDE!
TOMORROW I WILL BE YOUR KING! AND MARIA WILL BE MY QUEEN!
HA! HA! HA!

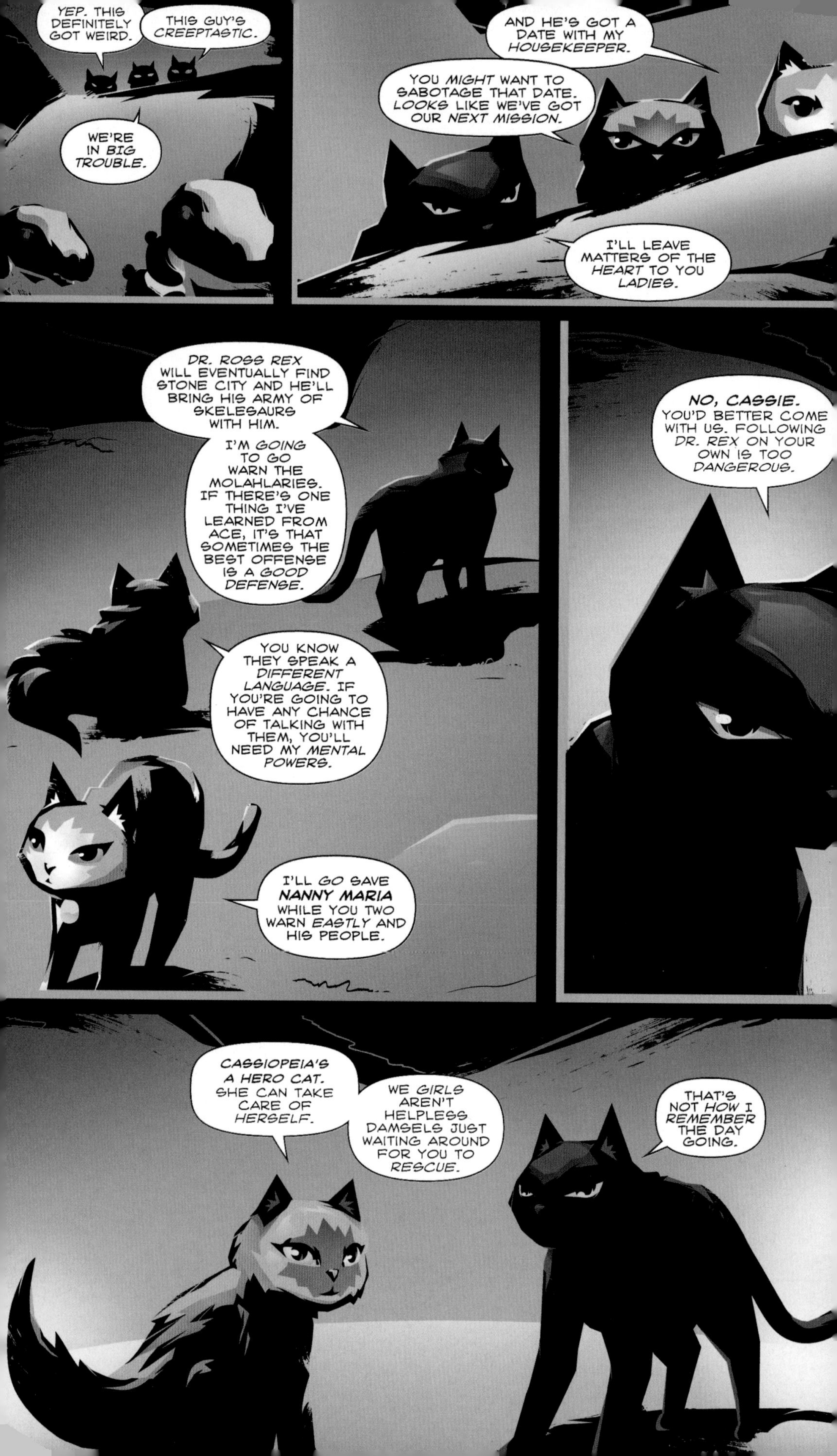
YEP. THIS DEFINITELY GOT WEIRD.
THIS GUY'S CREEPTASTIC.
WE'RE IN BIG TROUBLE.
AND HE'S GOT A DATE WITH MY HOUSEKEEPER.
YOU MIGHT WANT TO SABOTAGE THAT DATE. LOOKS LIKE WE'VE GOT OUR NEXT MISSION.
I'LL LEAVE MATTERS OF THE HEART TO YOU LADIES.
DR. ROSS REX WILL EVENTUALLY FIND STONE CITY AND HE'LL BRING HIS ARMY OF SKELESAURS WITH HIM.
I'M GOING TO GO WARN THE MOLAHLARIES. IF THERE'S ONE THING I'VE LEARNED FROM ACE, IT'S THAT SOMETIMES THE BEST OFFENSE IS A GOOD DEFENSE.
YOU KNOW THEY SPEAK A DIFFERENT LANGUAGE. IF YOU'RE GOING TO HAVE ANY CHANCE OF TALKING WITH THEM, YOU'LL NEED MY MENTAL POWERS.
I'LL GO SAVE NANNY MARIA WHILE YOU TWO WARN EASTLY AND HIS PEOPLE.
NO, CASSIE. YOU'D BETTER COME WITH US. FOLLOWING DR. REX ON YOUR OWN IS TOO DANGEROUS.
CASSIOPEIA'S A HERO CAT. SHE CAN TAKE CARE OF HERSELF.
WE GIRLS AREN'T HELPLESS DAMSELS JUST WAITING AROUND FOR YOU TO RESCUE.
THAT'S NOT HOW I REMEMBER THE DAY GOING.

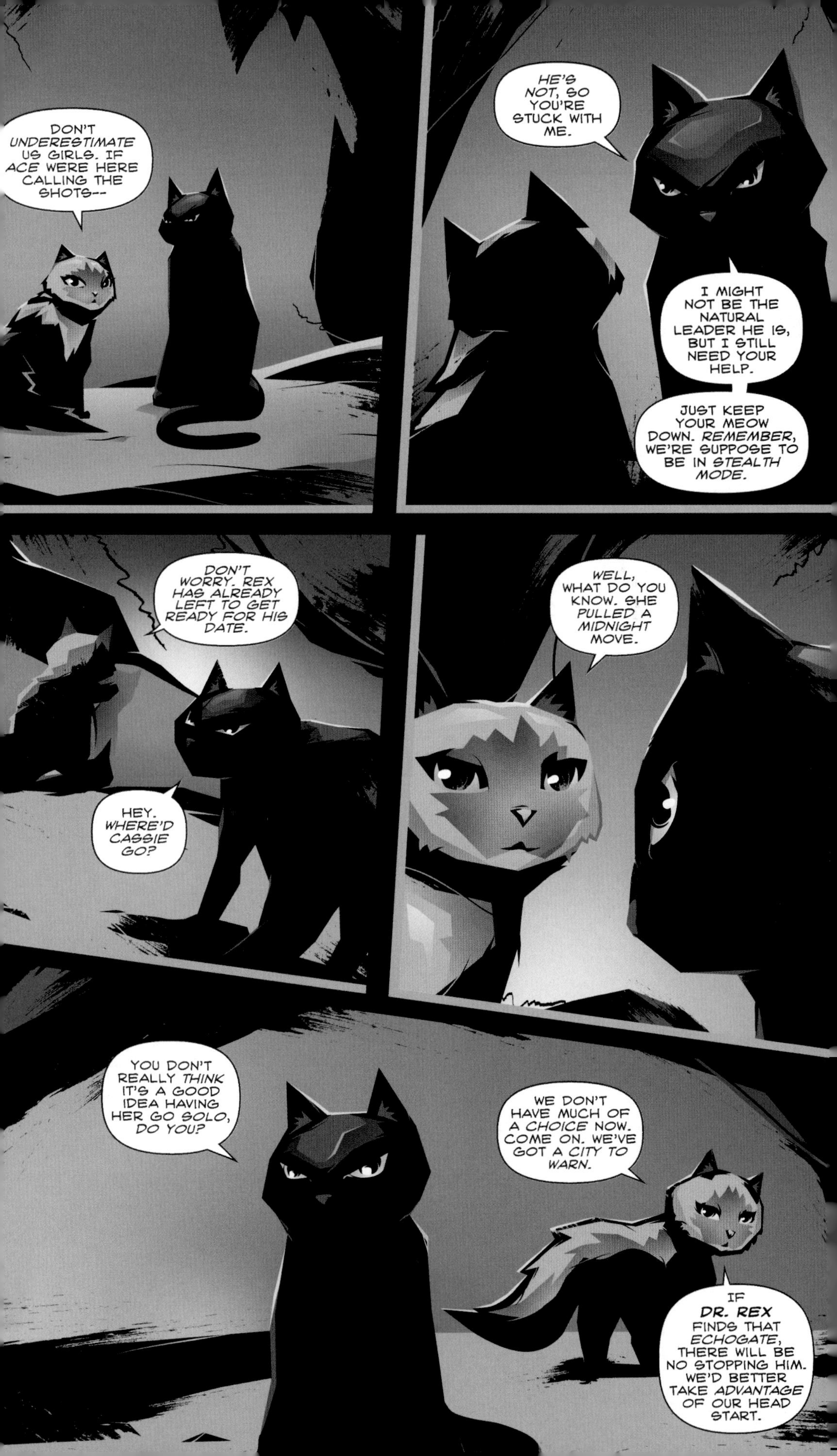

DON'T UNDERESTIMATE US GIRLS. IF ACE WERE HERE CALLING THE SHOTS--
HE'S NOT, SO YOU'RE STUCK WITH ME.
I MIGHT NOT BE THE NATURAL LEADER HE IS, BUT I STILL NEED YOUR HELP.
JUST KEEP YOUR MEOW DOWN. REMEMBER, WE'RE SUPPOSE TO BE IN STEALTH MODE.
DON'T WORRY. REX HAS ALREADY LEFT TO GET READY FOR HIS DATE.
HEY. WHERE'D CASSIE GO?
WELL, WHAT DO YOU KNOW. SHE PULLED A MIDNIGHT MOVE.
YOU DON'T REALLY THINK IT'S A GOOD IDEA HAVING HER GO SOLO, DO YOU?
WE DON'T HAVE MUCH OF A CHOICE NOW. COME ON. WE'VE GOT A CITY TO WARN.
IF DR. REX FINDS THAT ECHOGATE, THERE WILL BE NO STOPPING HIM. WE'D BETTER TAKE ADVANTAGE OF OUR HEAD START.

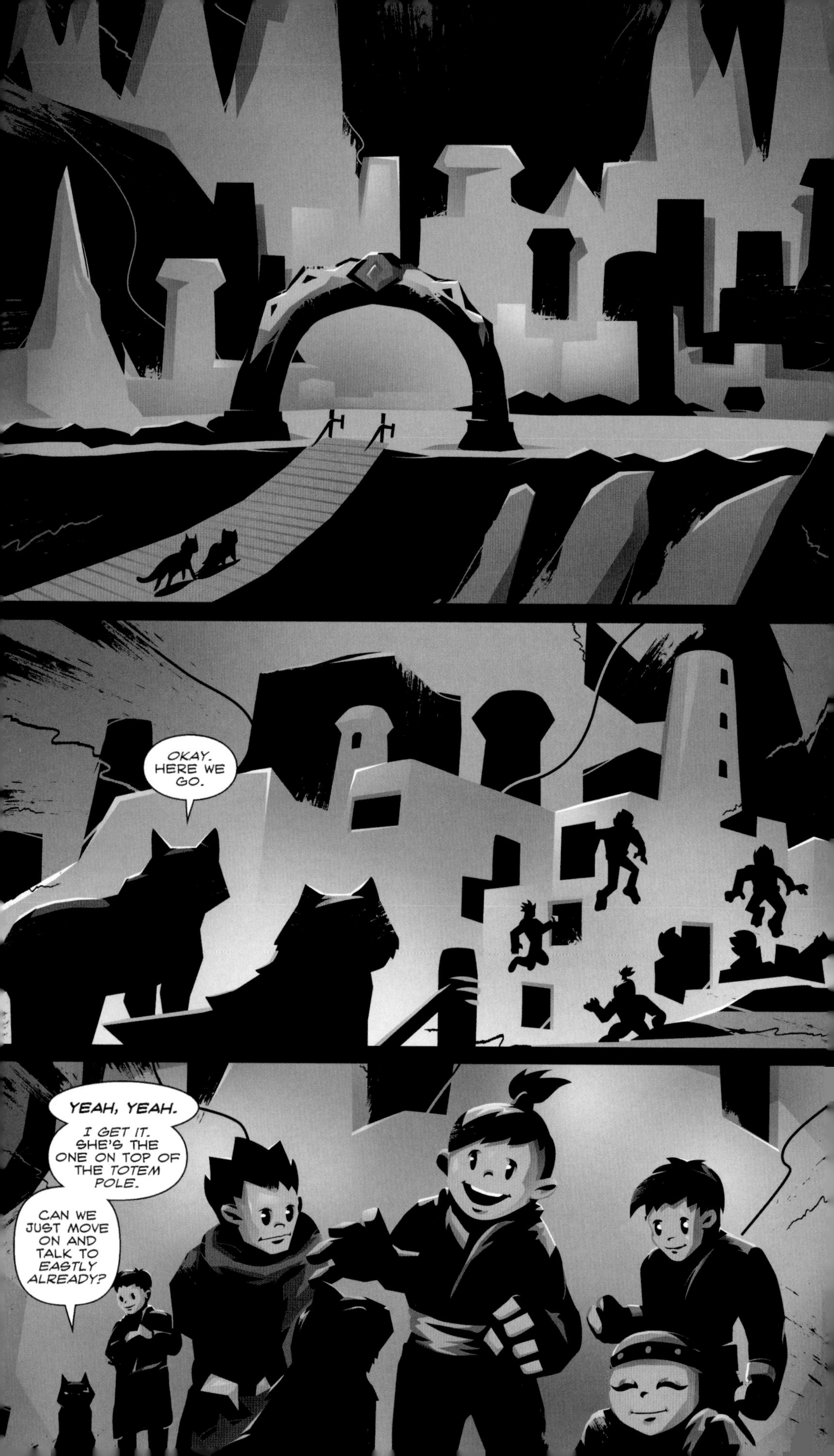
OKAY. HERE WE GO.
YEAH, YEAH.
I GET IT. SHE'S THE ONE ON TOP OF THE TOTEM POLE.
CAN WE JUST MOVE ON AND TALK TO EASTLY ALREADY?

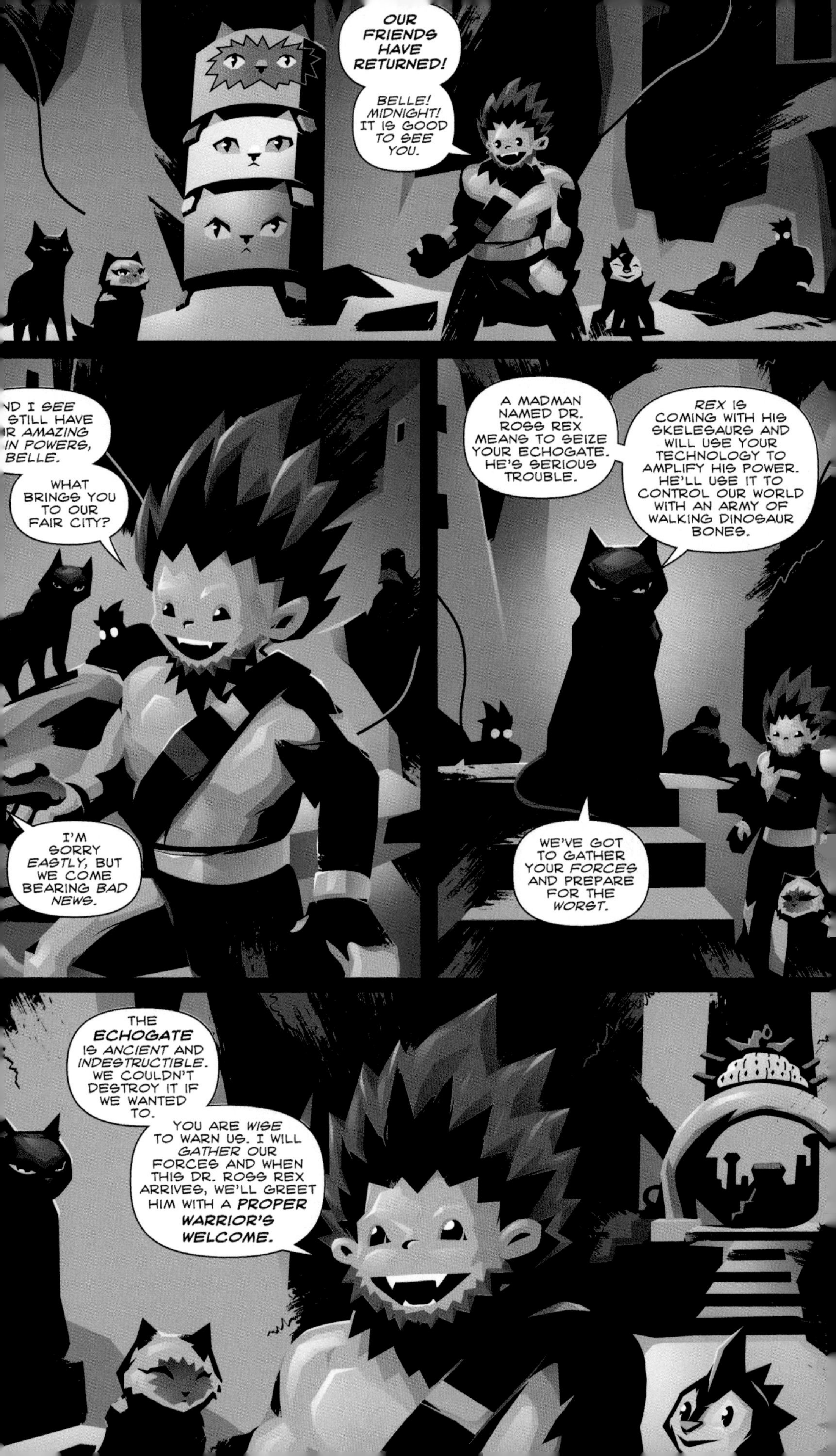

OUR FRIENDS HAVE RETURNED!
BELLE! MIDNIGHT! IT IS GOOD TO SEE YOU.
ND I SEE STILL HAVE R AMAZING IN POWERS, BELLE.
WHAT BRINGS YOU TO OUR FAIR CITY?
I'M SORRY EASTLY, BUT WE COME BEARING BAD NEWS.
A MADMAN NAMED DR. ROSS REX MEANS TO SEIZE YOUR ECHOGATE. HE'S SERIOUS TROUBLE.
REX IS COMING WITH HIS SKELESAURS AND WILL USE YOUR TECHNOLOGY TO AMPLIFY HIS POWER. HE'LL USE IT TO CONTROL OUR WORLD WITH AN ARMY OF WALKING DINOSAUR BONES.
WE'VE GOT TO GATHER YOUR FORCES AND PREPARE FOR THE WORST.
THE ECHOGATE IS ANCIENT AND INDESTRUCTIBLE. WE COULDN'T DESTROY IT IF WE WANTED TO.
YOU ARE WISE TO WARN US. I WILL GATHER OUR FORCES AND WHEN THIS DR. ROSS REX ARRIVES, WE'LL GREET HIM WITH A PROPER WARRIOR'S WELCOME.

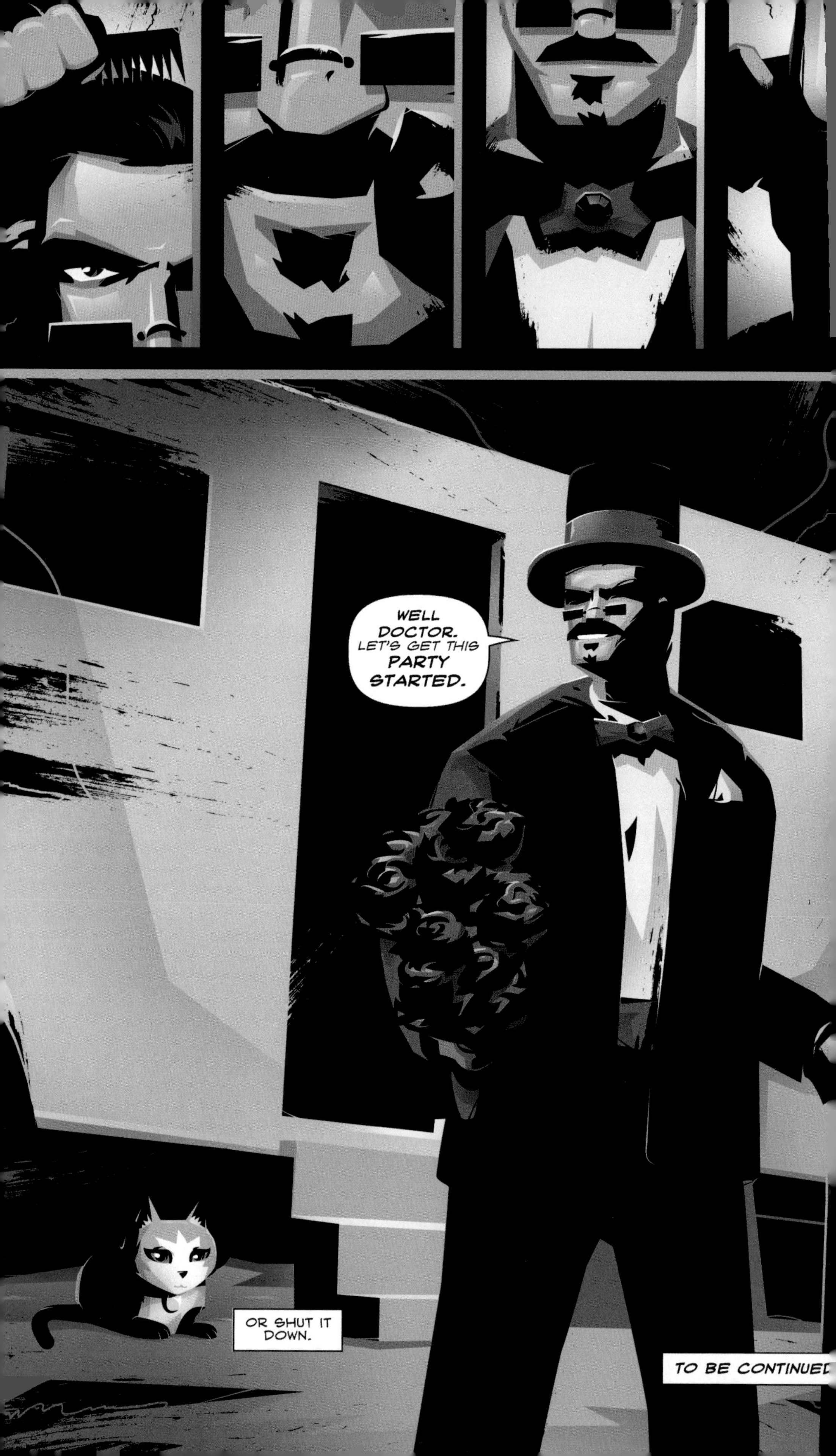
WELL DOCTOR. LET'S GET THIS PARTY STARTED.
OR SHUT IT DOWN.
TO BE CONTINUED

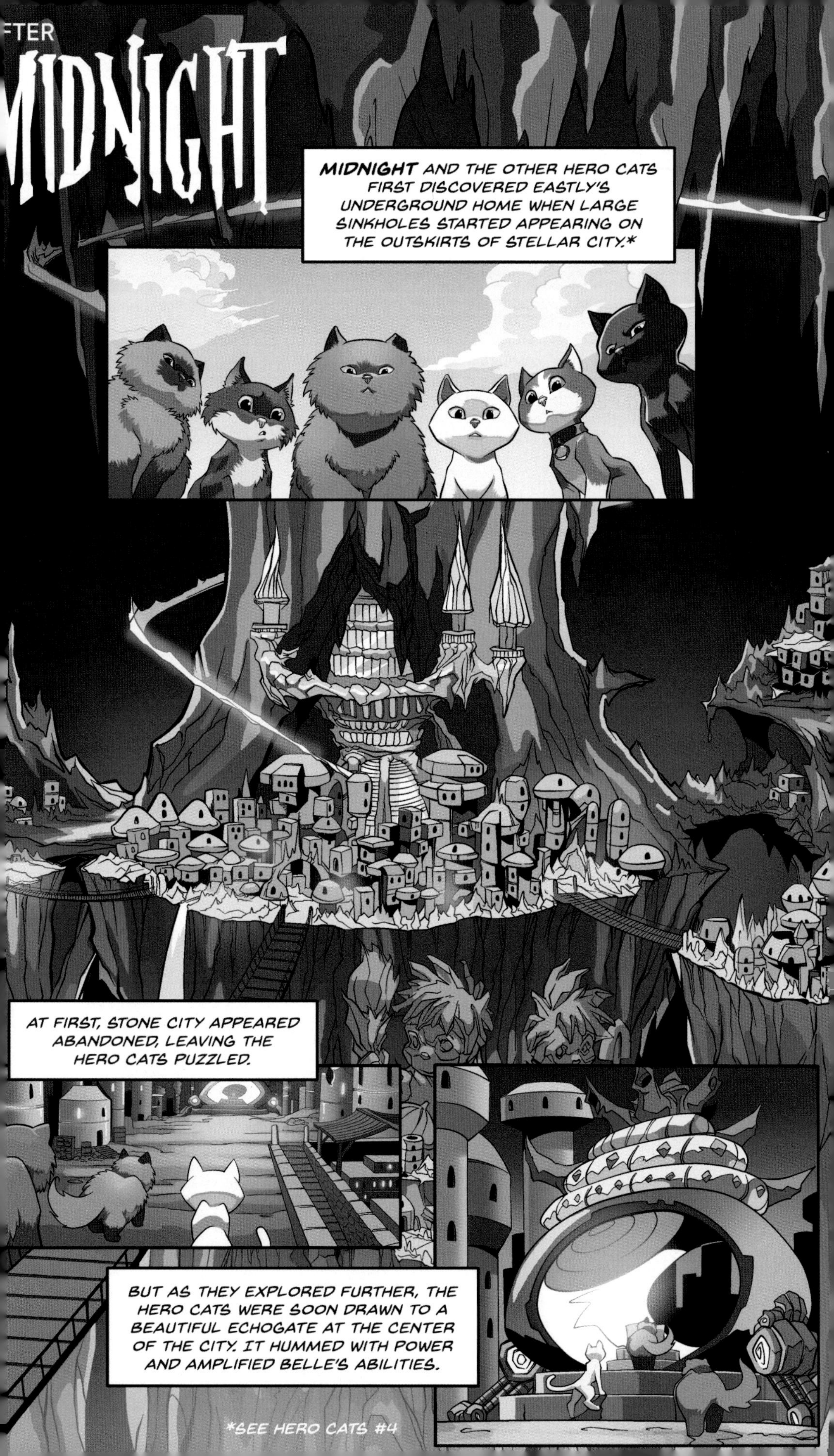
AFTER MIDNIGHT
MIDNIGHT AND THE OTHER HERO CATS FIRST DISCOVERED EASTLY'S UNDERGROUND HOME WHEN LARGE SINKHOLES STARTED APPEARING ON THE OUTSKIRTS OF STELLAR CITY.*
AT FIRST, STONE CITY APPEARED ABANDONED, LEAVING THE HERO CATS PUZZLED.
BUT AS THEY EXPLORED FURTHER, THE HERO CATS WERE SOON DRAWN TO A BEAUTIFUL ECHOGATE AT THE CENTER OF THE CITY. IT HUMMED WITH POWER AND AMPLIFIED BELLE'S ABILITIES.
*SEE HERO CATS #4

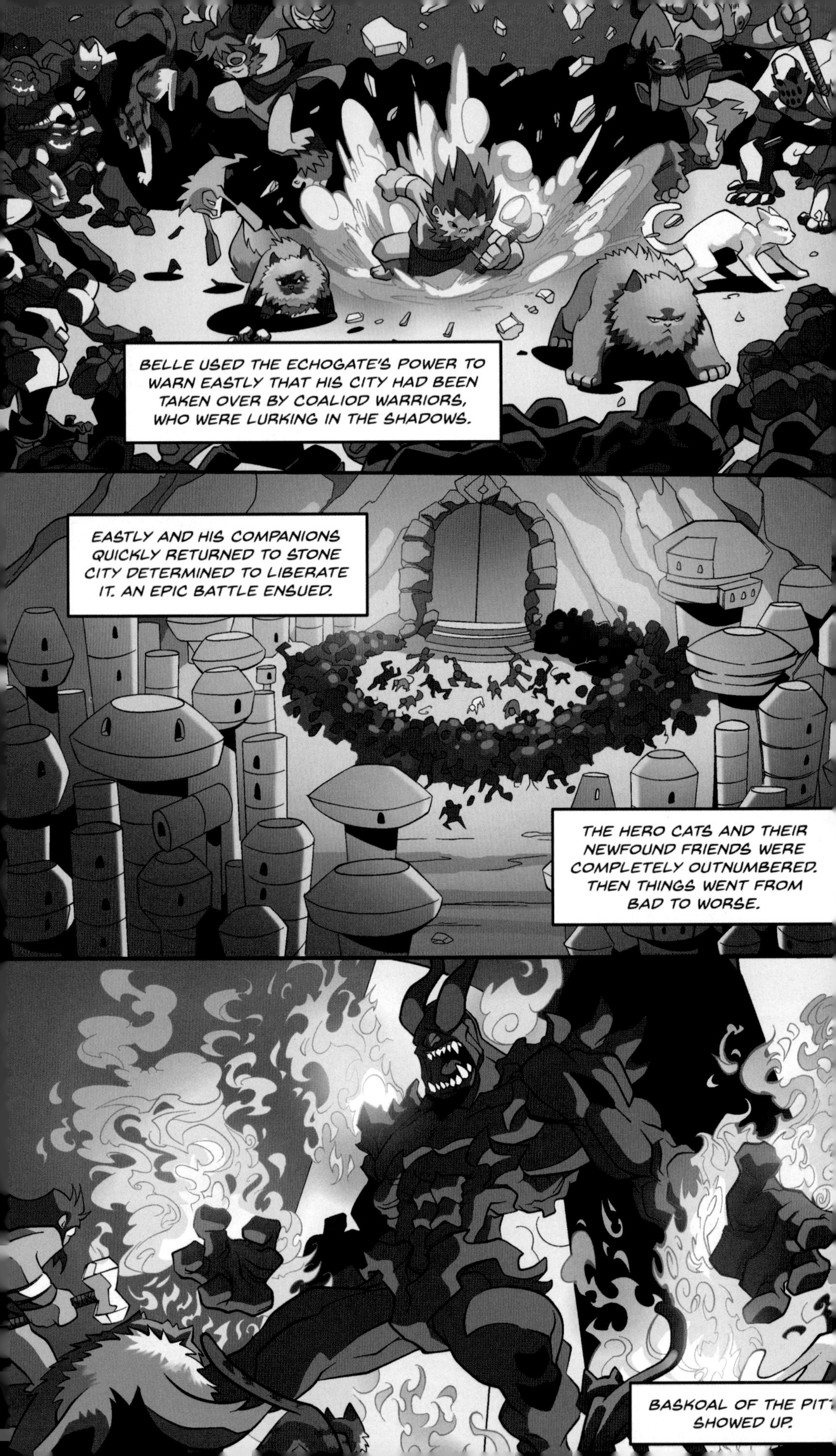
BELLE USED THE ECHOGATE'S POWER TO WARN EASTLY THAT HIS CITY HAD BEEN TAKEN OVER BY COALIOD WARRIORS, WHO WERE LURKING IN THE SHADOWS.
EASTLY AND HIS COMPANIONS QUICKLY RETURNED TO STONE CITY DETERMINED TO LIBERATE IT. AN EPIC BATTLE ENSUED.
THE HERO CATS AND THEIR NEWFOUND FRIENDS WERE COMPLETELY OUTNUMBERED. THEN THINGS WENT FROM BAD TO WORSE.
BASKOAL OF THE PIT SHOWED UP.

BUT BASKOAL AND HIS COALIOD WARRIORS WERE DRIVEN OFF A CLIFF BY MINDLESS BEASTS THAT BELLE WAS ABLE TO CONTROL CALLED WILD TERAH-TOMOOS.

THE HERO CATS DISCOVERED THE POWER OF THE ECHOGATE ON THAT DAY.

NOW DOCTOR ROSS REX IS DETERMINED TO USE THAT POWER TO AMPLIFY HIS OWN. IF THE HERO CATS CAN'T STOP HIM, THE WORLD WILL NEVER BE THE SAME!

UR STORY CONCLUDES IN
MIDNIGHT VOLUME 2 #3.

KYLE PUTTKAMMER   ALEX OGLE

HERO CATS:

MIDNIGHT

#3
VOLUME 2
$3.99

OVER STELLAR CITY

TION LAB ENTERTAINMENT

an Seaton - Publisher/SEO
wn Gabborin - Editor in Chief
on Martin - Publisher - Danger Zone
ole D'Andria - Marking Director/Editor
n Dietz - Social Media Manager
ielle Davison - Executive Administrator
d Cicconi - Nightshifts
wn Pryor - President of Creator Relations

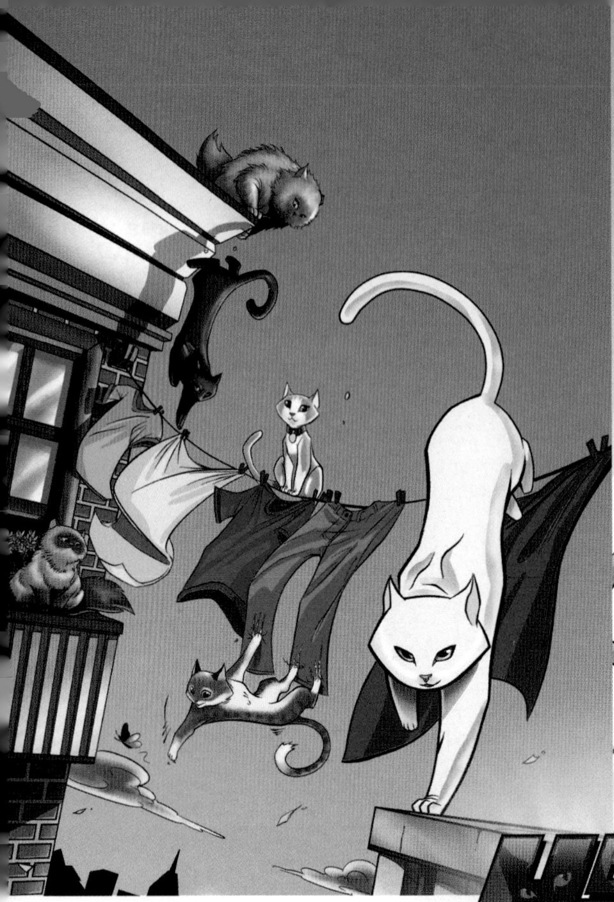

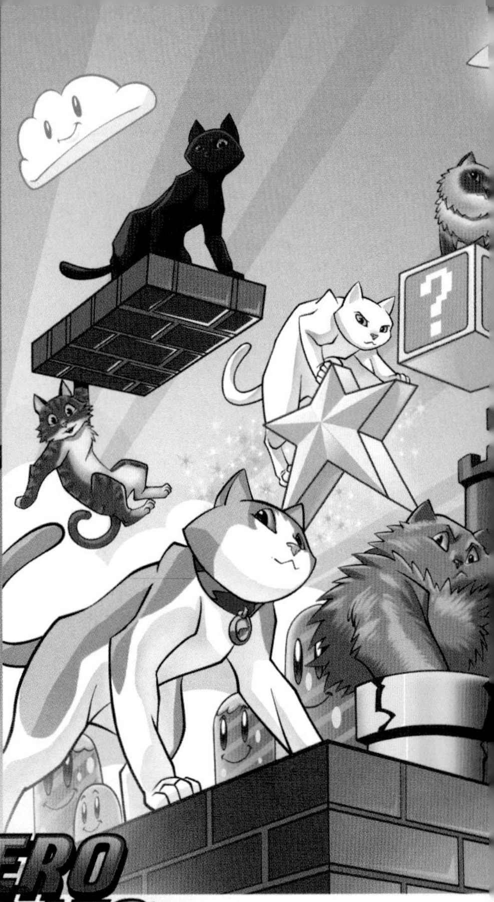

COVER GALLERY

HERO CATS Of Stellar City

COVER GALLERY

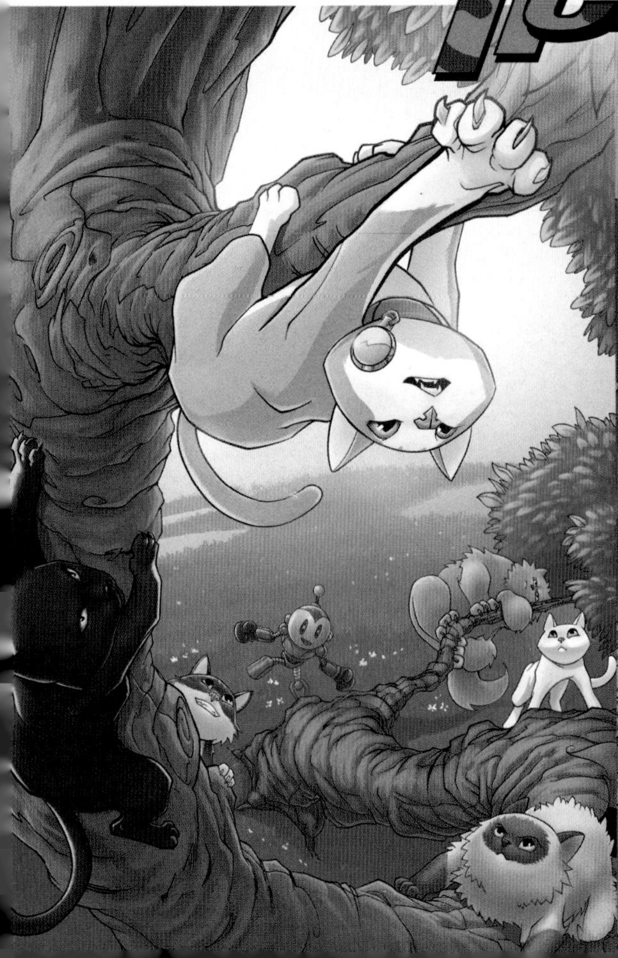

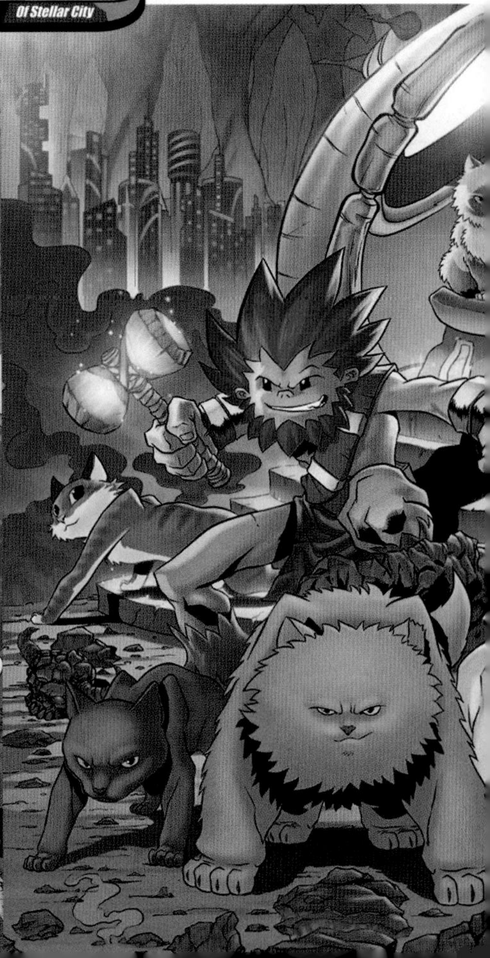

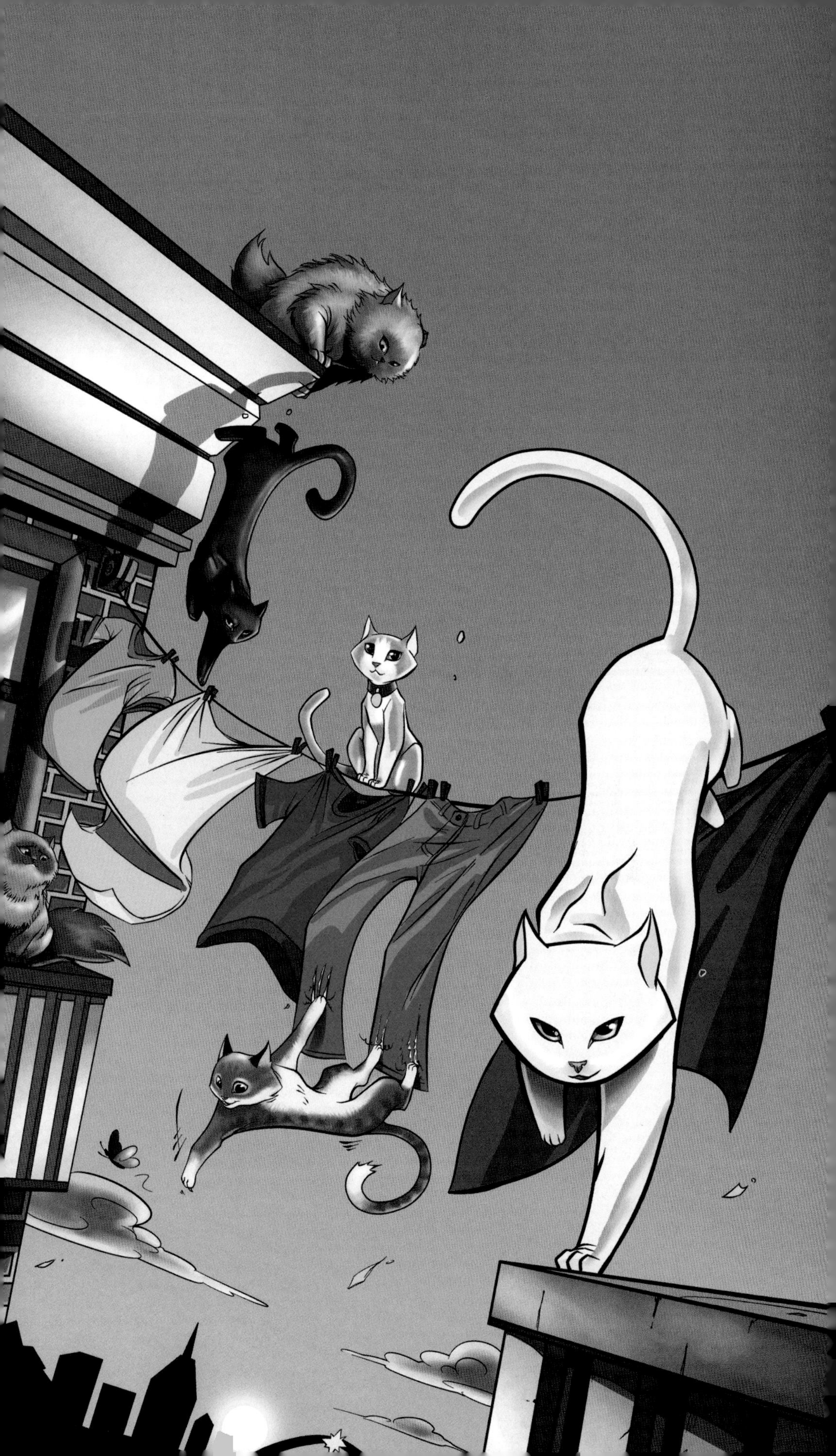

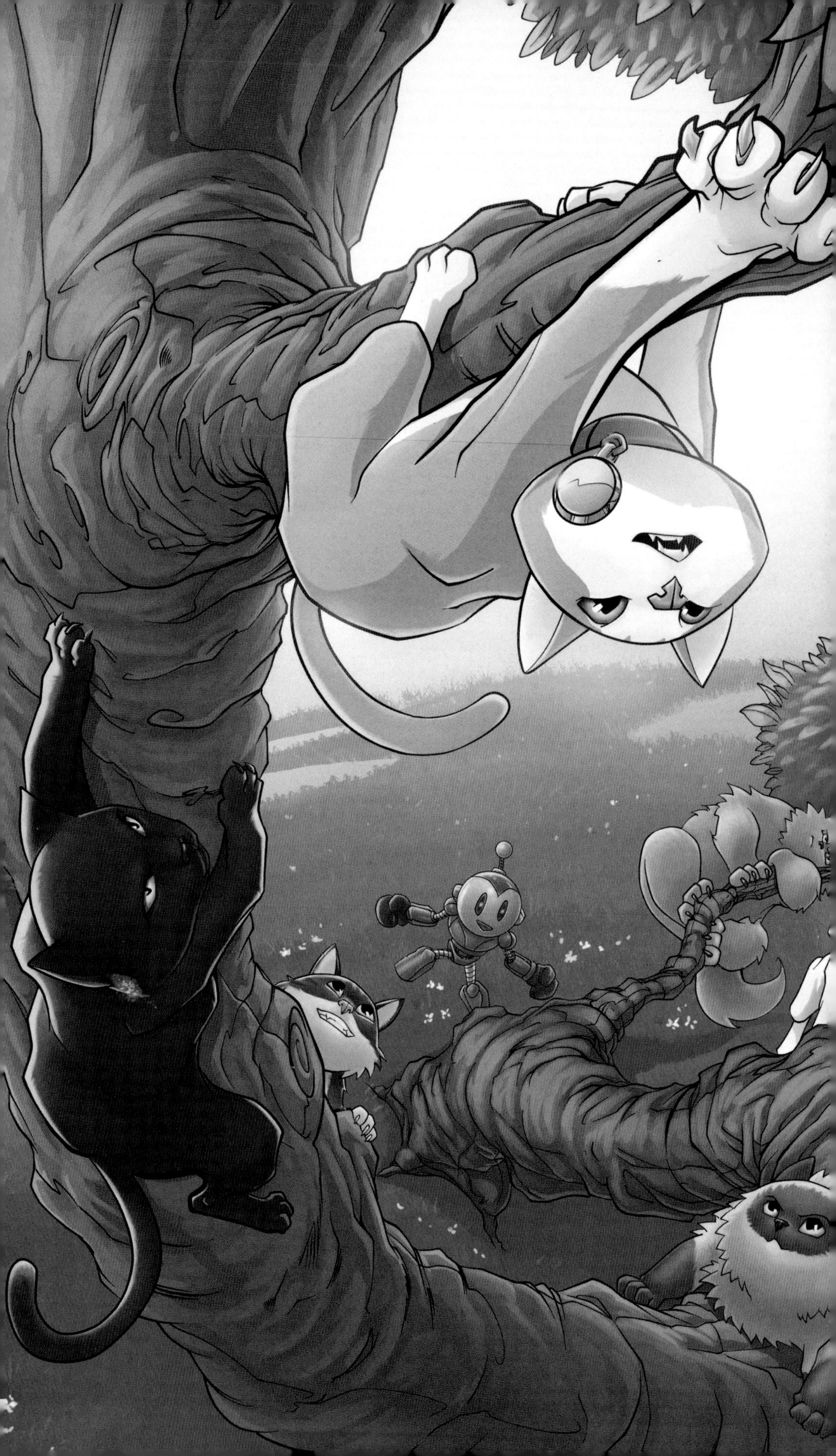

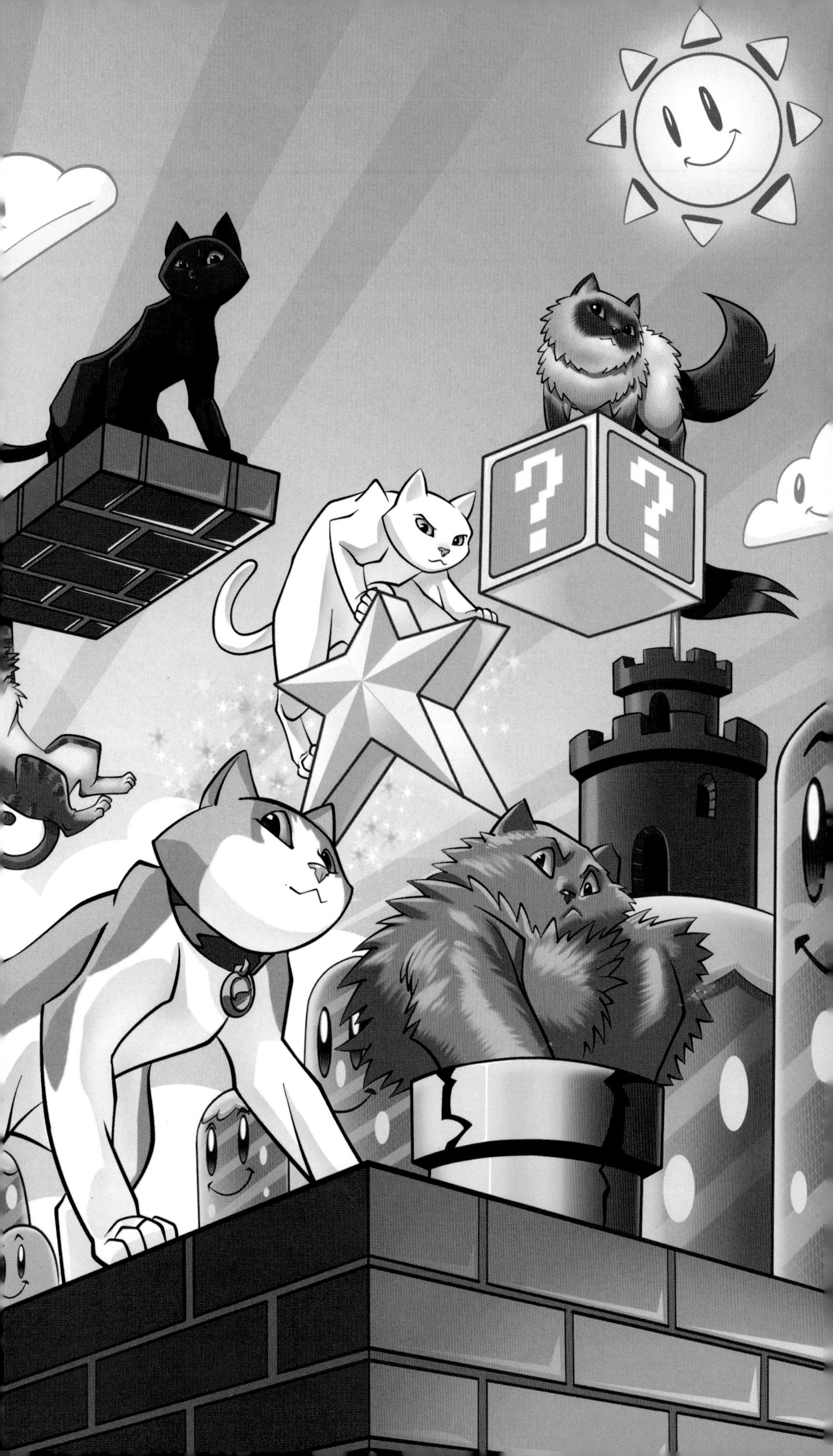

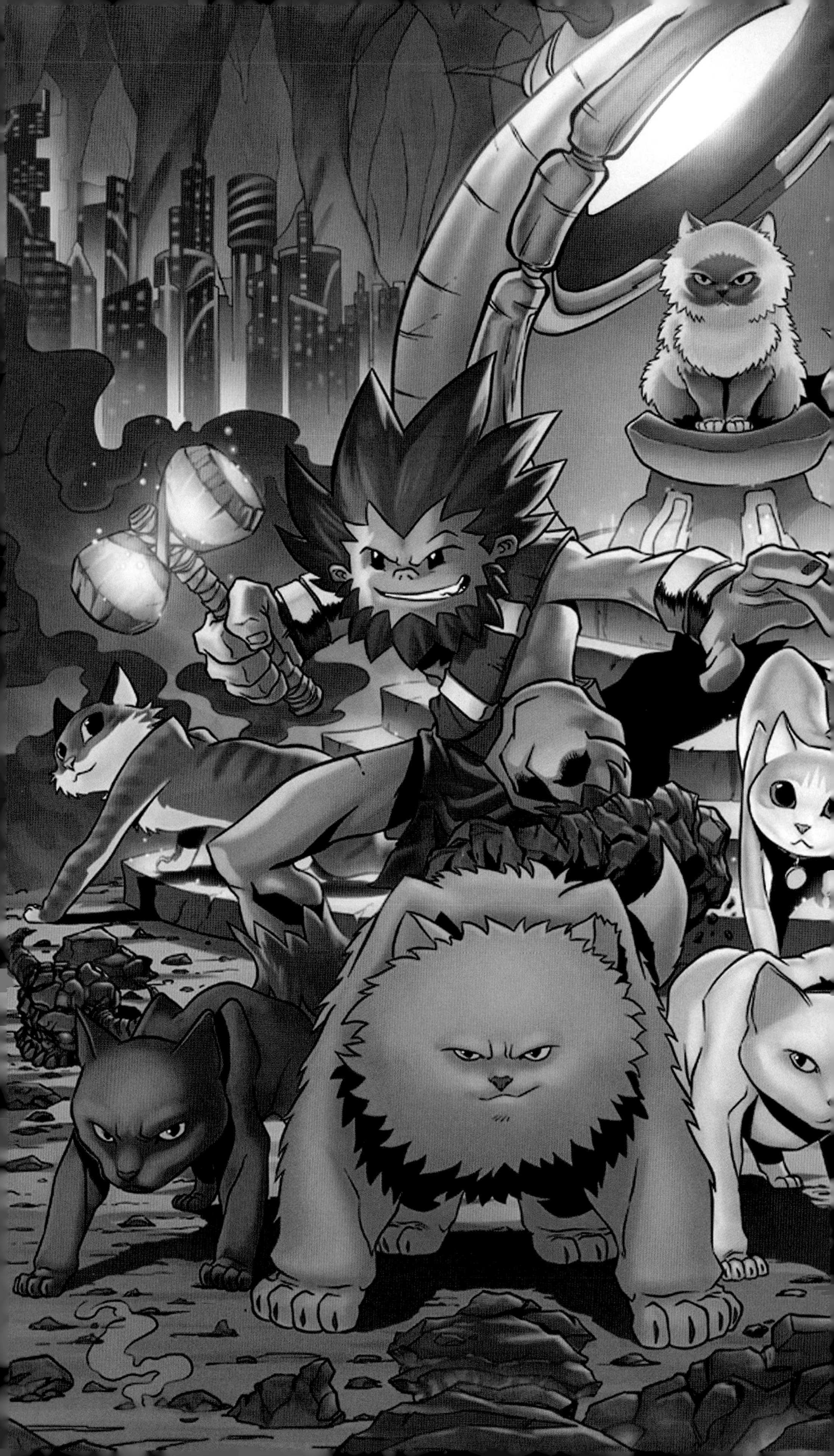

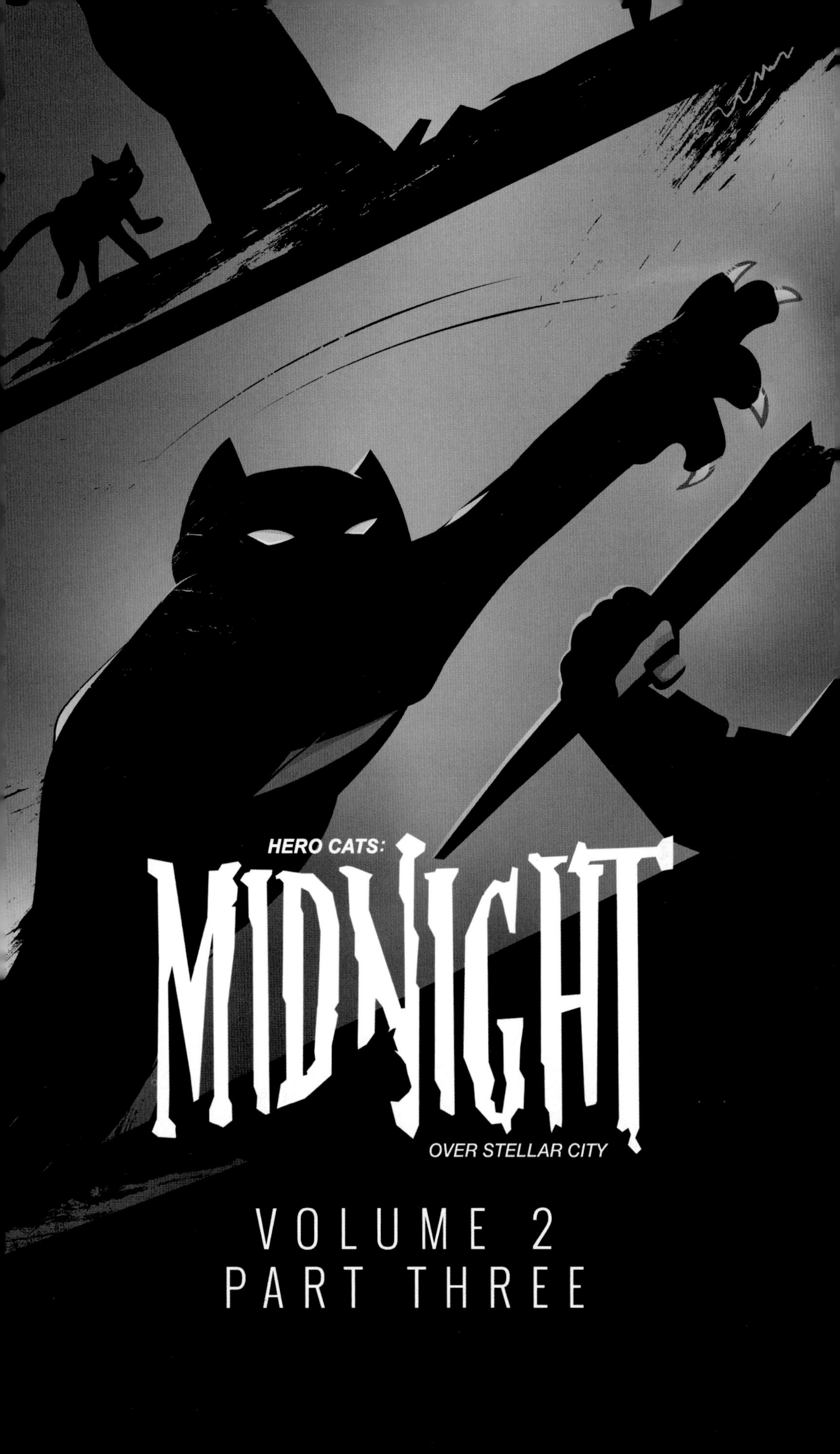
HERO CATS:
MIDNIGHT
OVER STELLAR CITY
VOLUME 2
PART THREE

THE CREATIVE TEAM

WRITTEN AND CREATED BY
KYLE PUTTKAMMER

ART AND LETTERS BY
ALEX OGLE

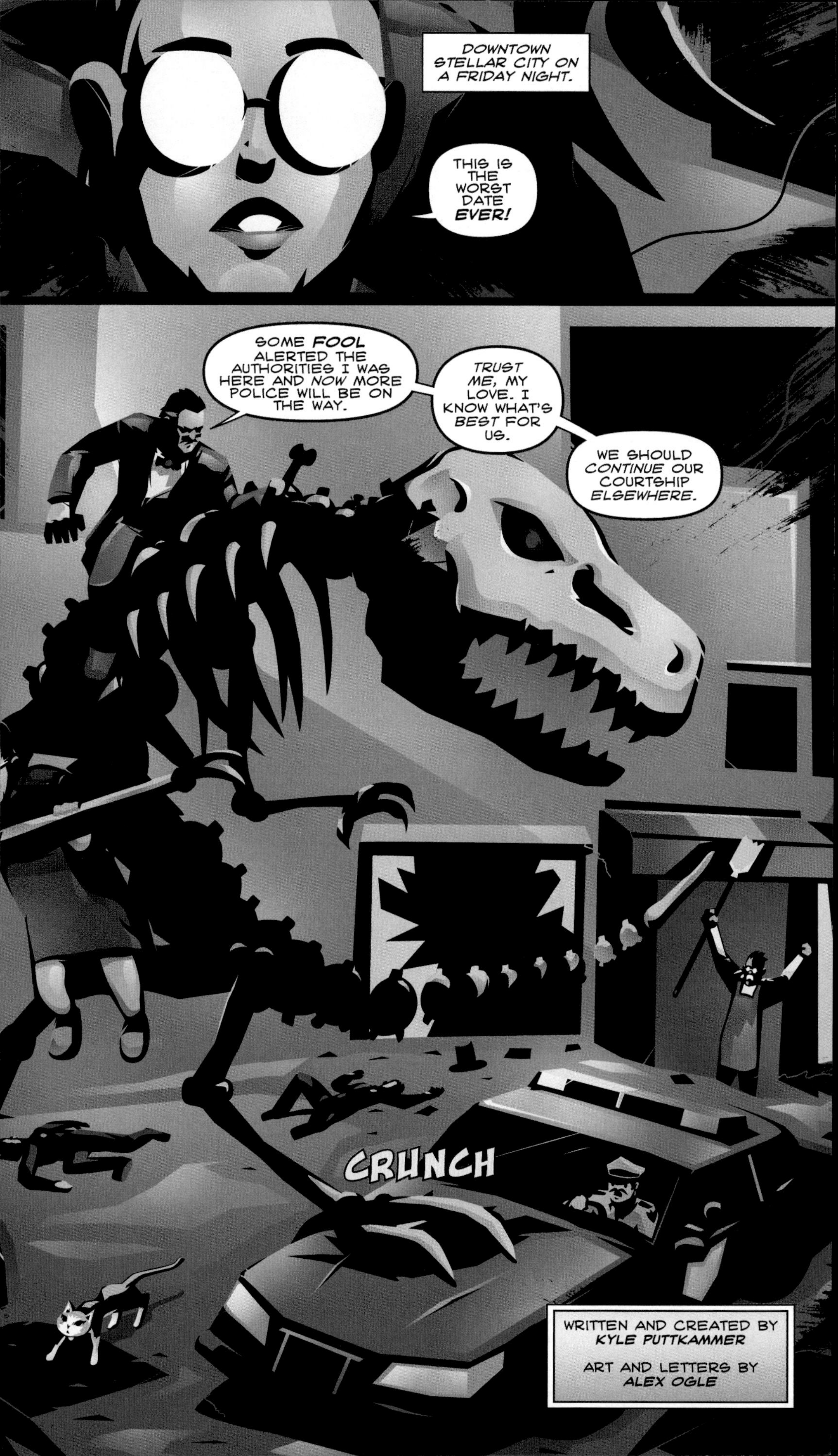
DOWNTOWN STELLAR CITY ON A FRIDAY NIGHT.
THIS IS THE WORST DATE EVER!
SOME FOOL ALERTED THE AUTHORITIES I WAS HERE AND NOW MORE POLICE WILL BE ON THE WAY.
TRUST ME, MY LOVE. I KNOW WHAT'S BEST FOR US.
WE SHOULD CONTINUE OUR COURTSHIP ELSEWHERE.
CRUNCH
WRITTEN AND CREATED BY KYLE PUTTKAMMER
ART AND LETTERS BY ALEX OGLE

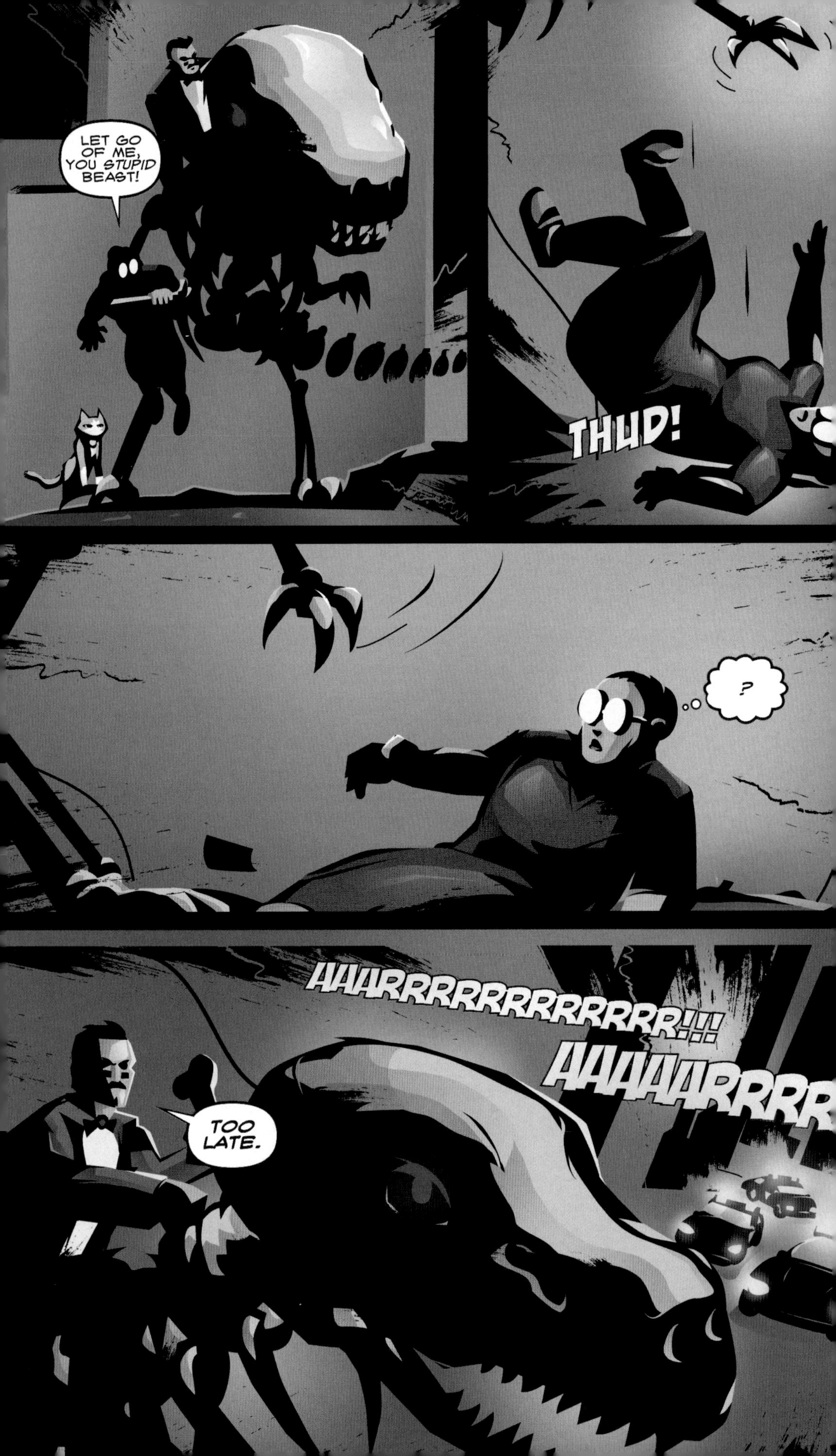
LET GO OF ME, YOU STUPID BEAST!
THUD!
?
AAARRRRRRRRRRRRRR!!!
AAAAARRRR
TOO LATE.

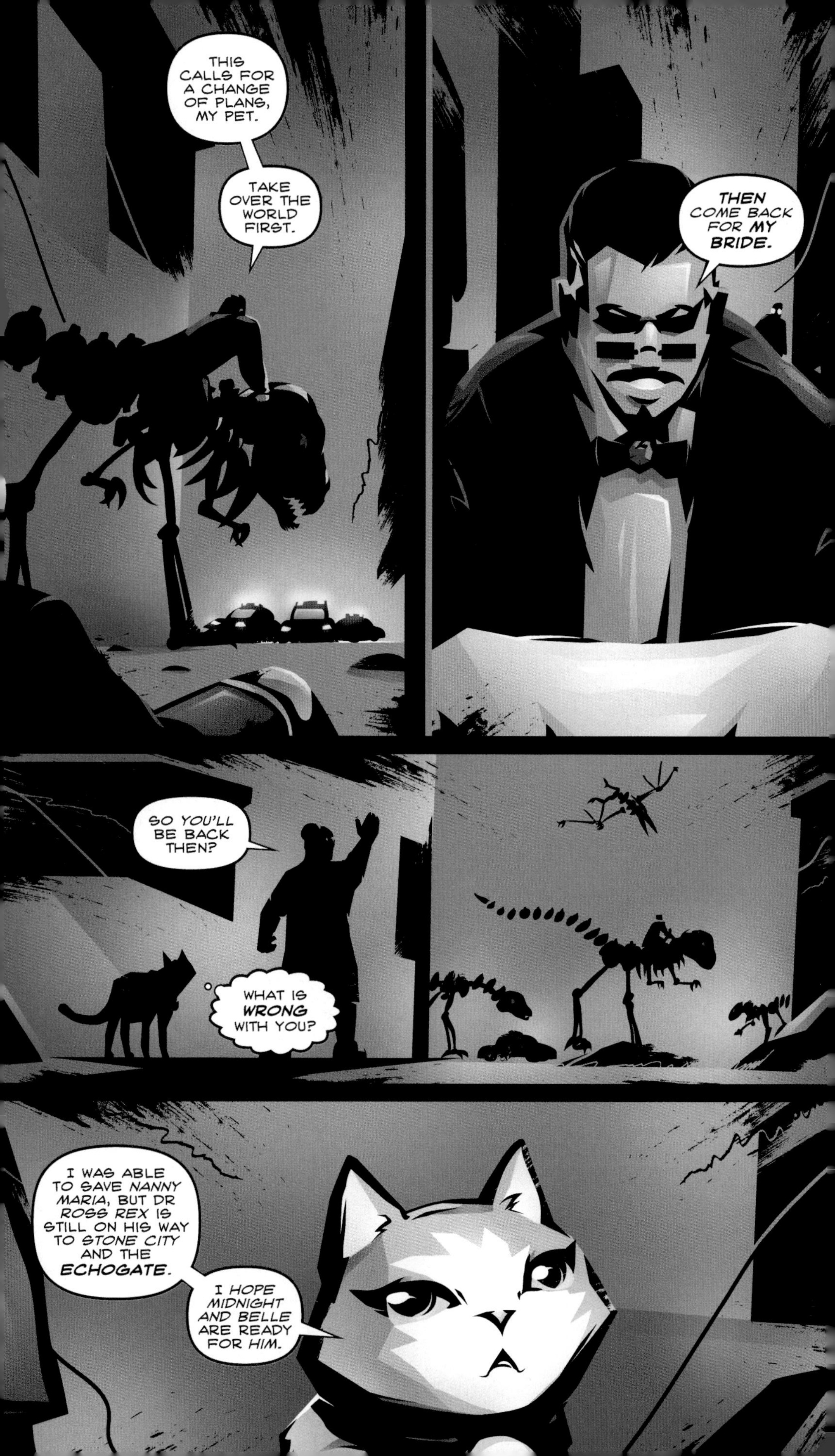

THIS CALLS FOR A CHANGE OF PLANS, MY PET.
TAKE OVER THE WORLD FIRST.
THEN COME BACK FOR MY BRIDE.
SO YOU'LL BE BACK THEN?
WHAT IS WRONG WITH YOU?
I WAS ABLE TO SAVE NANNY MARIA, BUT DR ROSS REX IS STILL ON HIS WAY TO STONE CITY AND THE ECHOGATE.
I HOPE MIDNIGHT AND BELLE ARE READY FOR HIM.

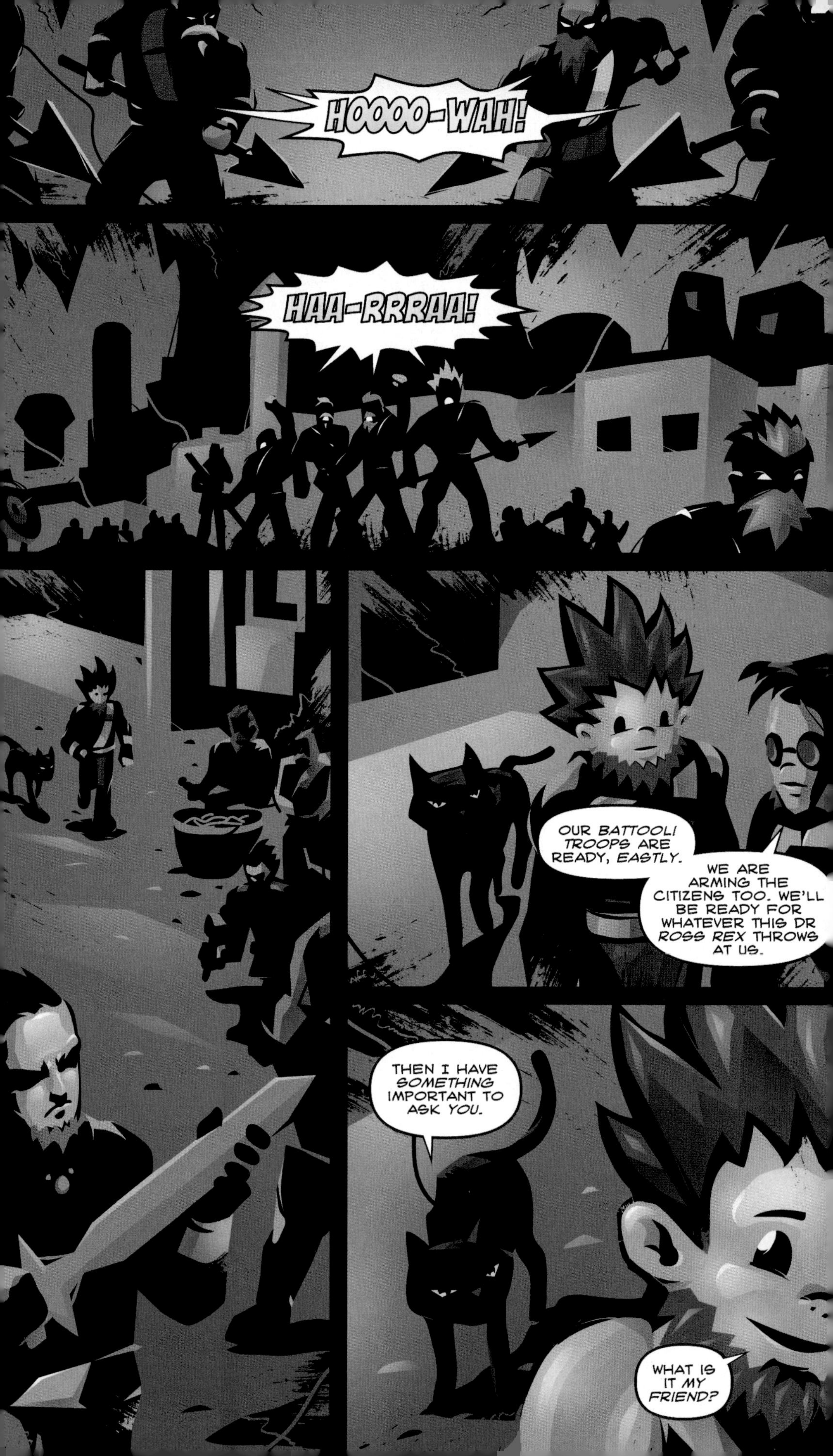
HOOOO-WAH!
HAA-RRRAA!
OUR *BATTOOLI TROOPS* ARE READY, *EASTLY*.
WE ARE ARMING THE CITIZENS TOO. WE'LL BE READY FOR WHATEVER THIS DR *ROSS REX* THROWS AT US.
THEN I HAVE *SOMETHING* IMPORTANT TO ASK *YOU*.
WHAT IS IT *MY FRIEND*?

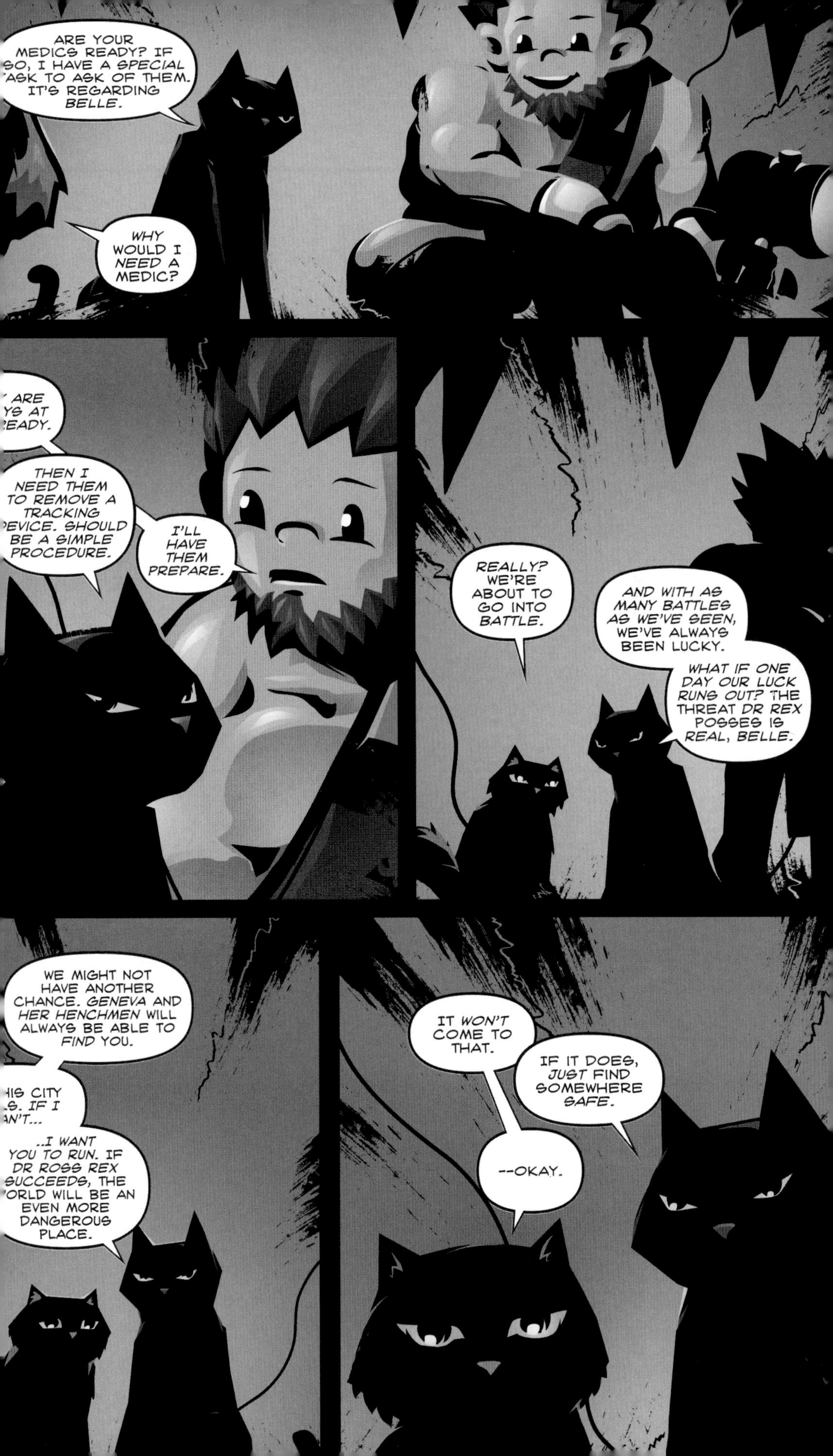
ARE YOUR MEDICS READY? IF SO, I HAVE A SPECIAL TASK TO ASK OF THEM. IT'S REGARDING BELLE.
WHY WOULD I NEED A MEDIC?
ARE
AT
EADY.
THEN I NEED THEM TO REMOVE A TRACKING DEVICE. SHOULD BE A SIMPLE PROCEDURE.
I'LL HAVE THEM PREPARE.
REALLY? WE'RE ABOUT TO GO INTO BATTLE.
AND WITH AS MANY BATTLES AS WE'VE SEEN, WE'VE ALWAYS BEEN LUCKY.
WHAT IF ONE DAY OUR LUCK RUNS OUT? THE THREAT DR REX POSSES IS REAL, BELLE.
WE MIGHT NOT HAVE ANOTHER CHANCE. GENEVA AND HER HENCHMEN WILL ALWAYS BE ABLE TO FIND YOU.
CITY
IF I
..I WANT YOU TO RUN. IF DR ROSS REX SUCCEEDS, THE WORLD WILL BE AN EVEN MORE DANGEROUS PLACE.
IT WON'T COME TO THAT.
IF IT DOES, JUST FIND SOMEWHERE SAFE.
--OKAY.

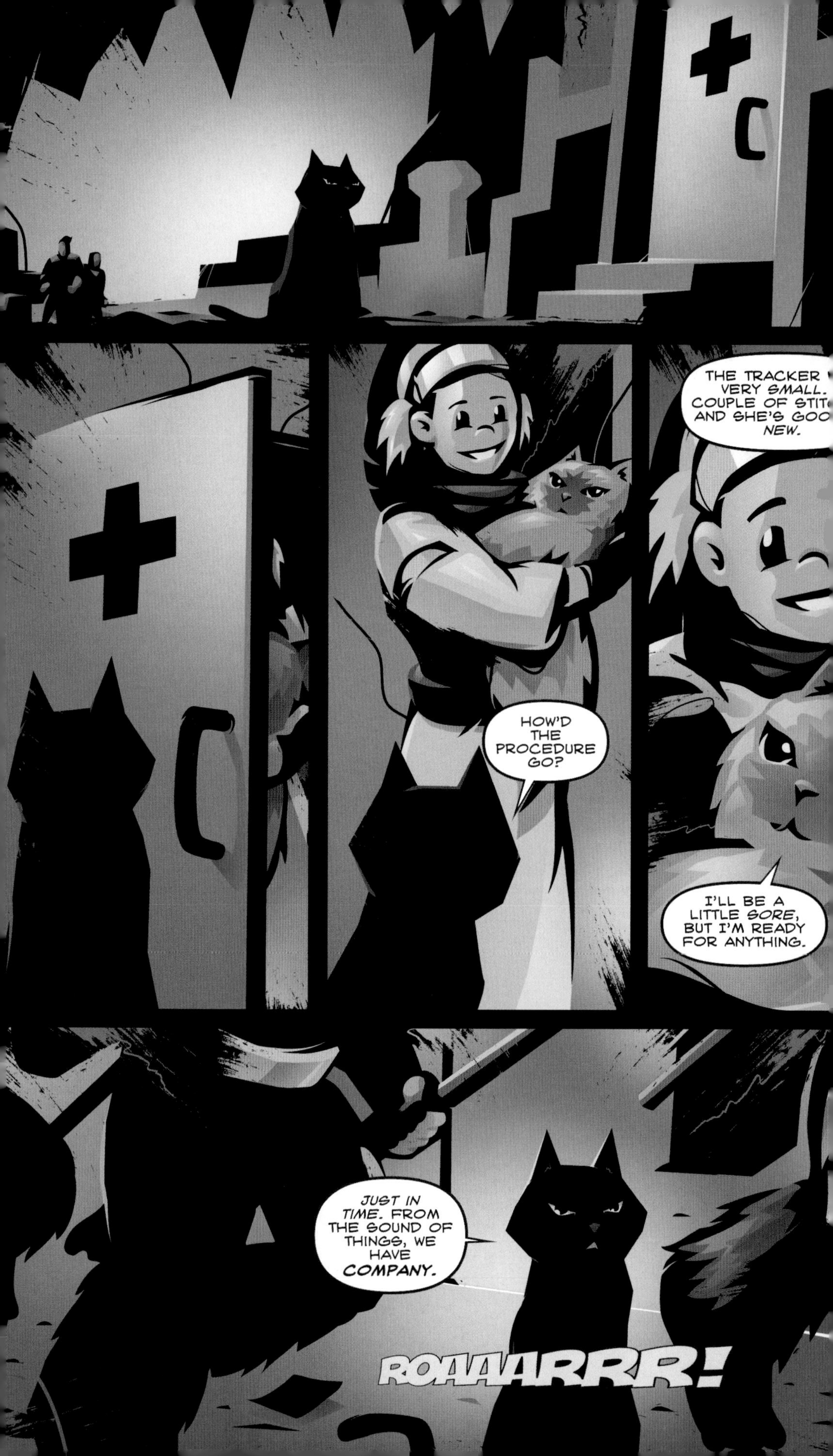
HOW'D THE PROCEDURE GO?
THE TRACKER VERY SMALL. COUPLE OF AND SHE'S NEW.
I'LL BE A LITTLE SORE, BUT I'M READY FOR ANYTHING.
JUST IN TIME. FROM THE SOUND OF THINGS, WE HAVE COMPANY.
ROAAARRR!

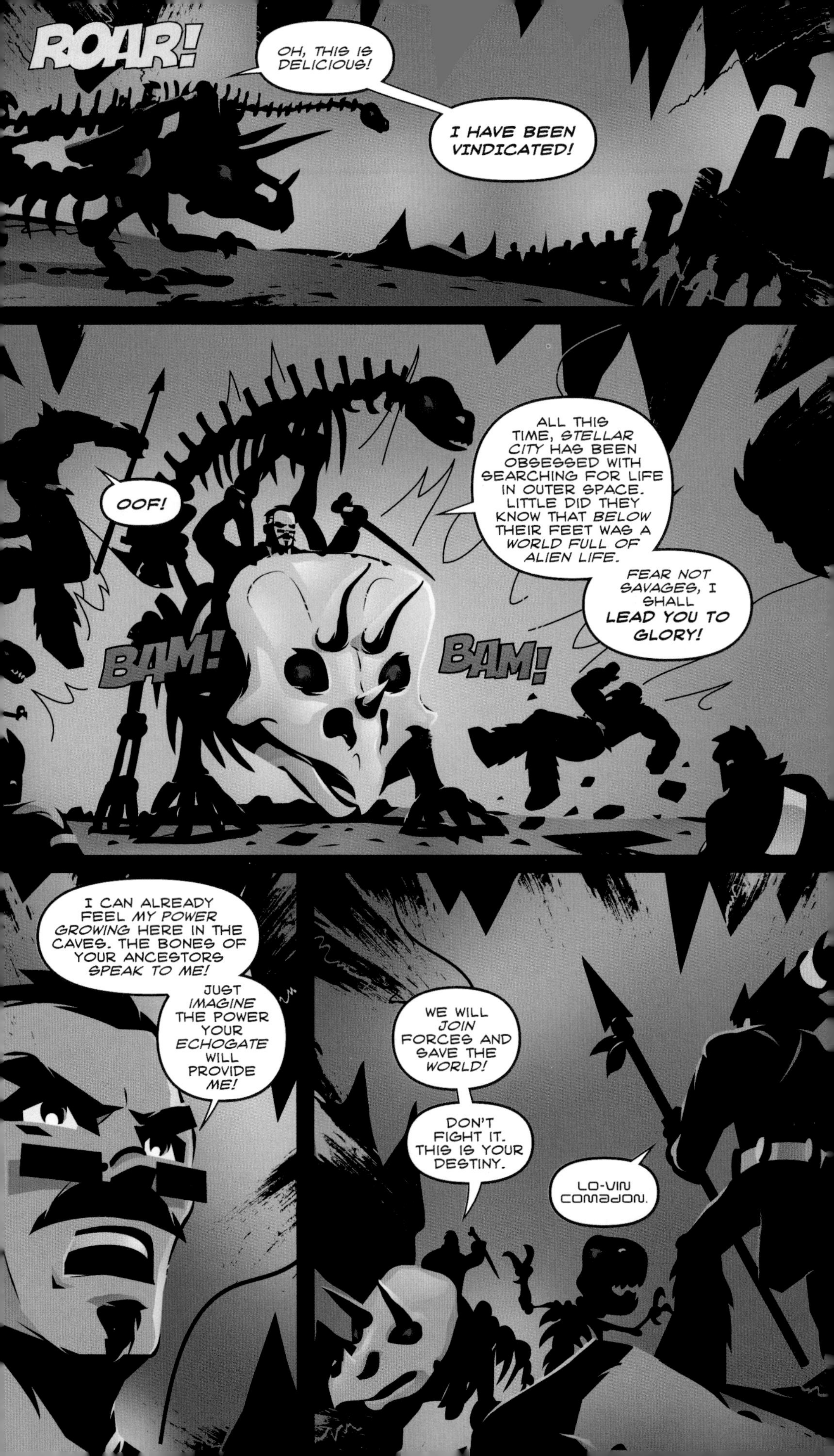
ROAR!
OH, THIS IS DELICIOUS!
I HAVE BEEN VINDICATED!
OOF!
ALL THIS TIME, STELLAR CITY HAS BEEN OBSESSED WITH SEARCHING FOR LIFE IN OUTER SPACE. LITTLE DID THEY KNOW THAT BELOW THEIR FEET WAS A WORLD FULL OF ALIEN LIFE.
FEAR NOT SAVAGES, I SHALL LEAD YOU TO GLORY!
BAM!
BAM!
I CAN ALREADY FEEL MY POWER GROWING HERE IN THE CAVES. THE BONES OF YOUR ANCESTORS SPEAK TO ME!
JUST IMAGINE THE POWER YOUR ECHOGATE WILL PROVIDE ME!
WE WILL JOIN FORCES AND SAVE THE WORLD!
DON'T FIGHT IT. THIS IS YOUR DESTINY.
LO-VIN COMADON.

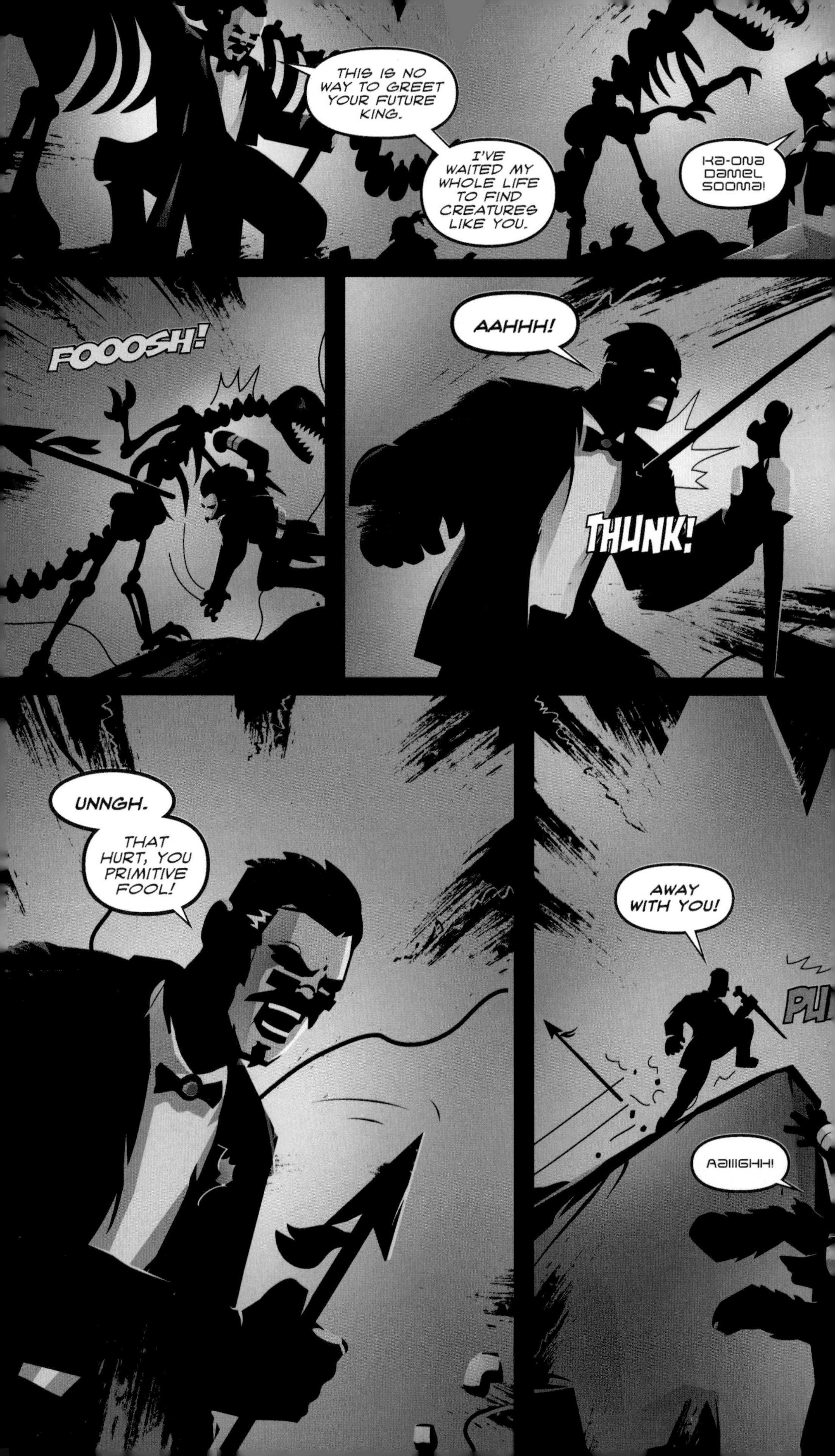

THIS IS NO WAY TO GREET YOUR FUTURE KING.
I'VE WAITED MY WHOLE LIFE TO FIND CREATURES LIKE YOU.
KA-ONA DAMEL SOOMA!
FOOOSH!
AAHHH!
THUNK!
UNNGH.
THAT HURT, YOU PRIMITIVE FOOL!
AWAY WITH YOU!
AAIIIGHH!

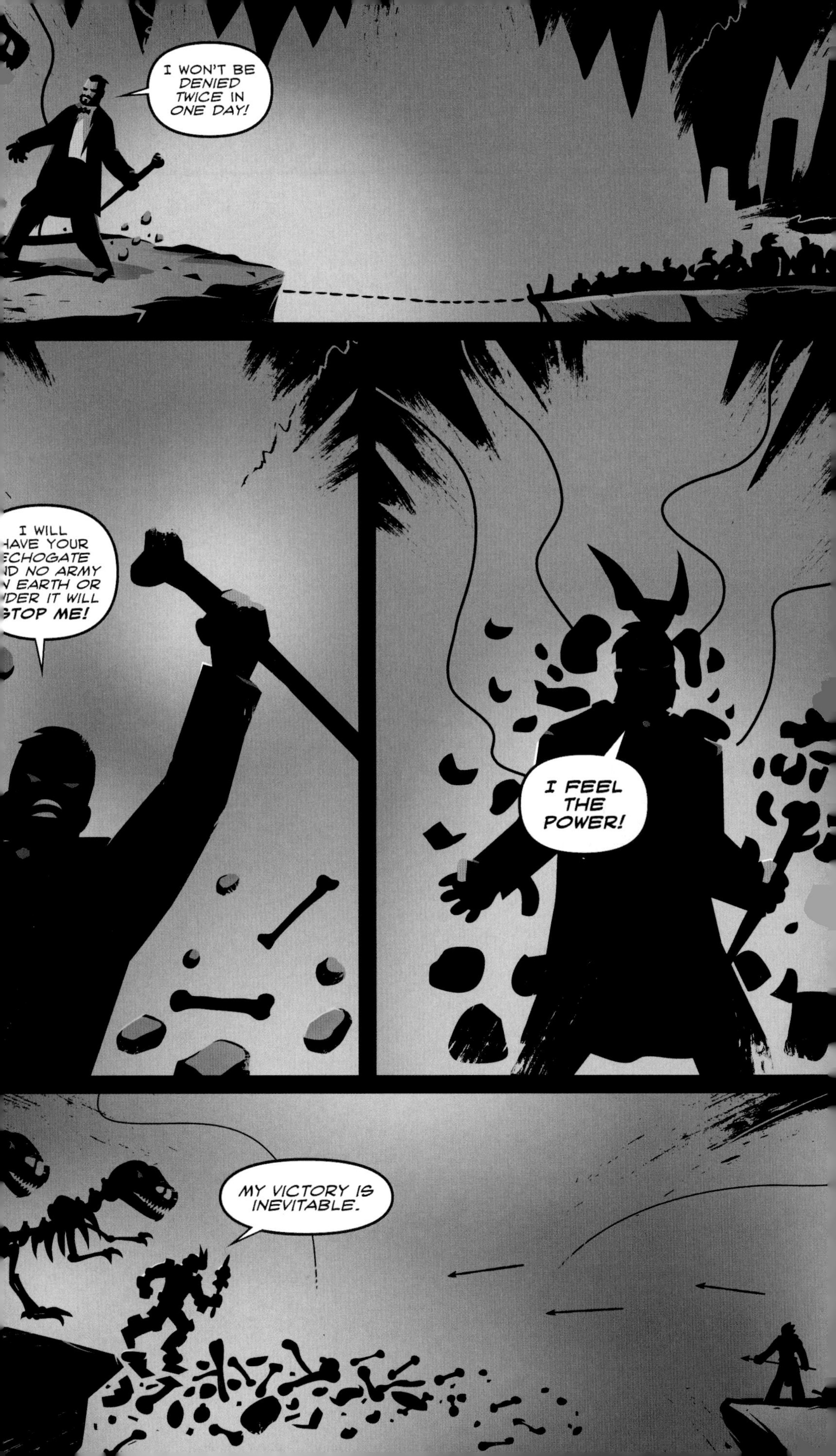

I WON'T BE DENIED TWICE IN ONE DAY!
I WILL HAVE YOUR ECHOGATE ND NO ARMY N EARTH OR DER IT WILL STOP ME!
I FEEL THE POWER!
MY VICTORY IS INEVITABLE.

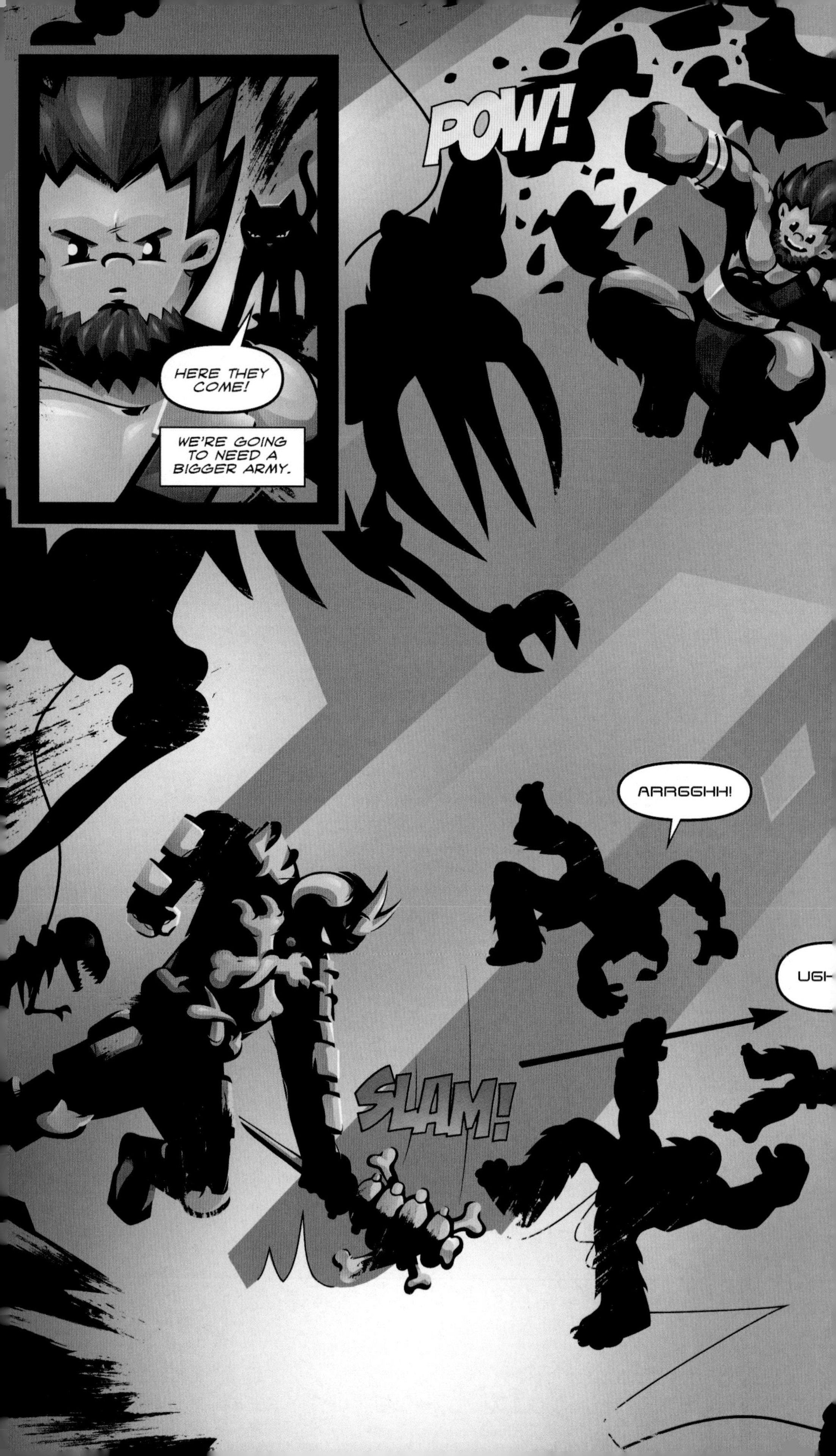
HERE THEY COME!
WE'RE GOING TO NEED A BIGGER ARMY.
POW!
ARRGGHH!
UGH
SLAM!

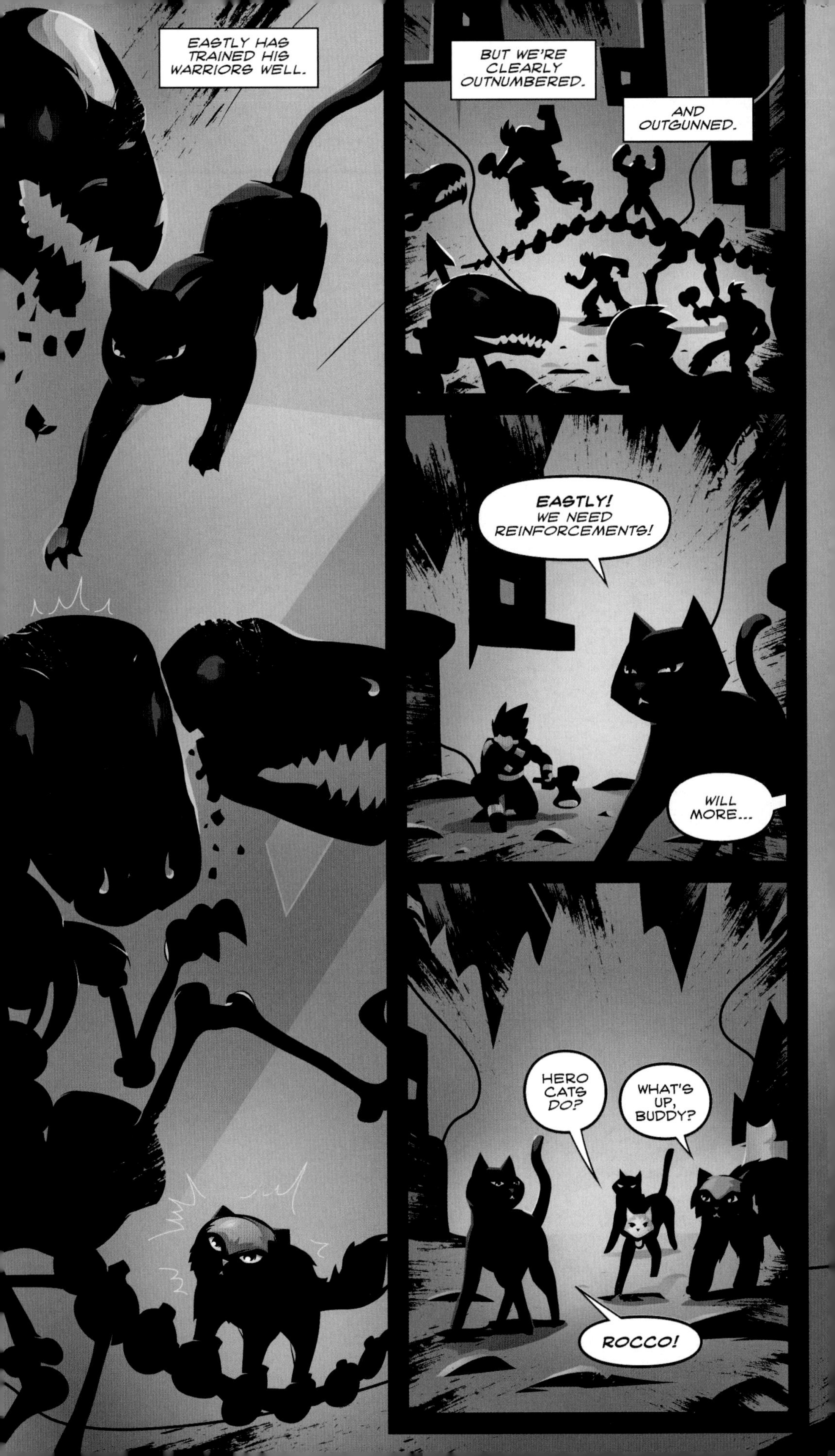
EASTLY HAS TRAINED HIS WARRIORS WELL.
BUT WE'RE CLEARLY OUTNUMBERED.
AND OUTGUNNED.
EASTLY! WE NEED REINFORCEMENTS!
WILL MORE...
HERO CATS DO?
WHAT'S UP, BUDDY?
ROCCO!

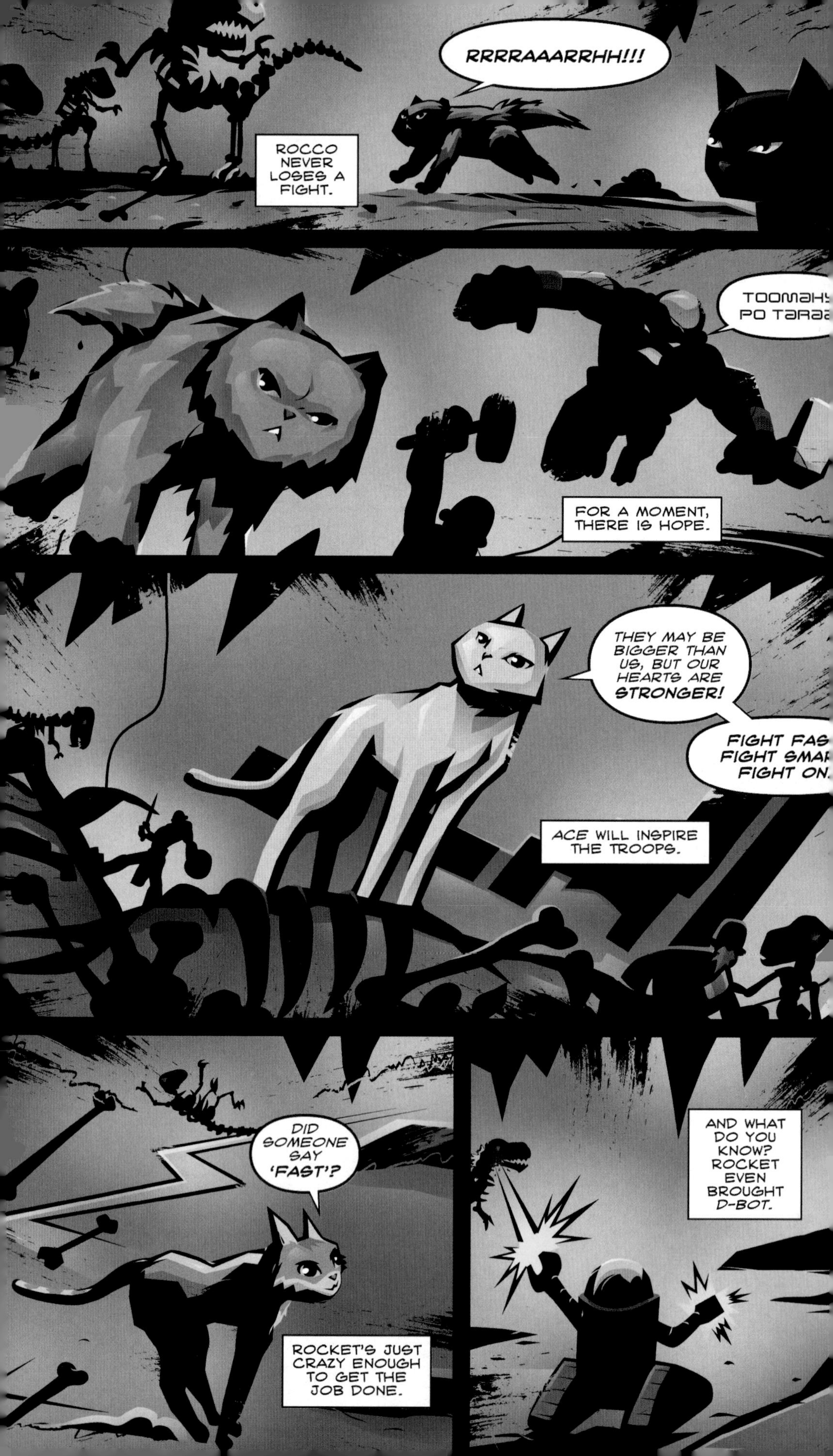
RRRRAAARRHH!!!
ROCCO NEVER LOSES A FIGHT.
FOR A MOMENT, THERE IS HOPE.
THEY MAY BE BIGGER THAN US, BUT OUR HEARTS ARE STRONGER!
FIGHT FAS
FIGHT SMA
FIGHT ON.
ACE WILL INSPIRE THE TROOPS.
DID SOMEONE SAY 'FAST'?
ROCKET'S JUST CRAZY ENOUGH TO GET THE JOB DONE.
AND WHAT DO YOU KNOW? ROCKET EVEN BROUGHT D-BOT.

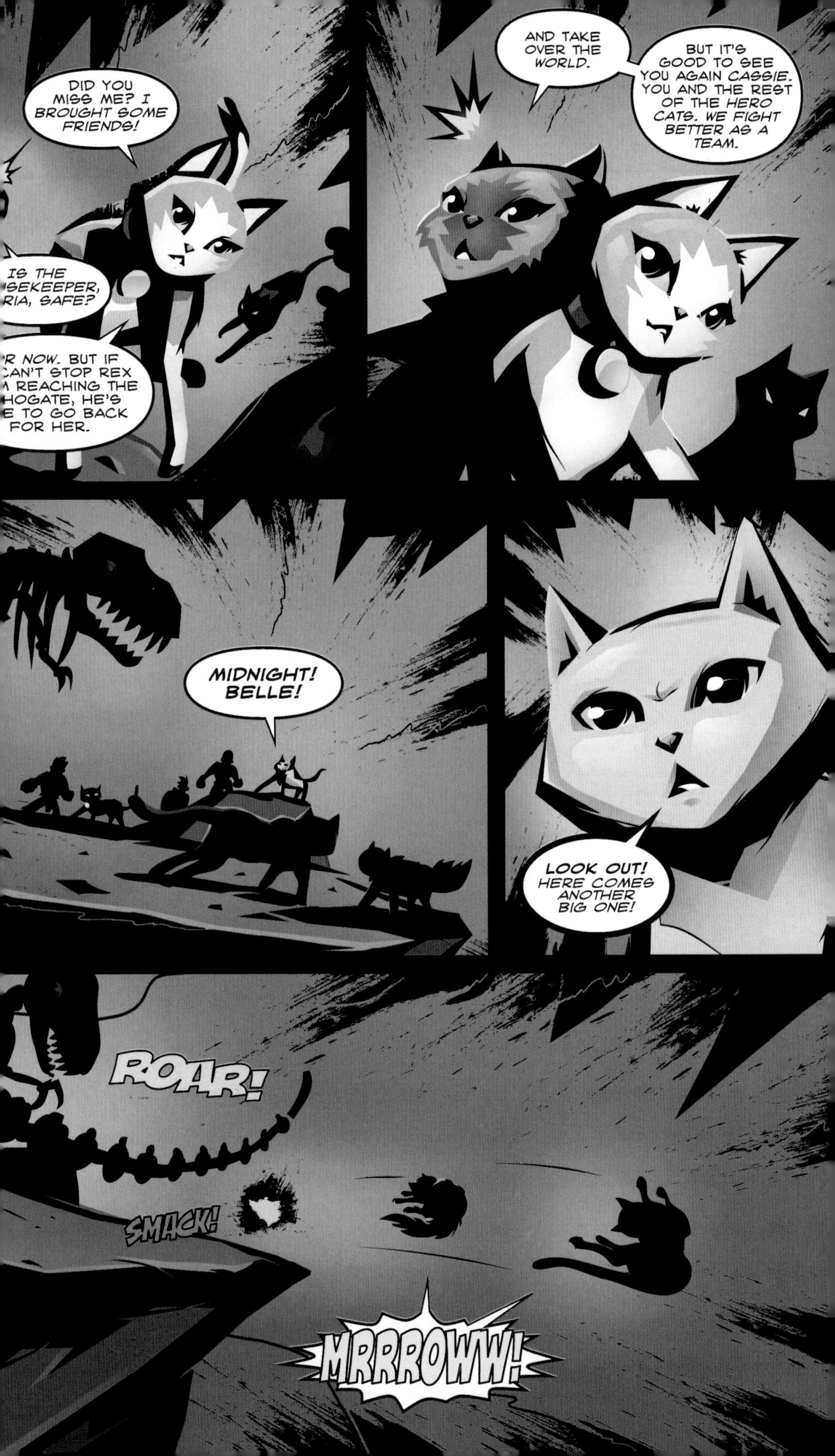
DID YOU MISS ME? I BROUGHT SOME FRIENDS!
IS THE SEKEEPER, RIA, SAFE?
R NOW. BUT IF CAN'T STOP REX M REACHING THE HOGATE, HE'S E TO GO BACK FOR HER.
AND TAKE OVER THE WORLD.
BUT IT'S GOOD TO SEE YOU AGAIN CASSIE. YOU AND THE REST OF THE HERO CATS. WE FIGHT BETTER AS A TEAM.
MIDNIGHT! BELLE!
LOOK OUT! HERE COMES ANOTHER BIG ONE!
ROAR!
SMACK!
MRRROWW!

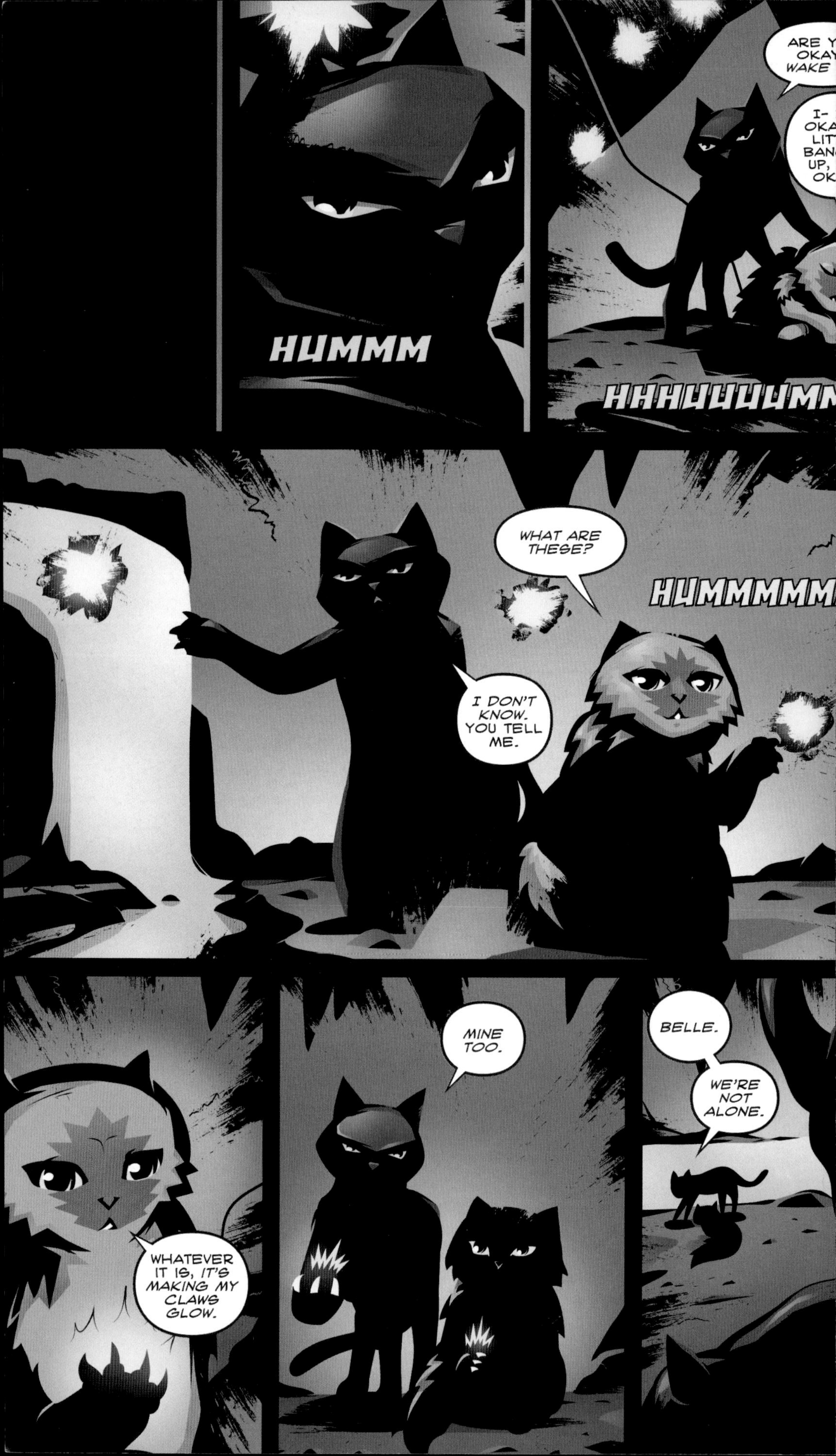
HUMMM
ARE Y OKAY WAKE
I- OKA LIT BANG UP, OK
HHHUUUUUMM
WHAT ARE THESE?
HUMMMMMM
I DON'T KNOW. YOU TELL ME.
WHATEVER IT IS, IT'S MAKING MY CLAWS GLOW.
MINE TOO.
BELLE.
WE'RE NOT ALONE.

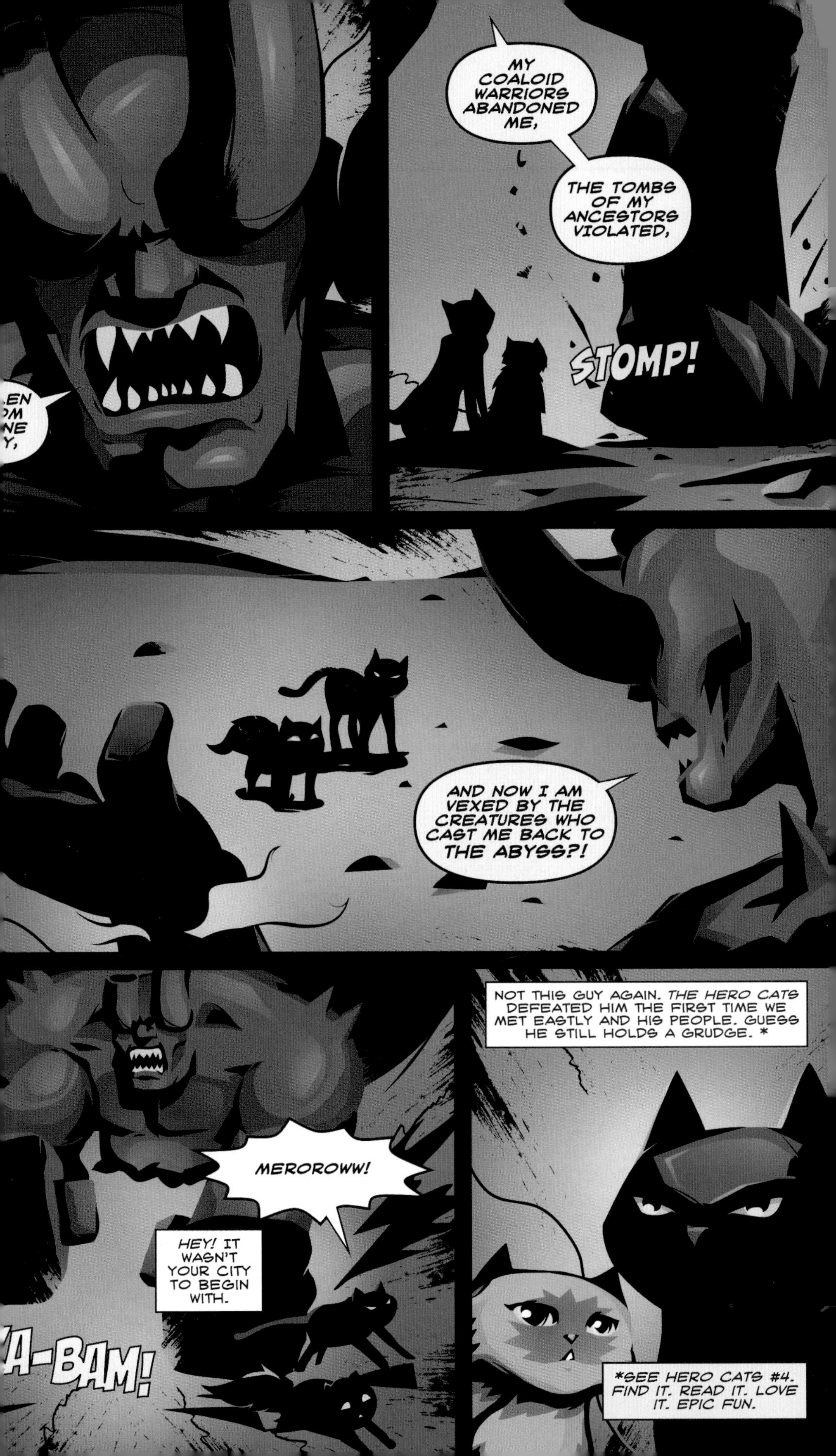
MY COALOID WARRIORS ABANDONED ME,
THE TOMBS OF MY ANCESTORS VIOLATED,
STOMP!
AND NOW I AM VEXED BY THE CREATURES WHO CAST ME BACK TO THE ABYSS?!
MEROROWW!
HEY! IT WASN'T YOUR CITY TO BEGIN WITH.
A-BAM!
NOT THIS GUY AGAIN. THE HERO CATS DEFEATED HIM THE FIRST TIME WE MET EASTLY AND HIS PEOPLE. GUESS HE STILL HOLDS A GRUDGE. *
*SEE HERO CATS #4. FIND IT. READ IT. LOVE IT. EPIC FUN.

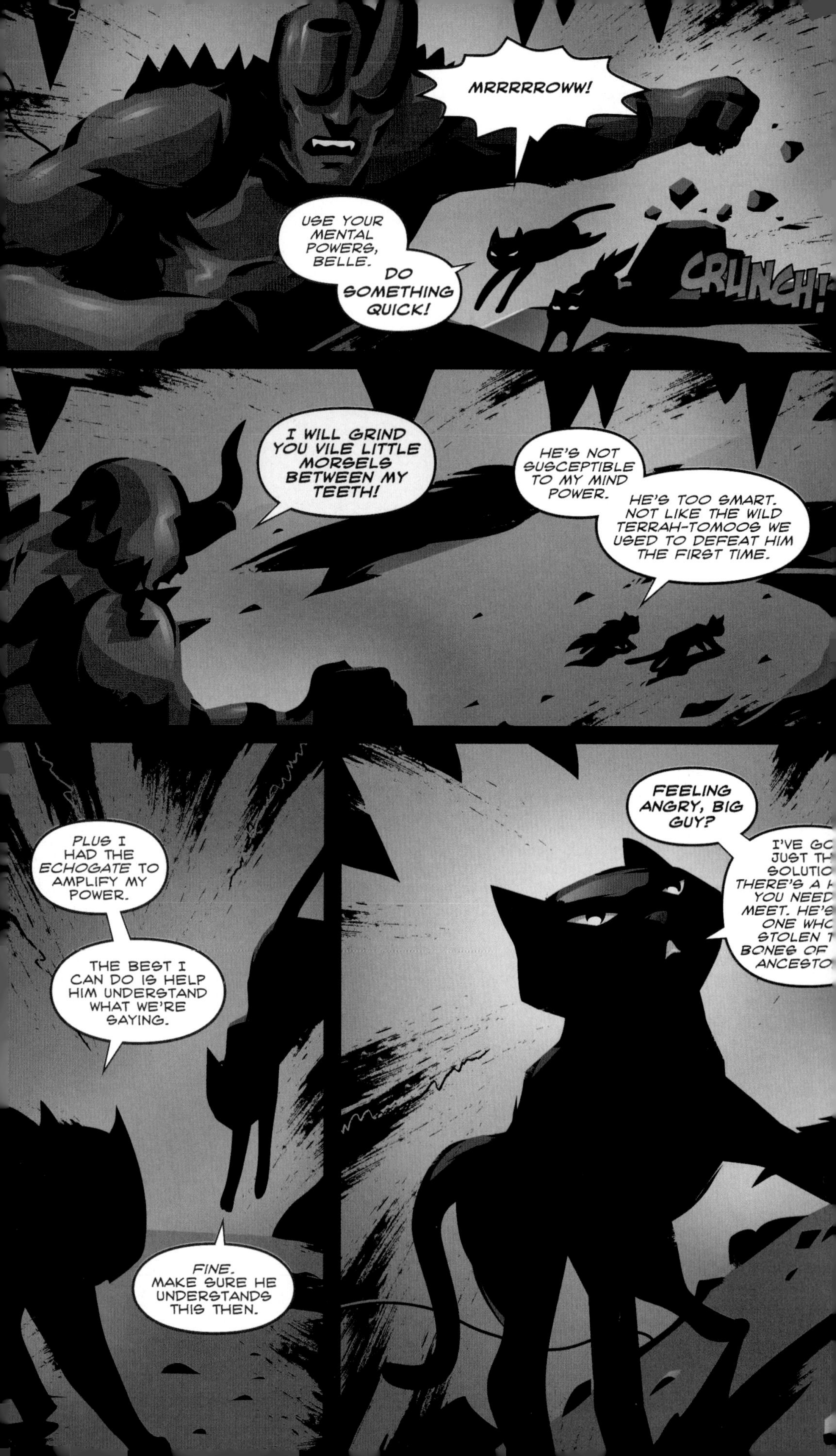
MRRRRROWW!
USE YOUR MENTAL POWERS, BELLE.
DO SOMETHING QUICK!
CRUNCH!
I WILL GRIND YOU VILE LITTLE MORSELS BETWEEN MY TEETH!
HE'S NOT SUSCEPTIBLE TO MY MIND POWER.
HE'S TOO SMART. NOT LIKE THE WILD TERRAH-TOMOOS WE USED TO DEFEAT HIM THE FIRST TIME.
PLUS I HAD THE ECHOGATE TO AMPLIFY MY POWER.
THE BEST I CAN DO IS HELP HIM UNDERSTAND WHAT WE'RE SAYING.
FINE. MAKE SURE HE UNDERSTANDS THIS THEN.
FEELING ANGRY, BIG GUY?

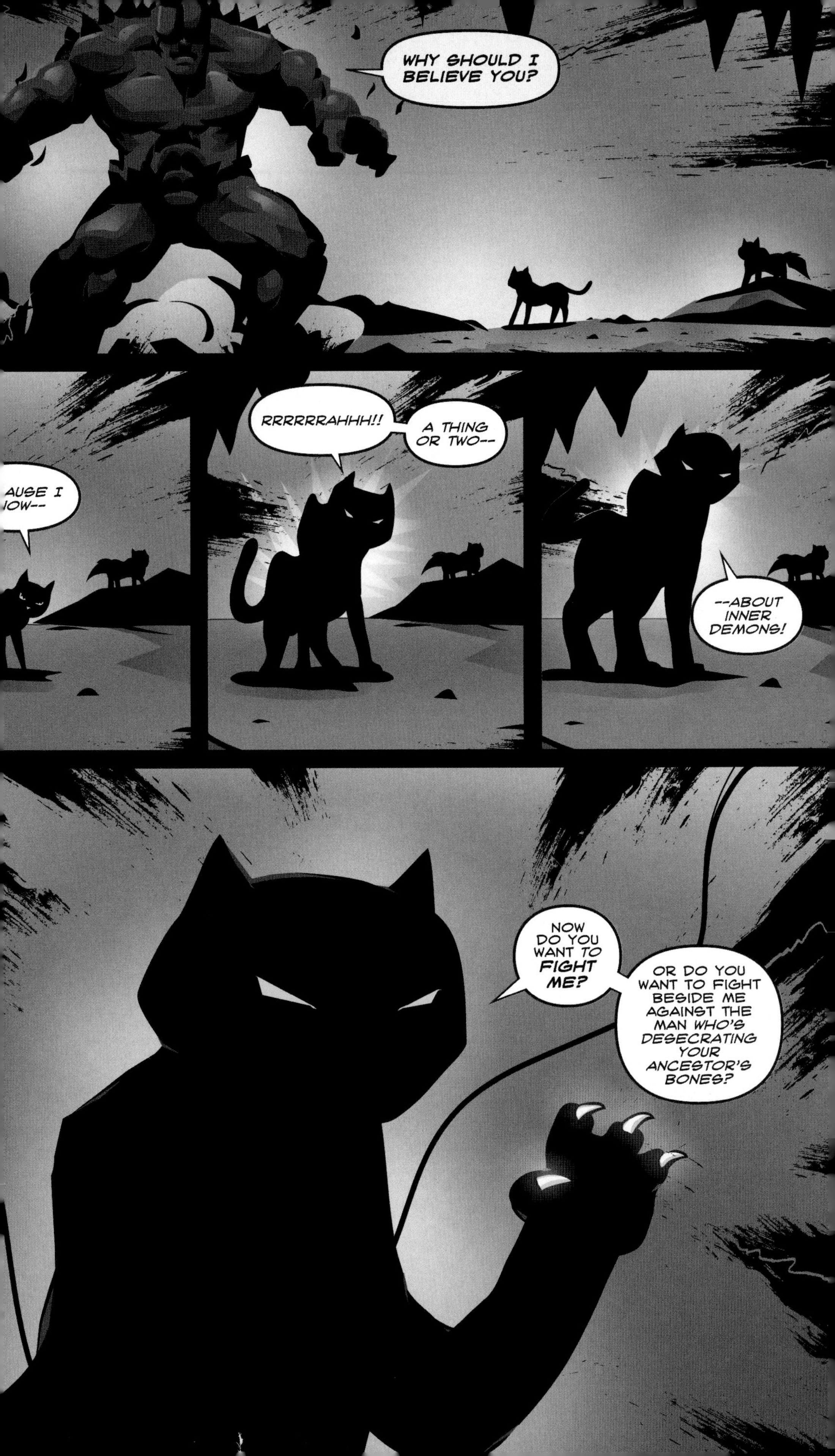
WHY SHOULD I BELIEVE YOU?
AUSE I
IOW--
RRRRRRAHHH!!
A THING OR TWO--
--ABOUT INNER DEMONS!
NOW DO YOU WANT TO FIGHT ME?
OR DO YOU WANT TO FIGHT BESIDE ME AGAINST THE MAN WHO'S DESECRATING YOUR ANCESTOR'S BONES?

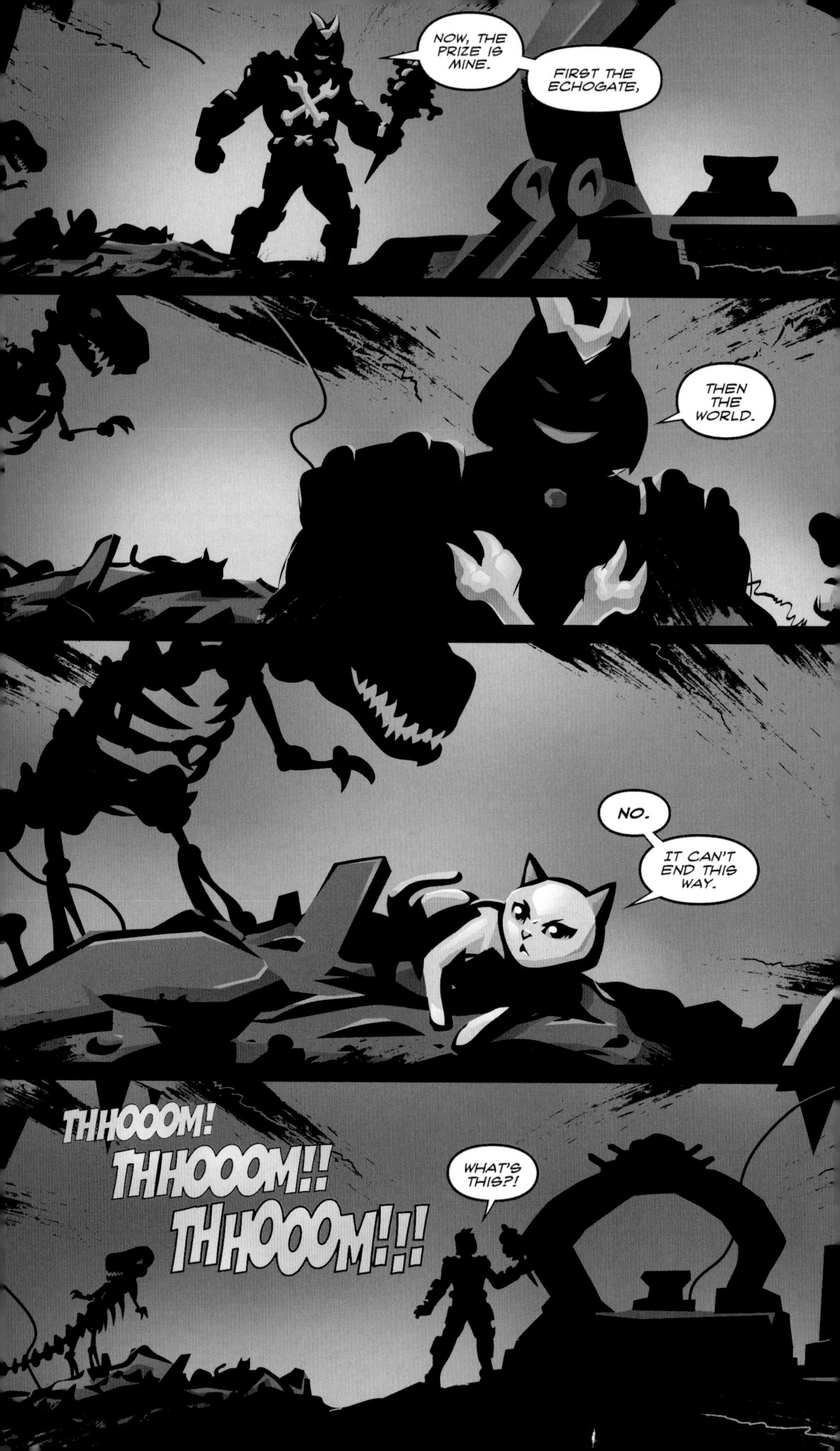
NOW, THE PRIZE IS MINE.
FIRST THE ECHOGATE,
THEN THE WORLD.
NO.
IT CAN'T END THIS WAY.
THHOOOM!
THHOOOM!!
THHOOOM!!!
WHAT'S THIS?!

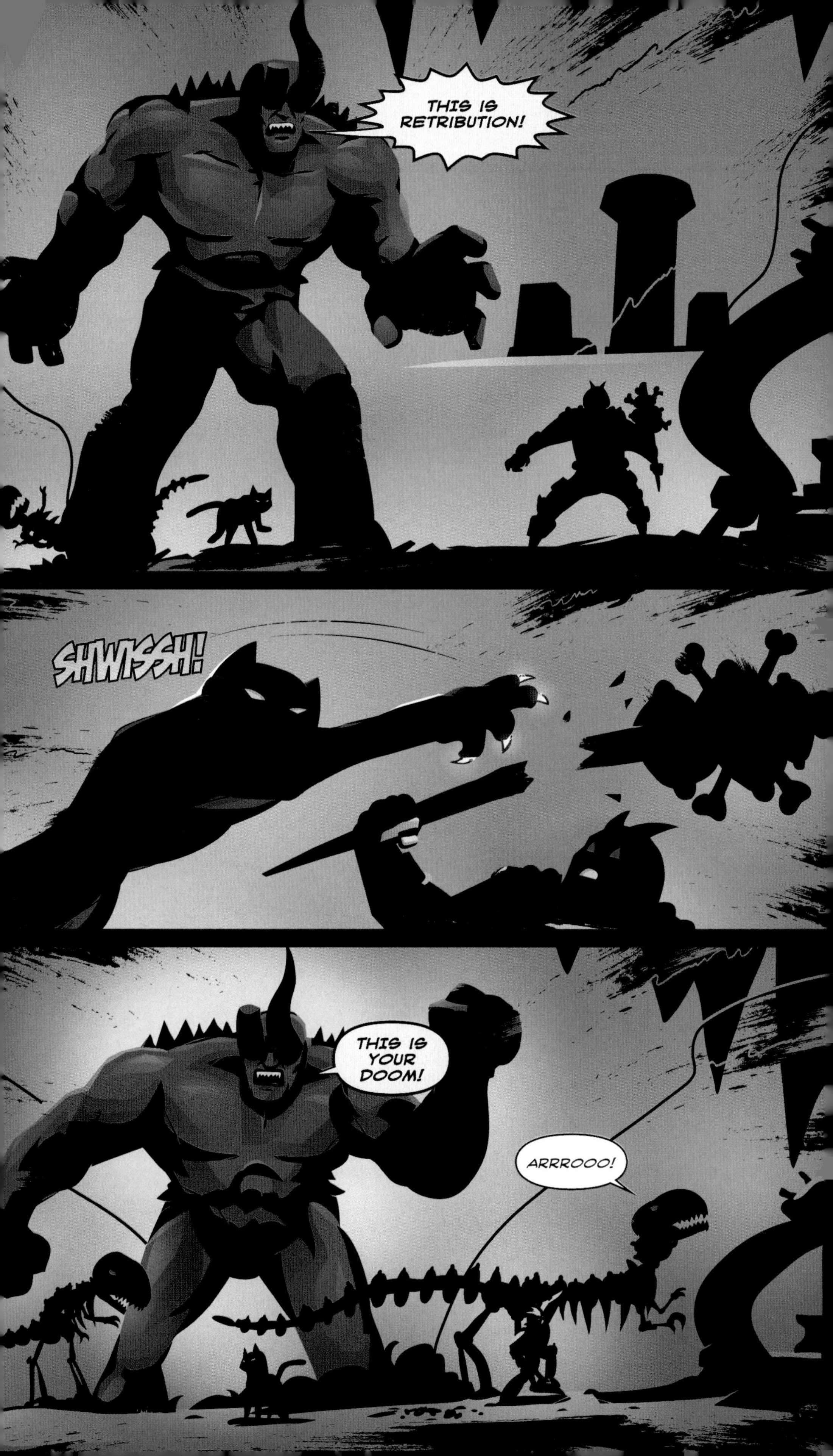
THIS IS RETRIBUTION!
SHWISSH!
THIS IS YOUR DOOM!
ARRROOO!

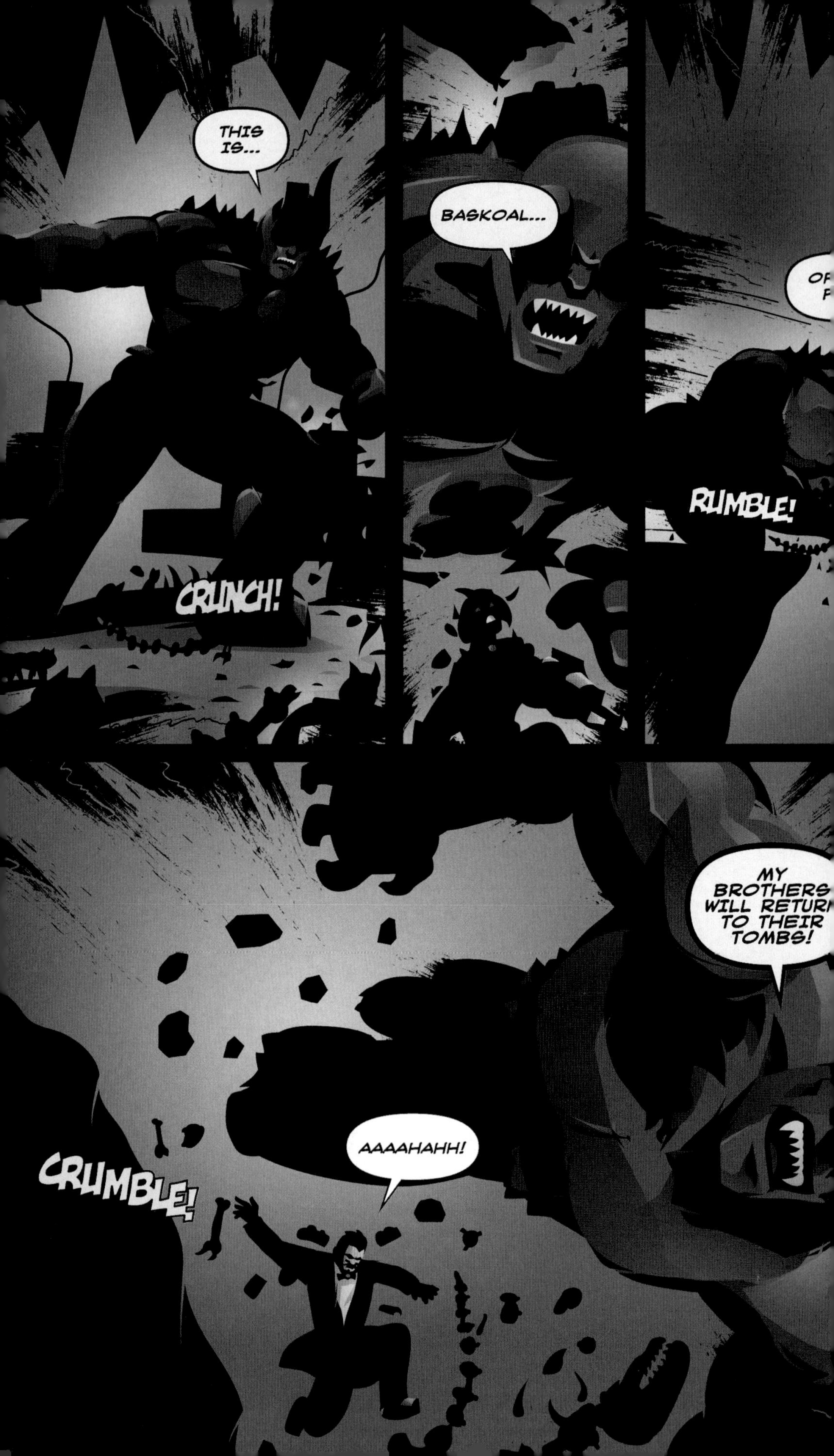
THIS IS...
CRUNCH!
BASKOAL...
RUMBLE!
MY BROTHERS WILL RETUR TO THEIR TOMBS!
CRUMBLE!
AAAAHAHH!

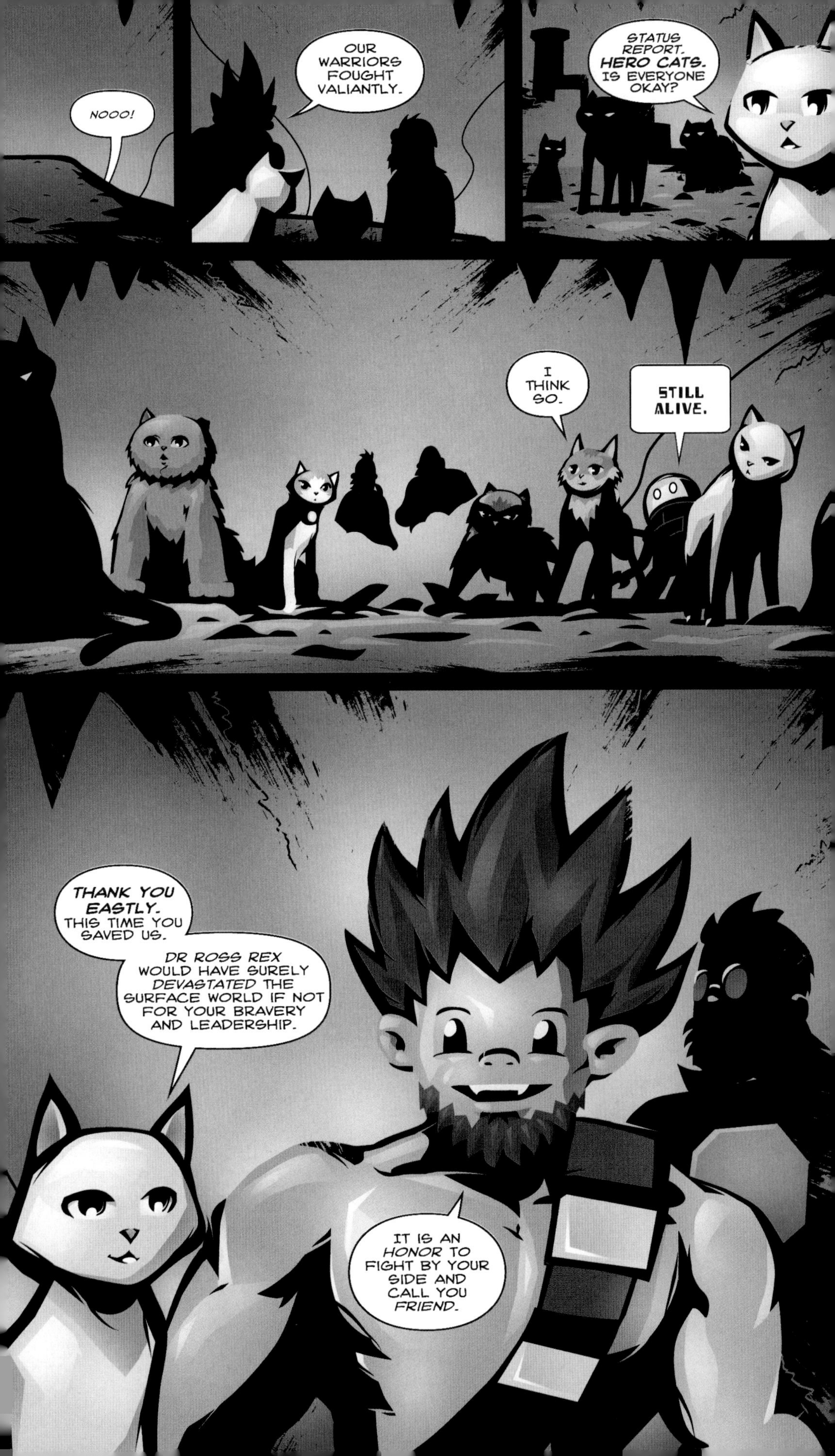
NOOO!
OUR WARRIORS FOUGHT VALIANTLY.
STATUS REPORT. HERO CATS. IS EVERYONE OKAY?
I THINK SO.
STILL ALIVE.
THANK YOU EASTLY. THIS TIME YOU SAVED US.
DR ROSS REX WOULD HAVE SURELY DEVASTATED THE SURFACE WORLD IF NOT FOR YOUR BRAVERY AND LEADERSHIP.
IT IS AN HONOR TO FIGHT BY YOUR SIDE AND CALL YOU FRIEND.

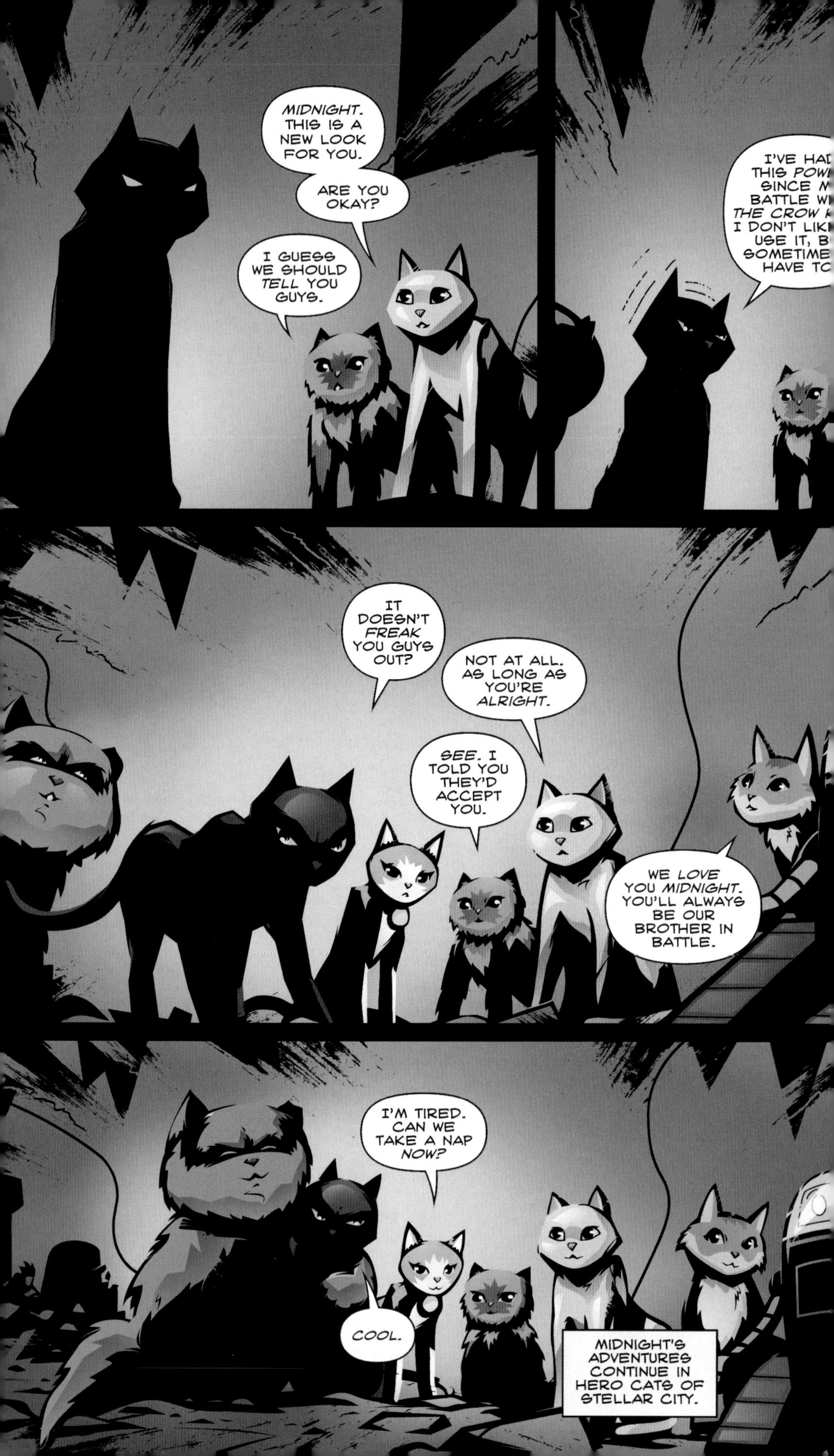

MIDNIGHT. THIS IS A NEW LOOK FOR YOU.
ARE YOU OKAY?
I GUESS WE SHOULD TELL YOU GUYS.
THIS SINCE BATTLE THE CROW I DON'T USE IT, HAVE
IT DOESN'T FREAK YOU GUYS OUT?
NOT AT ALL. AS LONG AS YOU'RE ALRIGHT.
SEE. I TOLD YOU THEY'D ACCEPT YOU.
WE LOVE YOU MIDNIGHT. YOU'LL ALWAYS BE OUR BROTHER IN BATTLE.
I'M TIRED. CAN WE TAKE A NAP NOW?
COOL.
MIDNIGHT'S ADVENTURES CONTINUE IN HERO CATS OF STELLAR CITY.

MIDNIGHT WANTS YOU TO DO HIM A FAVOR.
HE WANTS YOU TO TELL ALL YOUR FRIENDS ABOUT HIM!

**FIND OUT MORE ABOUT HERO CATS
AT WWW.HEROCATSONLINE.COM**

CTION LAB ENTERTAINMENT
ryan Seaton - Publisher/SEO
hawn Gabborin - Editor in Chief
son Martin - Publisher - Danger Zone
icole D'Andria - Marking Director/Editor
m Dietz - Social Media Manager
anielle Davison - Executive Administrator
had Cicconi - Nightshifts
hawn Pryor - President of Creator Relations

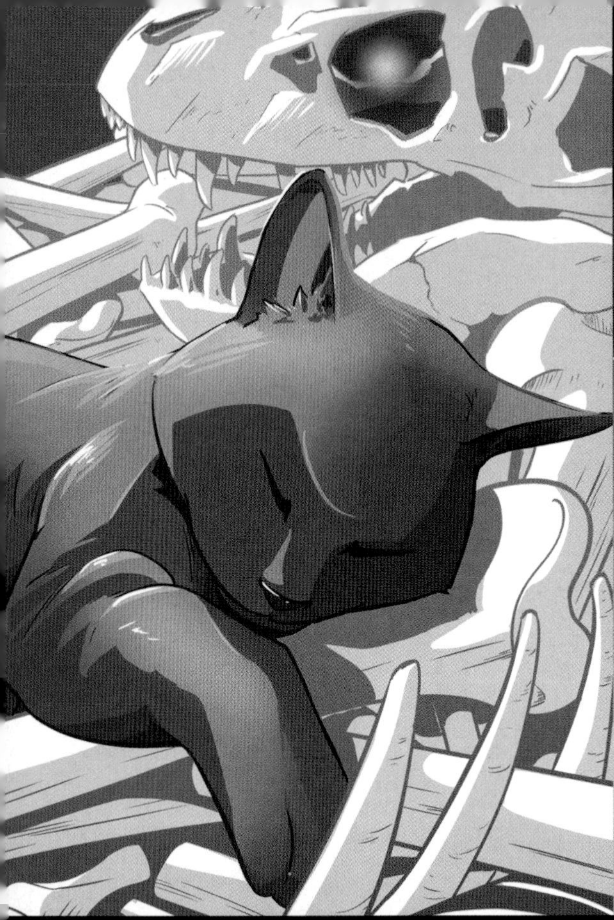

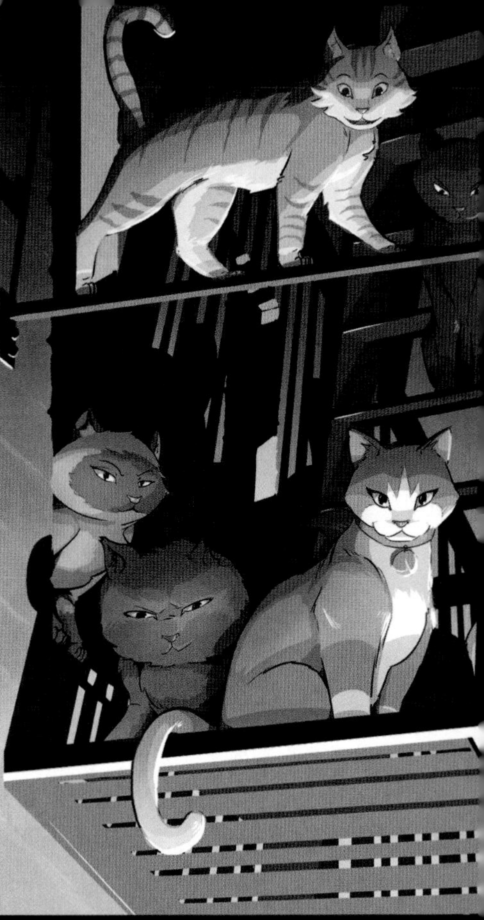

THE CAT GALLERY

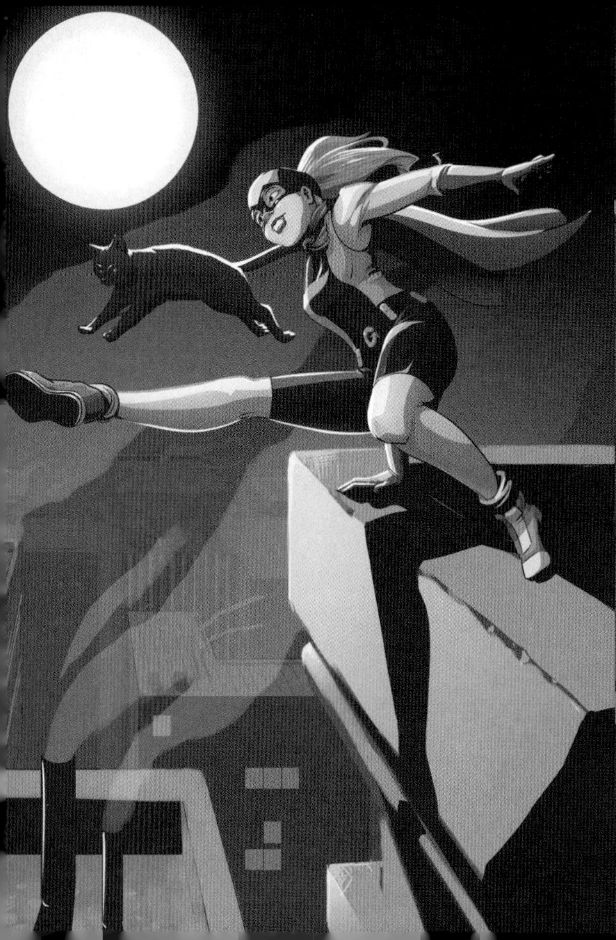

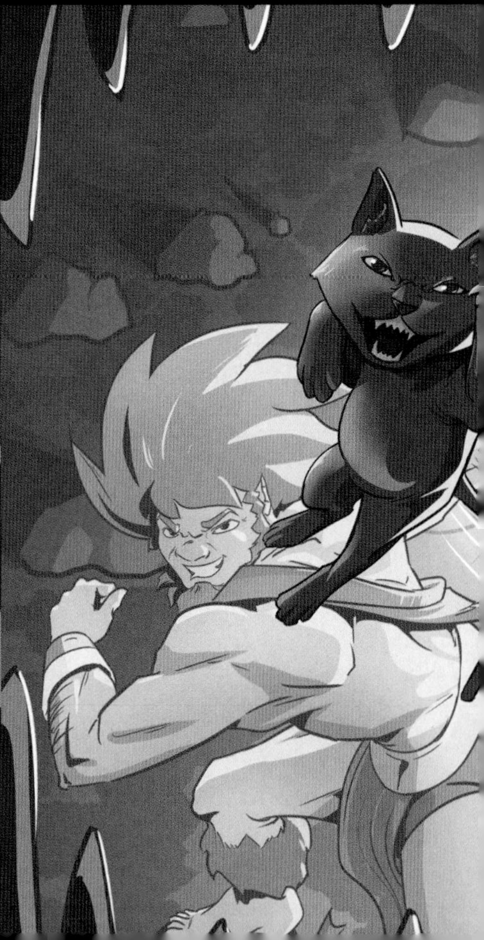

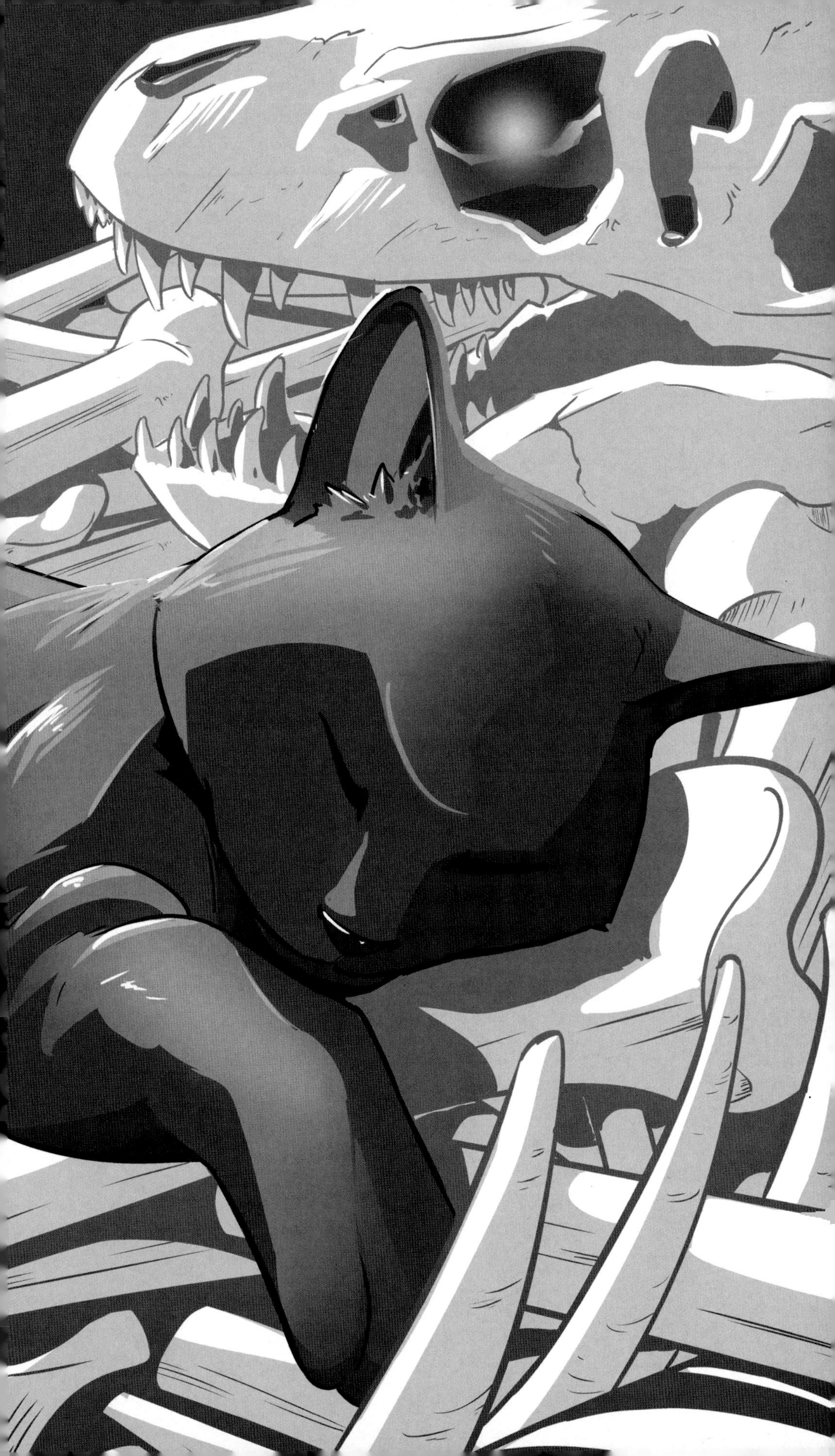

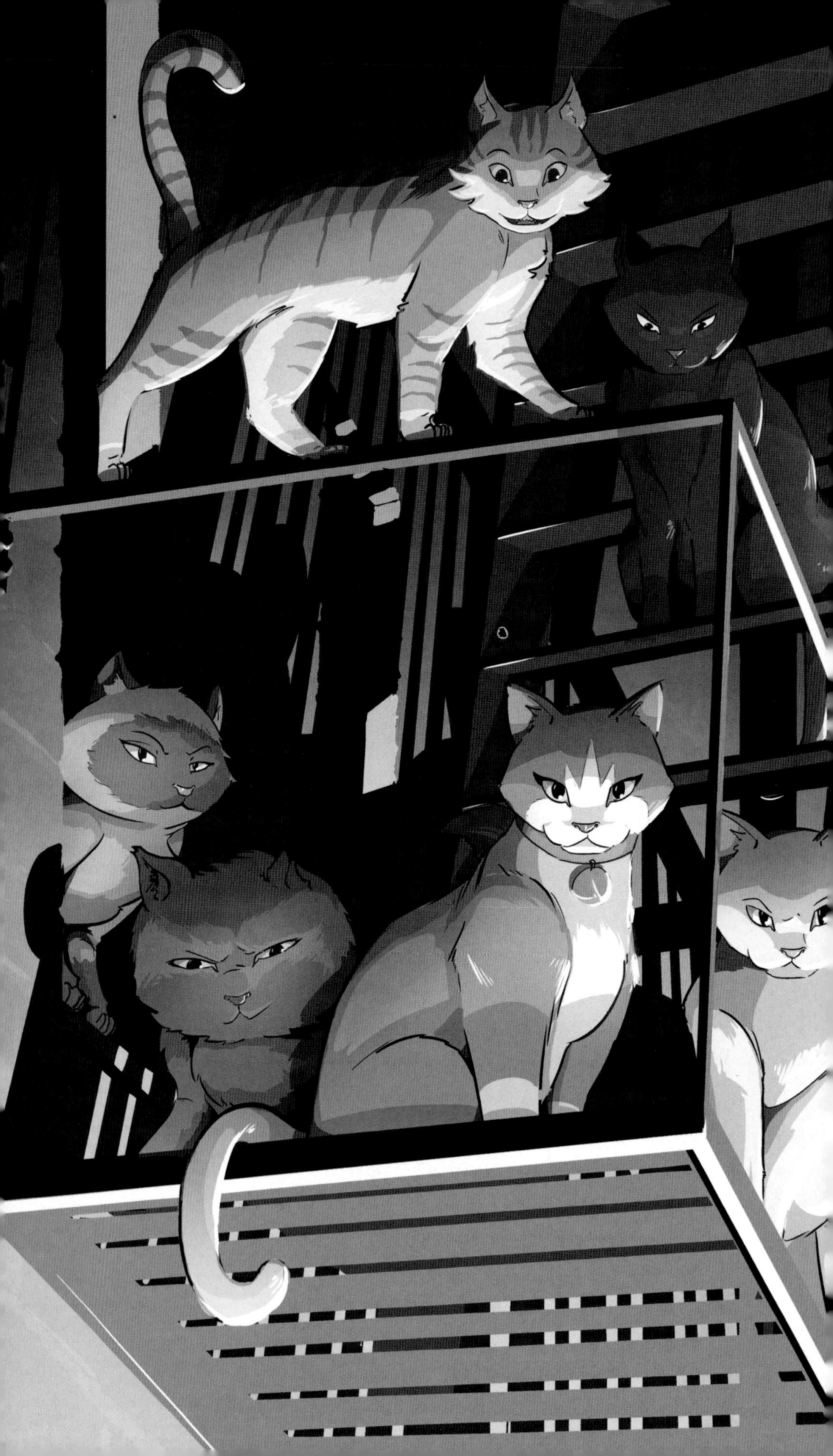

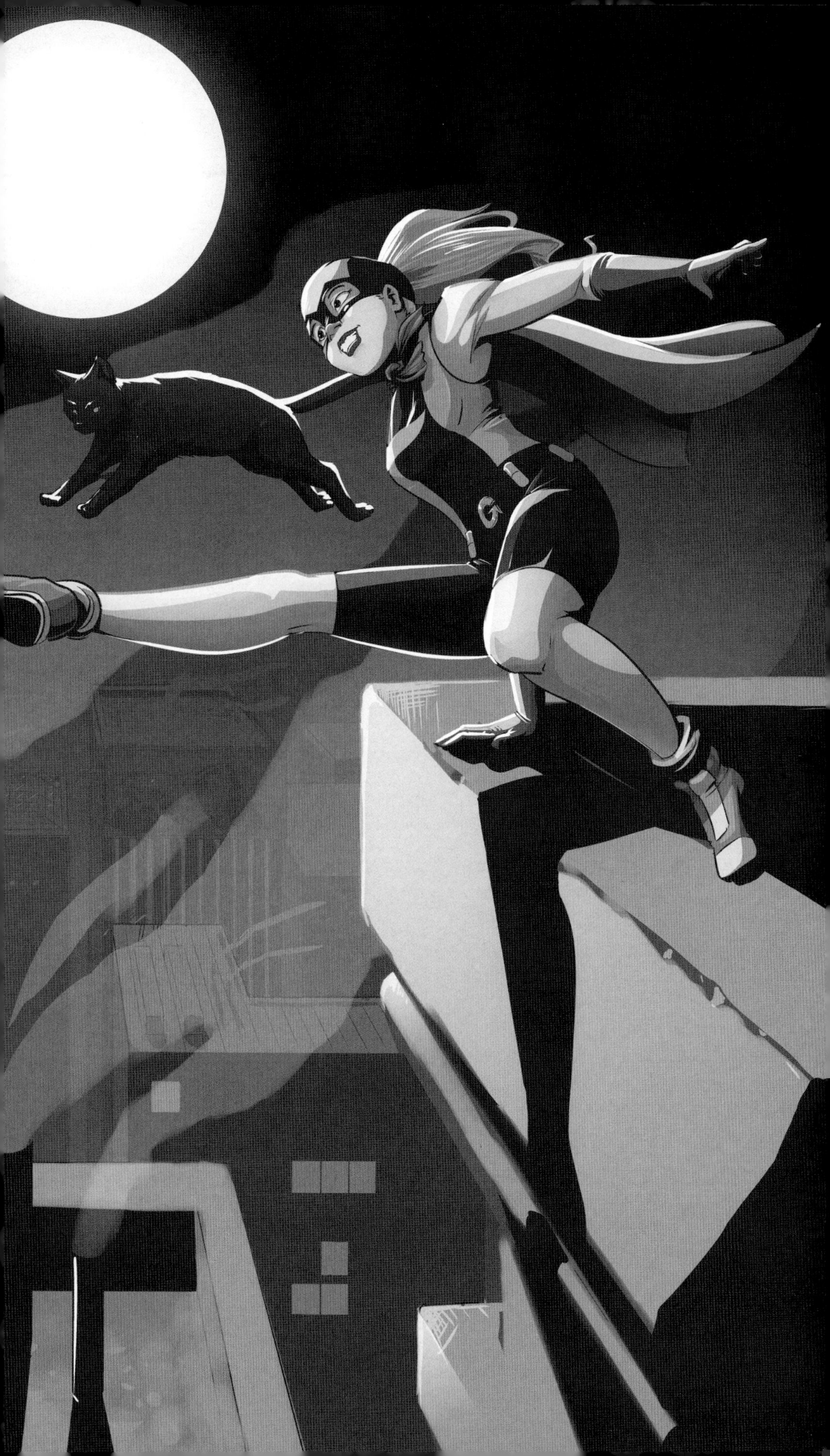

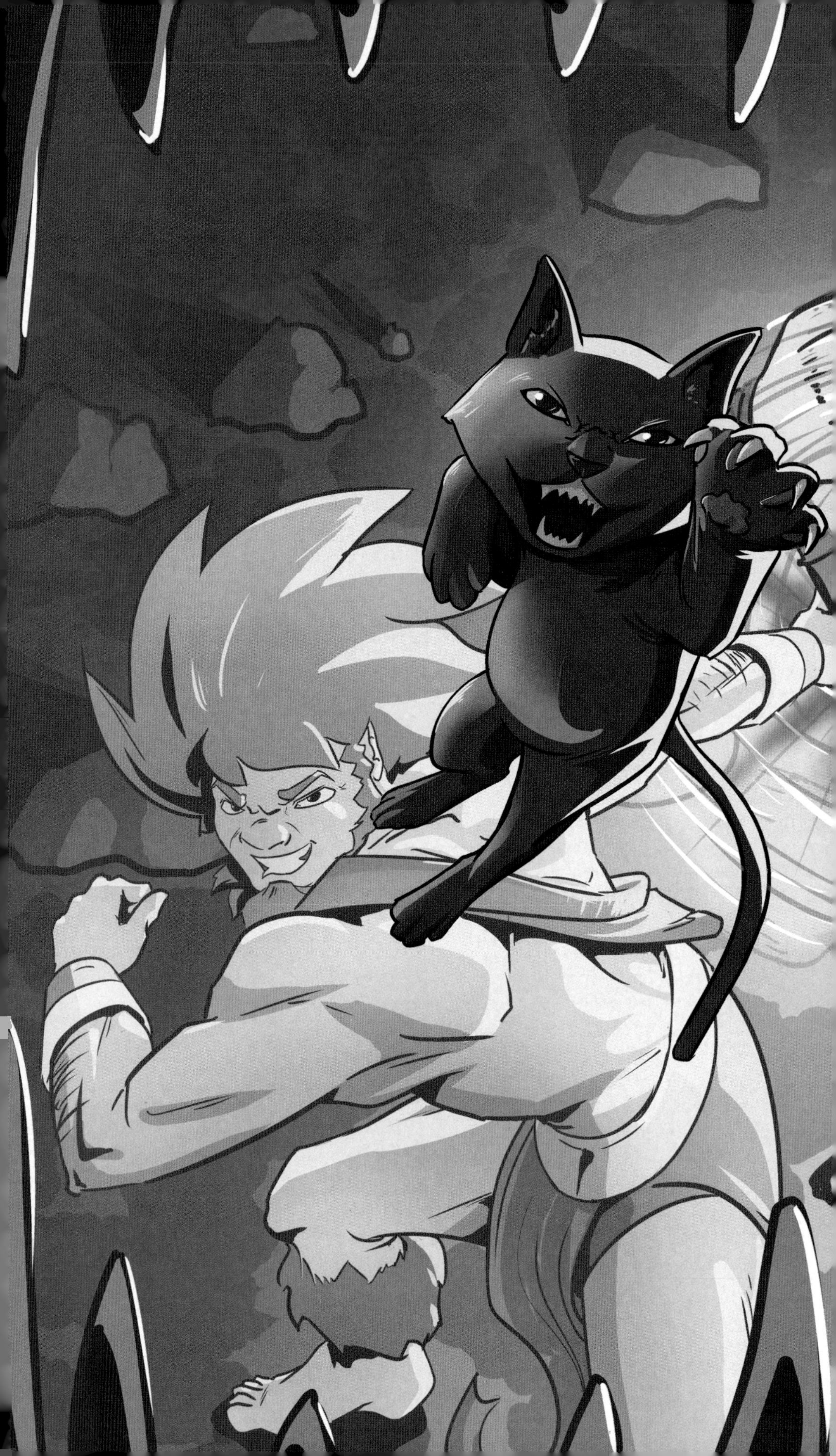

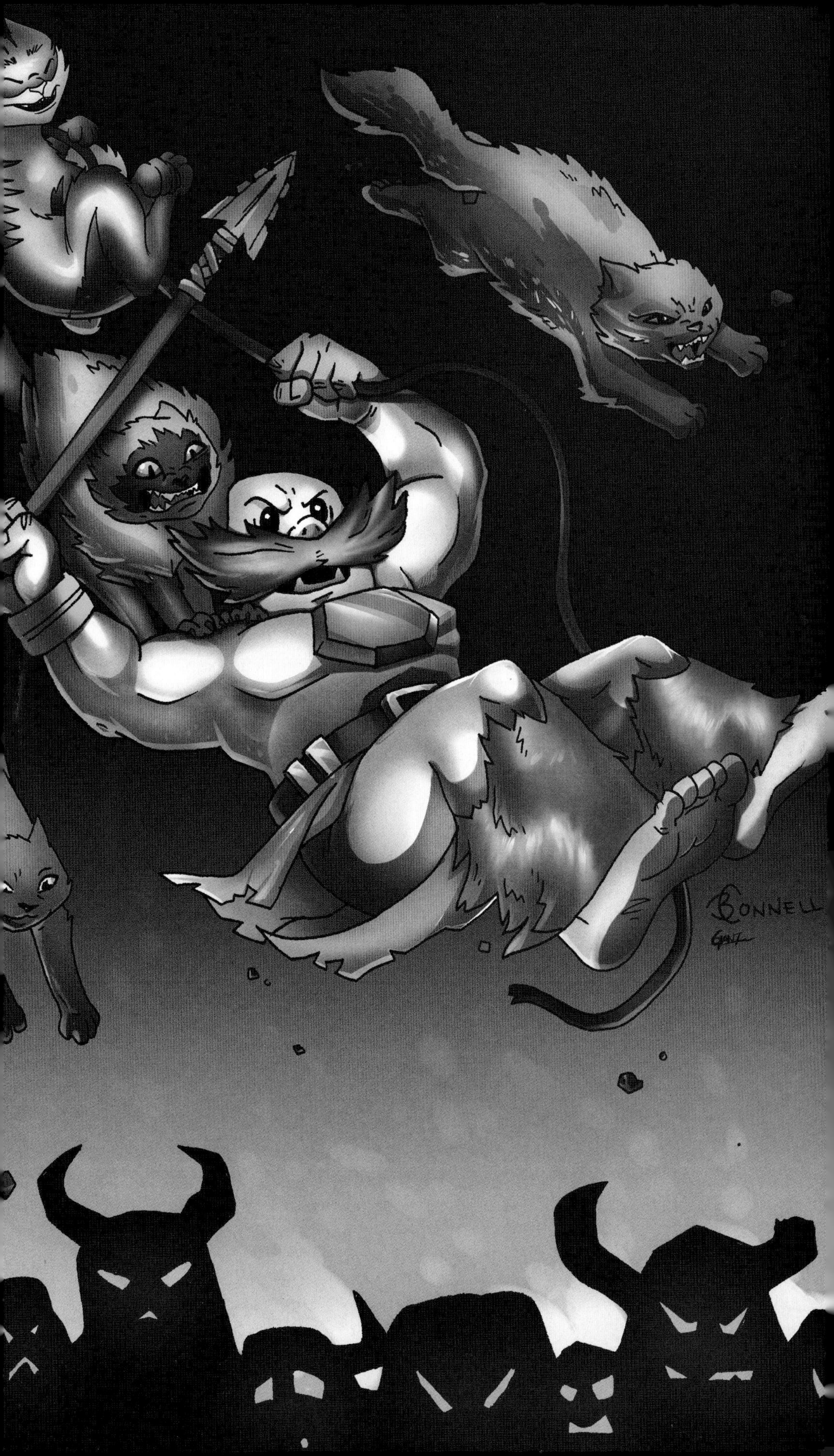
BONNELL

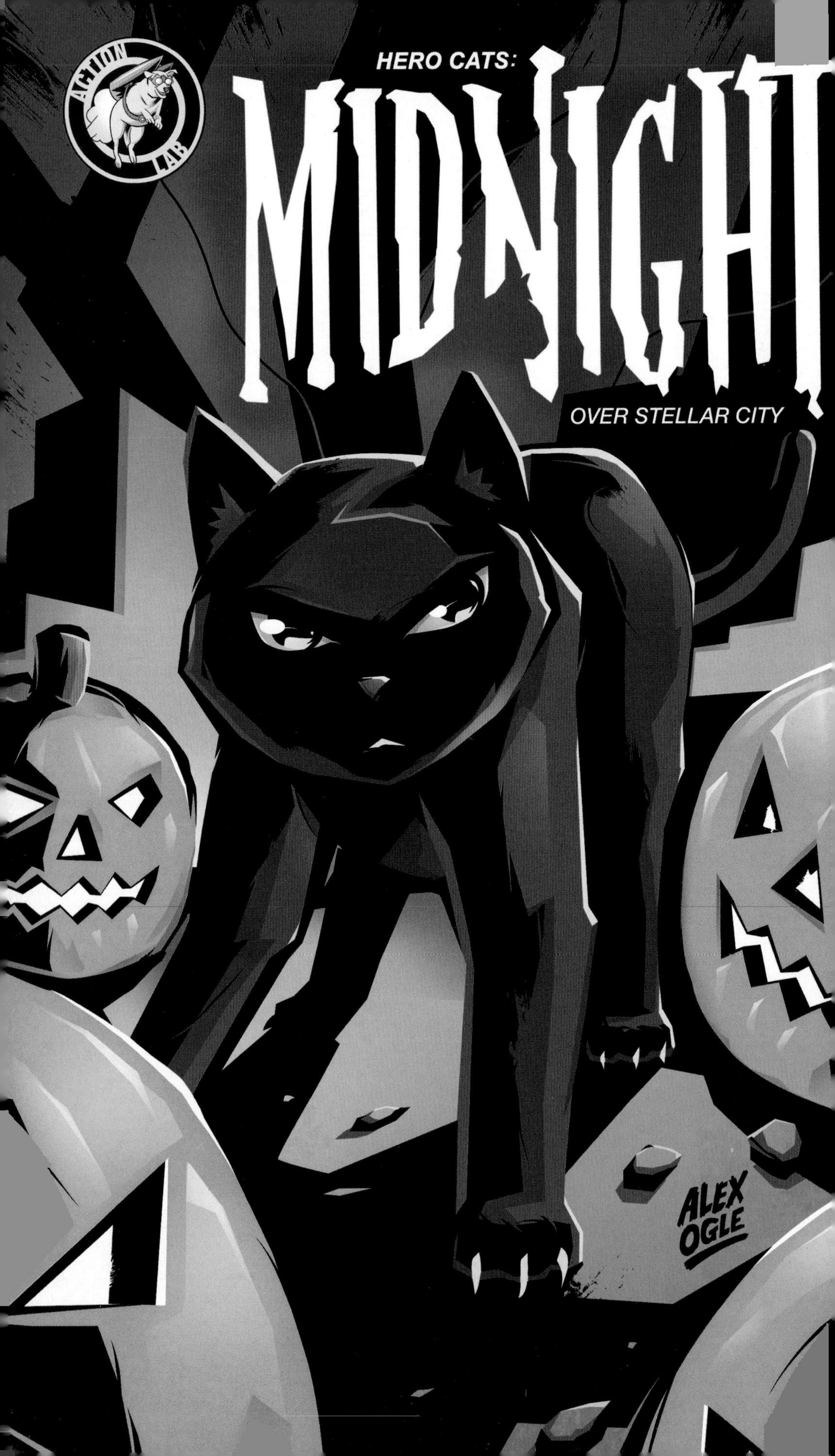
ACTION LAB
HERO CATS:
MIDNIGHT
OVER STELLAR CITY
ALEX OGLE